To Dance One More Day

Rachel Jones

Clean Reads
www.CleanReads.com

TO DANCE ONE MORE DAY
Copyright © 2014 RACHEL JONES
ISBN 978-1-62135-588-5
Cover Art Designed by AM Designs

This is a work of fiction. Names, places, characters, and events are fictitious in every regard. Any similarities to actual events and persons, living or dead, are purely coincidental. Any trademarks, service marks, product names, or named features are assumed to be the property of their respective owners, and are used only for reference. There is no implied endorsement if any of these terms are used. Except for review purposes, the reproduction of this book in whole or part, electronically or mechanically, constitutes a copyright violation.

To my husband, Randy,
who has always been my Prince Charming.

One

Jillian opened and closed her eyelids several times, taking in the darkness accompanied by an eerie silence. She dragged her head from side to side, trying to clear away the fuzziness surrounding her consciousness. Her head hurt. How long had she been knocked out? A minute? Ten minutes? Feeling something warm on her cheek, her fingers followed the sticky trail up to her right temple, touching the gash that caused blood to spill down her face. Without moving, she listened to pieces of refuse falling to the floor around her, making thumping sounds. She shifted her body, and tiny bits of confetti-like debris sprinkled down around her, creating a powdery film of dust on her skin. With guarded motions, she touched her arms and torso, assessing for other injuries. Moving her legs, she let out a sigh of relief when she discovered it was not painful. A ballerina with injured legs couldn't be a ballerina.

What in the world had happened? She had stopped at Mancini's to pick up some takeout for a late lunch and decided to run into Goodwin's Pharmacy next door for toilet paper and shampoo. "God, please help me," she prayed as she lay on the floor in the dark.

She called out, "Is anyone there?"

Someone moaned. "Over here—I'm hurt."

The woman took in short breaths as she began to sob. Jillian struggled to shift her body, crying out in pain. She moved her right hand over her left shoulder and discovered something protruding from her shoulder blade. Her initial reaction was to pull it out, but instinct guided her hand to move away before she acted on impulse. Taking a deep breath and gritting her teeth, she moved to a sitting position. Attempting to keep her voice even, to sound braver than she felt, she called out, "I'm Jillian, what's your name?"

"Cathy—Strickland. There's something heavy on my right leg. I can't move it."

Holding her left arm immobile, Jillian stood up on trembling legs. With caution, she moved in the direction of the voice, but the scattered rubble surrounding her blocked her path.

"Oh—I just felt a gush. I think my water broke."

"It's okay. I'm sure someone will come for us soon." Working hard to keep the sob in her throat from escaping, she sat down on the floor. Her head pounded as she held her arm close to her body. She couldn't focus on the pain; she had to remain calm.

The crying gnawed at Jillian's heart as she tried to assess their situation. And then Cathy screamed, claiming her full attention.

"What's wrong?"

Cathy sobbed. "That was—a hard contraction. I can't go into labor here."

In an authoritative voice she had used many times with her students, Jillian took command of the situation. "You've got to calm down."

"It—hurts so much." She screamed again.

"Take some deep breaths for me." Jillian wanted to go to her but it was too dangerous to move around in the dark.

"My baby's too small."

Jillian wanted to cry but knew she had to take hold of her emotions and figure out a plan. Hearing a loud sound in the distance, she jerked her head up from its bowed position, her eyes following in the direction of the sound as muffled voices reached her ears.

"Listen! Someone's coming. I told you someone would come."

Alan Armstrong sat in the back of the ambulance waiting for the area to be secured and deemed safe to enter. He had been assigned to accompany the first responders into what was left of the building that had housed a pharmacy. The trauma center had categorized the explosion a catastrophic event and sent a small team of medical personnel to the site to provide care to the victims ASAP.

While he had time to think, he questioned his motive for volunteering. When Franklin Witt had been approached to go and had hesitated, Alan had stepped up and volunteered. Being the newest trauma surgeon at Bradley Medical Center, he had wanted to show he was a team player. Or did he want to make Franklin look bad? He hadn't liked the guy from the first time he'd laid eyes on him. He preferred to think he was doing this to rack up as much trauma experience as possible, even better it was in the field. In a year or two, he wanted to find the right place where his skills would benefit a large rural area, where the need was greatest. His father would be alive today if he had received medical treatment sooner. But his plane had gone down in an area where there was no available doctor or hospital for miles, and his body had not been able to hold out for the help he needed to survive.

The waiting ended as the signal to proceed was given. *Please God, let there be survivors.* Alan would take injured patients over dead bodies any day. Securing his backpack in place, he followed the two men as they jumped from the ambulance. Tension he'd felt in his neck and shoulders as he had waited followed him into the hole of the mangled building. The team members picked their way through the rubble, creating a path for a quick return out, if needed. They moved deeper into the shell of the building left by the blast and heard a scream.

"Sounds like we have at least one patient. Can we move any faster?"

"No sir, we have to be careful so we won't get trapped in here too."

The screaming stopped. Alan wasn't sure what it meant. Moving at a snail's pace was a challenge as the familiar rush of adrenaline raced through his body, urging him to move faster. Another scream pierced the darkness.

"Come on, Mark, keep moving toward the screaming," said the lead EMT to his partner.

A female voice quavered, "Over here, please help us."

"Johnny, we need to split up. The screaming came from the right, and the voice came from over there to the left." Emphasizing his words, he pointed his flashlight to the left.

Alan's mind went into prioritizing mode. It was obvious he needed to go to the screaming patient first. "Who's moving toward the screaming? I'm going with you."

"Come on, Doc, you're with me. Mark, radio out to the captain and give him an update before you move ahead. And be careful."

"You too, man."

The EMTs lifted the stretcher into the back of the ambulance. Alan followed behind, jumping up into the narrow space. His patient cried out as another contraction racked her body. He was used to having more room in the trauma bay at the hospital. There was a sense of security working at the trauma center. All the latest technology was there in the form of sophisticated equipment and educated, skilled personnel who performed the tasks needed to stabilize a patient. But now it was just he and Johnny. Even in the January weather, he could feel sweat trickle down the center of his back.

"Ma'am, I know it's hard, but try to breathe with the contraction. You need to take control of the pain, and we're going to help you." Losing no time, he moved to her side and palpated her pulse, counting one hundred and twenty-six beats.

Johnny pumped up the cuff on her arm and listened for the thumping sound of her heartbeat as he measured her blood pressure. "BP is eighty-nine over forty-seven. There's an IV start kit in the compartment above my head. Fluids are to my right." He pointed while he gave directions.

A first responder ran up to the back of the ambulance. "Hey, Johnny, they're bringing out the other woman. She's ambulatory. Can we send her in with you?" Mark appeared with his arm around the woman's waist, moving her with caution toward the ambulance.

"Sure. Let's get her in so we can move." He reached down as Mark lifted her up to him. Her shoulder was jostled during the maneuver, and she cried out in pain. Johnny guided her to the bench against the right side of the ambulance's interior. "Will you be okay if I move over there to help the doc?"

"Yes, please help Cathy. I'll be okay."

The doors closed with a bang. Grabbing the edge of the shelf above her with her right hand, the woman shut her eyes as a double thump sounded on the window. With lights flashing and siren blaring, the ambulance driver sped off.

Alan glanced across his patient to make a visual assessment of the other woman. She had a gash on the right side of her forehead but seemed to be holding her own. Still he should have a closer look. "Let me know if her vitals change," he said to the EMT as he crossed the small space to the other woman.

Bending his knees, he steadied himself in front of her. The blood from the gash on her forehead had clotted. "How are you doing?"

Her eyelids fluttered upward and startling green eyes, the most gorgeous, green eyes he had ever seen, stared back at him. The churning of his stomach took him by surprise, causing a momentary lapse in his thought process. Running his hand through his hair, he gave himself time to redirect his mind to the emergent situation in the ambulance.

"I'm a doctor. Is it okay if I take a quick look at you?"

She consented with a nod of her head. "Is Cathy going to be alright?"

"I think she's in labor. We're just minutes away from the hospital, and we'll take good care of her. Let's concentrate on you." He flashed his penlight across her pupils and was relieved to see they were equal in size and reactive to the light. "Does your head hurt? Is your vision blurred?"

"My vision is fine, but my head is throbbing."

He moved her hand down from the shelf. He touched her shoulders to help her lie back on the bench seat, and she jerked away. "Please don't touch my shoulder." Her voice was shrill and the color of her face changed from pale to white. She crumpled forward, falling into Alan's chest.

The tight space of the ambulance kept him from losing his balance. "I'm sorry, but this may hurt. I need to determine the extent of your injury."

He touched her left shoulder, moving his hand down her back until he felt the protrusion from her scapula. Even though he used a careful approach, she cried out in pain, pulling away from him. Not wanting whatever was there to be pushed in any deeper, he gripped her arms to stop her from moving.

"Okay, I'm stopping. Let me help you lie back on this bench on your right side. Ready?" he asked as he moved her. Crying out again, her head rolled back as she lost consciousness. Alan noted she was breathing without difficulty. Passing out was a godsend, taking her away from her pain.

The pregnant patient claimed his attention when she moaned. "My poor, little baby." Another contraction started, and he heard her pull in a deep breath.

Alan remained at the green-eyed woman's side, pulling a belt across her abdomen to hold her in place on the bench. "Johnny, another blood pressure after the contraction passes," he called out.

"Hey, Doc, we've got a problem. BP is sixty-eight over twenty-nine." Alan heard a touch of panic in his voice.

He gave a quick glance at the patient on the bench then moved back to the stretcher. "All right, Cathy. Stay with me." Alan entered the zone, the place where he sought extreme mental focus on his objective. There was no one or nothing else in the zone, just Alan and his patient. His eyes became riveted on the body in front of him.

Cathy's face was ashen, her eyes bright. "I—can't—breathe." She closed her eyes, and her limp arm fell to the side of the stretcher.

Alan placed his index and middle fingers on her carotid artery. "No pulse. Start compressions." He opened the AED. They worked in synchronized motions without talking.

Alan called out, "Clear." He pushed the discharge button. Cathy's chest jumped forward from the shock. There was no response. "Clear." Her chest jumped again. Still no response. Alan clenched his jaw as thoughts of the worst possible outcome entered his mind. "Again, clear!"

Cathy's body rebounded back on the stretcher with a thump. Johnny moved his fingers upward and touched her neck. "I'm sorry, Doc. No pulse."

"Tell your driver to stop." With decisive movements, he unzipped his mobile trauma bag, and pulled out a kit of sterile instruments.

"We're a block away from the hospital. Why would we stop?"

"Tell him to stop *now* and put on some clean gloves. Our patient is gone, but we're going to try and save her baby."

The ambulance jerked to a stop. He knew the baby's best chance for survival was for it to be delivered within five minutes of initiating CPR, and he was running out of time. Alan made the first incision through the skin. There was no time for precision. His vertical movements were quick, slicing through the fat layer, fascia, and peritoneum. The objective was clear in his mind. Get to the uterus ASAP.

"Johnny, find the foil bag so we can keep this baby warm."

Stopping just long enough to take a deep breath, Alan made a careful cut along the uterus, hoping to avoid cutting the baby. He dropped the scalpel on Cathy's chest. Johnny moved it out of the way. Alan used his hands to tear apart the opening in his patient's abdomen. He reached in and pulled the baby out to its new, unpleasant, even harmful environment. He clamped the cord and watched for spontaneous breaths, but saw none. He cut the cord with a quick motion, and flipped the blue baby over to rub its back with a dry towel. Judging the weak cry, Alan knew the baby needed to pull more air into its lungs. He continued to rub, applying slightly more pressure and the cry became stronger as the baby's skin became pink.

"Let's move," shouted Alan as he handed the baby to Johnny. Slumping beside the stretcher, a painful lump rose in his throat. "I'm sorry," he murmured to his lifeless patient. He pulled the blanket over her exposed body.

Within minutes, the ambulance doors were opened by waiting hospital personnel. Alan jumped down, and gave an abbreviated report to the team reaching for the baby. As the stretcher bearing Cathy's body was removed from the ambulance, he ordered, "Wait over there," pointing to the left side of the vehicle. He watched as the green-eyed woman was placed on a stretcher. He quickened his pace to accompany his unconscious patient and motioned for the others to follow.

Once inside, Alan called to his coworker. "Ron, can you take over here? I need to go with my other patient."

"I'll handle this. Just do whatever you need to." Moving to the head of the stretcher, the tall, black doctor assumed the patient's care.

"I owe you," Alan said over his shoulder as he followed the charge nurse to the bay where Cathy's body was being taken.

"I'm sorry about your patient, Dr. Armstrong," said the nurse. "I'll keep you posted on how the baby's doing and let you know when we make contact with her next of kin."

Giving a dismissive nod, his eyes focused on the still, covered form on the stretcher. Weariness set in. With his back against the wall, Alan slid down on the floor and pulled his knees up to his chest. He grabbed his hair in clumps.

The frustration he always experienced when he lost a patient, made him replay the scene over and over in his mind. It felt surreal, but as he raised his head, one look at the stretcher brought his focus back to reality. He had done all that was humanly possible to save Cathy. It just hadn't been enough. He stood up and moved to the supply cabinet. The creaking of the glass door was the only sound in the room. Alan reached inside and pulled out several packs of suture. He removed the blanket from Cathy's body then began to sew her abdomen together. He wouldn't leave her body gaping open.

A patient care tech crept into the room. "Dr. Armstrong?"

"What is it?" he asked, without looking up from his task.

"I'm supposed to get the patient ready for her family."

Using meticulous skill, he pulled edges of skin together with a running stitch. "I'll be finished here in a few minutes, and then you can help me."

An hour later, Alan walked out of the trauma bay and pounded his fist against his thigh to keep from hitting the door. The man inside would remember this day forever. On this January day, his life had been turned upside down in a matter of hours. Leaving for work that morning, he had been married, on the verge of becoming a father, and now he was a widower with a preterm baby daughter in the NICU. Alan wondered again if he could have done something more to change the outcome. Deep down he knew the answer was no.

Alan sat down at a table in the back corner of the cafeteria. He took a drink of strong, hot coffee. The exhaustion brought with it a sense of déjà vu, memories of long shifts he had endured when he was an intern and during his residency.

He had been on shift about ten hours when he had volunteered to ride out to the explosion site with the first responders, about four or five hours ago. Alan was tired and knew if he sat too long, he would fall asleep. He also knew he should eat something, but the food on his plate remained untouched.

"I heard about your run today—sorry about your patient."

Looking up, Alan motioned to the chair across from him. "Hey, Tim, how's your day going?"

The anesthesiologist sat down. "*Hmph.* Better than yours, I'm sure. Think you can chalk this one up as the toughest day you've had here at Bradley Medical?"

"Professionally, I think it ranks as my toughest day ever." He took a tasteless bite of his sandwich. "Hey, you were in the ER this morning. Can you tell me what happened to the other woman we brought in with my deceased patient? She was unconscious when they moved her from the ambulance."

"It was pretty chaotic for a while. Which one was she?"

"Left scapula injury, a gash on her right temple." He stared across the room, not focusing on anything in particular. "She has green eyes—beautiful, green eyes."

"What? No hair color, no measurements?"

Alan glared at his friend. "I was focused on Mrs. Strickland the majority of the time."

"But you were still able to notice the beautiful, green eyes of another patient. I'm impressed."

Alan stood up and reached for his tray.

Tim laid a hand on his arm. "Just trying to lighten things up."

Alan settled back down into his chair.

"Check around with the nurses. They might be able to help you find your mystery patient. It's sad about Mr. Mancini. He was such a nice man. My wife and I went to his restaurant on our first date. Taking her to a place with ambiance and wine, I guess I was trying to impress her. We met Mr. Mancini that night, and we've been going back there for twelve years. I was listening to the news earlier, and they said the cause of the explosion is still under investigation, but they suspect a gas leak of some kind." He sighed. "Break time's over. I've got to head back to the OR, but I'll leave you with this. It all balances out. You can't always win."

"Are you talking medicine or life?"

"Both. Hope you find your lady with the green eyes. Got to go."

Alan sipped his coffee as the overhead paged blared, "Dr. Armstrong to the ER—Dr. Armstrong to the ER."

Alan pushed through the doors marked *Staff Only*, hurrying up to the main desk with a sense of urgency. "Someone paged me."

The blond-haired nurse at the desk stood up. "Dr. Armstrong, you're needed in trauma room two."

He nodded and moved down the corridor. Pushing the curtain aside he asked, "What's the problem?"

"This is Ms. Russell, a victim from the explosion. Dr. Compton asked me to page you when he was called away to a code. The CT scan of her head was negative, and the x-ray of her shoulder is on the counter. He was just about to assess her wound when the code was called."

The patient faced the opposite wall, but Alan recognized the wound. A jolt zipped through his body. A slight smile played on his lips. He had found his mystery patient.

He walked around to the other side of the stretcher. "Ms. Russell, I'm Dr. Armstrong. I'm not sure if you remember, but I was in the ambulance with you."

The eyes that met his gaze were cold, her words staccato. "I remember."

Rubbing the back of his neck, he questioned her demeanor in silence. "I need to take a look at your shoulder again so we can decide what to do." He performed a quick assessment, but as before, the pain made her cry out. Turning to the nurse he said, "Give her five milligrams of morphine while we wait for an OR."

"Five milligrams of morphine," she repeated. "I'll be right back."

Alan picked up the x-ray and pushed it against the wall-mounted light box. "You have a piece of metal jammed against your shoulder blade. You're lucky it didn't shatter the bone."

The nurse returned and pushed the morphine into the patient's IV line. "This case is scheduled in OR ten. They're cleaning it as we speak."

Alan handed the chart to the nurse. "I've written some pre-op orders." Circling back around to face the patient, he said, "We'll be taking you to the OR soon to fix your shoulder."

He focused on her eyes, the green irises already appearing glassy from the medication. Still, he was drawn to them. She closed her eyes without answering.

Walking out the door he said, "Page me when the OR is ready."

Two

Jillian's attention darted to her hospital room door. The knock was followed by the entrance of the one person she didn't want to see. The doctor from yesterday, the one with the rough hands.

"Good morning, Ms. Russell. How are you feeling today?"

Her knee-jerk reaction to his presence made her shift away from the handsome man as he approached the bed. "I don't want to see you. My shoulder hurts enough without you touching it again."

His forehead creased into a frown. "The morphine's not controlling your pain?" He pressed the nurse call light.

"I didn't say the pain medicine isn't helping."

A knock sounded, and the nurse stepped into the room. "Did you need something? Oh, Dr. Armstrong, I didn't know you were here for rounds."

"We may need to increase the morphine dose on Ms. Russell's pump."

"*Excuse me.* I was saying the pain medicine helps. I just don't want you to touch my shoulder. In fact, can I have another doctor assigned to me? In a hospital this size there's got to be another doctor who can take care of me."

The wounded expression on his face made her realize she had done it again—speaking without thinking. He was probably a competent doctor who hadn't meant to hurt her during his examinations yesterday. But she couldn't take back her words.

The nurse moved toward the door. "Dr. Armstrong, may I see you outside please?" Addressing Jillian, she said, "I'll be back soon."

Jillian settled on her right side and drew in a cleansing breath. Just talking about her pain seemed to make it more evident. Pushing the button on the morphine pump, she closed her eyes, waiting for the relief it would bring.

She supposed she should be grateful the doctor had been with the EMTs to take care of her and Cathy. He seemed nice enough. But each time he had examined her shoulder, he had caused her so much pain, she couldn't let him touch her again. Another doctor was a good idea.

She wondered how Cathy was doing, if her baby had been born. Shifting against the pillow for a more comfortable position, she thought about asking the nurse to take her to Cathy's room so she could check on her. The morphine was making her drowsy. So maybe she would ask later.

⁓

Wearing a frown, Alan followed the nurse into the nurses' station. "I don't understand why she's being so obstinate about her treatment."

"At least she's not refusing treatment. She just wants another doctor."

"I'll turn her care over to Dr. Witt and make the call now."

Alan pulled his cell phone out of his pocket, settling into a chair as he tapped the screen of his phone. He would prefer to hand her over to someone else, but Dr. Witt was the on-call physician for the day.

"Franklin, Alan Armstrong. I need a favor. I've got a patient requesting a different doctor. Last name is Russell, and she's in Room G54."

"What's the problem?"

"I guess you could call it a personality conflict. Can you add her to your patient list? I didn't have the chance to assess her before she asked for someone else."

"I'm almost finished with my rounds. I'll be by soon."

"Thanks, Franklin. I appreciate it."

"Don't worry, I'll remember this the next time I need a favor."

"I'm sure you will." *Jerk.*

Opening the chart labeled *Russell, Jillian G54*, he flipped to the progress notes section and paused before writing a single word. *What did I do to make her so upset with me?* His cell phone vibrated in his pocket.

A smile encompassed his face as he read the text message. *I'm in labor. Sometime today you'll become an uncle.*

His mind shifted to the task at hand. The sooner he entered his progress note, the sooner he could turn Jillian Russell's chart over to Franklin. He'd have preferred to follow her case through, until she was discharged from the hospital. But patients have a say in their care and who provides the care, so he had to let go. It would have been a challenge to spend time with the beautiful, green-eyed woman. He liked challenges. Sighing, he began to write.

Even though his morning and afternoon had been hectic, Alan walked with a bounce in his step, navigating the hallway of the labor and delivery unit. He gave a knock before pushing on the door of the hospital room. His sister, Jenny, held her newborn son against her chest while he dozed. Mark, his brother-in-law, snapped pictures of the new addition to the family.

"Look at you. You're a mom! How are you doing?" He kissed her on the top of her head. And then he frowned. "Are you in pain? I can make it better."

"Alan, I'm fine. I couldn't be any better. The epidural worked great and hasn't worn off, so I'm good."

Alan turned to his brother-in-law and gave him a hearty slap on the back. "You're one lucky man. First you sweep away my beautiful sister, and now you've got this handsome guy," he said, touching the sleeping baby's soft hand.

As happy as he was for Jenny and Mark, thoughts of Cathy Strickland crept into his head. It would take time for him to be able to push her death into the recesses of his mind and lock it away. He believed things happened for a reason. That yesterday had just been some random act with devastating consequences was not a possibility in his thought process. There was a reason—and he might never know what it was—Cathy Strickland hadn't survived the explosion. And there was a reason he had crossed paths with Jillian yesterday and then was pulled away from her today.

Alan stood beside the labor bed, staring down at his nephew. He touched his soft cheek with his thumb, glad his nephew's entrance into the world had been more gentle and serene than the baby girl's delivery had been yesterday.

"You know, if you want one of these little guys, you need to start dating. You've had about a year to settle into your job, now I'm going to start pushing."

"Jenny, don't turn into Mom. I left New York because she became too stifling after Dad died. And my time here is temporary. You know I'll be moving on in a year or two. Even if I wanted to date, I don't need your help. Besides, David Kennedy has been trying to push some redhead on me."

"You've never dated a redhead. Good for David. I'm glad Mark introduced you when you moved here."

He remained silent, his eyes focused on his nephew.

"Oh, Alan, shake things up and live a little. *Date the redhead.*"

"We'll see. I've got to go, time for rounds. He reached for her free hand and kissed it. I'll check on you later but call me if you need anything at all."

"Thanks. Love you, big brother."

Three

The sofa in Jillian's office was covered with pillows and a fluffy comforter. "Barbara Ann Brooks, please stop fussing over me like a mother hen."

"I will not. It's been two weeks since—"

"It's okay, you can say it. I'm not going to fall apart. It's been two weeks since the explosion."

"Right, I'm going to make sure you rest in the middle of the day until you're released from your doctor's care." In a quiet voice she added, "I don't know what I'd do if anything happened to you. You're my best friend."

Her injuries had become inconsequential once she found out Cathy had died. Thinking about it now made her shiver. Pushing her thoughts of Cathy aside, she focused on her friend.

"It's okay, Barb. I just happened to be in the wrong place at the wrong time. I'm healing just fine. Look." She moved her left arm up and down, careful not to wince but wanting to put her mind at ease. "I'm more concerned about this huge scar on my forehead. I hope it fades over time."

Barbara continued to glare at her.

"You win. I'll rest for thirty minutes, but I'm teaching my class this afternoon."

"The scar's not so big. Now remember, the doctor said fatigue can bring on your migraines again. So, forty-five minutes every afternoon, or you won't be allowed to stay for rehearsal tomorrow night."

Jillian sighed. "Yes, mother hen, you push a hard bargain." Her lips curved into a smile. She settled back against the pillows and pulled the comforter up to her waist. It felt good to have someone care. She'd been careful to keep people at a distance after moving to Charlotte six years ago. Everyone of importance had abandoned her at some point in her life through desertion or death. Mother, Father, Grandmother, even her husband and child—gone.

And then last year her best friend from childhood moved from Dixon to Charlotte. Barbara was a phenomenal assistant who usually knew when Jillian needed her space. Though she closed her eyes, her thoughts refused to be quieted. What other things did she miss? She missed performing. To be so good at something then to have it ripped out of her life! Would she ever find the same satisfaction as when she executed a stunning *grand jete* or a *pirouette a la seconde?* She had hoped so, but in six years' time, it hadn't happened.

The explosion had rocked her world in both the figurative and literal sense. In the last two weeks her thoughts gravitated to the loneliness of her personal life she had allowed to occur. For the first time since moving to Charlotte, Jillian allowed herself to dwell on the sadness of her life. It was time to let it go. But it would mean pulling down the barriers she had placed around her to keep her heart safe. She didn't know if she could do it.

※

Alan pulled his black SUV into a parking space near the entrance to the North Carolina Ballet Company. Several of the old cotton mill buildings in this part of the city had been brought back to life and caused much excitement to the surrounding community. The Highland, Mecklenburg, and Johnston mills had all been converted to apartments, condos, and townhouses. These renovations had infused the area with new residents, which in turn had spurred the revitalization process.

The area now boasted art galleries, music venues, restaurants, and the home of the North Carolina Ballet Company.

On the drive to the studio, Alan had paused at the intersection of North Davidson and East Thirty-Sixth Street, admiring the muted red, green, orange, and purple buildings. Though the paint added a new dimension to the buildings, it did not detract from the original brickwork or the history behind the buildings' existence. He was pleased the ballet company was located in the historic arts district of NoDa, short for North Davidson, just two miles from downtown Charlotte. The recent articles and local media attention updating the project had been free publicity for the company.

Alan shut off the motor and stared ahead. The two-story structure in front of him had no doubt once housed a textile or cotton mill. It had long windows, about eight feet in length with rounded arches across their tops. The blinds were open and gave a nice view of the class in progress. Little ballerinas-in-training appeared to be five or six years old, he couldn't say for sure. He strained to make out the features of the redheaded woman at the far end of the room and thought about getting out of his SUV for a closer look. But he didn't want to be branded a Peeping Tom this first trip to the studio.

Alan believed in supporting the arts. He'd seen his parents' copious donations of time and money to many organizations and knew he had inherited his sense of civic responsibility from them. So when David told him about a vacancy on the board of the North Carolina Ballet Company—and by coincidence the owner was also the redhead he wanted to introduce him to—Alan had been intrigued. His schedule at the hospital had been time-consuming, the first six months in particular. But now he felt he could slow down a little. His reputation as a skilled trauma surgeon was established, and it was time to put his personal life under a microscope.

The vacancy had been unexpected and needed to be filled right away. Board members were volunteers with plenty of work to go around, so losing one was sure to put a hardship on the other members' spare time. But it wasn't until

David mentioned the name, Jillian Russell, that his interest was altogether engaged. So he'd given in to David's request that he join the board, killing two birds with one stone. He could support the arts and maybe he could get to know this green-eyed woman. Acting in the capacity of board member would enable him to interact with Jillian. Then maybe she'd agree he was an okay guy. If she didn't agree, then their relationship would remain on a civic level.

It was forty-seven degrees outside, according to the radio announcer. David's gray coupe pulled in beside him. Alan's mouth formed a half-smile. He had met David right after moving to Charlotte. Who knew the man he'd picked as his financial advisor would become such a good friend. The feeling of camaraderie he remembered having with his fraternity brothers and also with the students in med school surfaced soon after they'd met.

Alan exited the warmth of his SUV. A gust of wind hit him from behind. Winter was his least favorite season, and the promise of spring was weeks away. He flipped the collar of his jacket up as he greeted David. "Hey, man. So, we have to do this?"

"It's unfortunate, but we have to—bad news should be given in person. Being a doctor, you should know this."

Alan moved toward the building and wondered how she would react to their news. The loss of federal grant money would place a hardship on the company's finances. He couldn't relate—money had never been an issue for him or his family, for which he was grateful. He had gone to the best schools and moved in an upper class social circle his whole life. If he performed an honest assessment of himself, he'd admit to having been somewhat spoiled in his youth. Becoming a doctor had revealed a side of him that, as a teenager, had been hidden. Part of the reason he was successful was because he cared about the whole patient, trying to make each of their lives better, not just resolving their medical issues.

At age thirty-six, Alan remained single by choice. He enjoyed the company of women. The steady stream of blondes and brunettes through his life over the past several years had attested the fact. But none of these women had captured his heart like Reagan Whitmore, his first love. And he had been careful not to mislead them into thinking he wanted anything more than the moment at hand. Also, the death of his father had pushed his life in a direction, which was not conducive to family life.

Moving toward the studio, he said, "Let's do this." He opened the door, and they stepped inside.

The reception area was warm and welcoming, a sharp contrast to the cold outside. A light smell of vanilla wafted through the air. Original brick walls had been painted white. Black frames held pictures of famous dancers: Nureyev, Fonteyn, Baryshnikov, Pavlova, as well as others. The wall collage was a mixture of artists in full costume in performance posture and artists in rehearsal attire, their focus intent on polishing their craft. An attempt to inspire the students was apparent to Alan as he glanced around the walls. These pictures brought back memories of his sister, Jenny. In particular, the first costume she'd worn, which, in his mind, had transformed her from a dance student into a ballerina.

David stepped inside behind Alan. He rubbed his hands together and moved toward the reception desk. "Hey, Barbara, is Jillian in her office?"

"She's just finishing a class in Studio A."

"This is Alan Armstrong, our new board member. Alan, this is Barbara, Jillian's assistant."

Barbara's eyes sparkled with warmth. "Hello, Mr. Armstrong. It's nice to meet you."

Alan nodded. "Please, call me Alan."

"Come this way, Alan." David moved to the left of Barbara's desk.

"Nice meeting you," Alan called out as he followed David through the door. They stopped at the studio door, watching parents and little ballerinas flood the hallway in a mass exodus from Studio A.

"Here we go." David moved ahead with determination to do his job, his lips pulled together in a thin line.

※

Jillian lingered behind, thinking about her students. This was the best group of seven-year olds she had taught since opening the school. She enjoyed teaching all ages, but this group was the highlight of her week. Sighing, she wondered if maybe it had something to do with the fact Lily would have been seven this year. Brushing the thought away, she moved to the piano and focused her attention on arranging the music for the dance company's rehearsal the next night.

Her school of ballet was impressive, but her dance company was her crowning glory. Expanding her lungs to their fullest she exhaled, feeling a sense of pride and accomplishment. The North Carolina Ballet Company, now in its fifth year of existence, continued to experience growing pains and would for several years to come. As they grew in number, they also grew in depth and dimension, becoming a cohesive group of artists excited to tell many stories through dance. Their progress was measured by the reputation they enjoyed for offering professional performances to the surrounding communities.

"You have a good-looking group of ballerinas, Jilly," remarked David as he crossed the studio floor, followed by Alan.

The familiar voice brought a smile to her face. She had met David soon after moving to Charlotte when she was searching for a financial advisor. They had spent a lot of time together working on the financial end of setting up her school. When she took the plunge a year later, with David's encouragement, and started the North Carolina Ballet Company, he'd been her biggest fan. Feeling she could trust him with her life, she was grateful he had accepted her invitation to be a part of the company's initial board of directors.

Turning around at the sound of the tenor voice, her eyes darted from her friend to the familiar form standing beside him. Her smile disappeared.

"You!" Jillian took a step back. "What are you doing here?"

"What's wrong?" David's gaze bounced back and forth between his friends. "Do you two know each other?"

Her eyes remained fixed on the doctor as if she were seeing him for the first time. He was tall, about six feet she estimated, with thick brown hair, and he had the most gorgeous, deep-set brown eyes. It was like looking into pools of chocolate, and she was finding it hard not to stare. She shifted her gaze to her friend. "I recall seeing him at the hospital, after the explosion."

"Oh, come on, Ms. Russell. I performed the surgery on your shoulder and I was your doctor for two days—until you fired me. And all you have to say is, 'I recall seeing you'?"

"If memory serves, it was a day and a half. And I'd prefer not talking about anything having to do with the explosion, if you don't mind."

"I see. Well, I hope your recovery is going well."

"Yes it is, thank you."

Narrowing his eyes at Jillian, David stepped forward. "Jilly, I'd like to introduce our newest member of the board, Alan Armstrong, in case you forgot his name. Maybe you should start over, like you've never met."

She shot a look to kill at David. *Well, I can play this game.* Smiling she extended her hand in the doctor's direction. "Mr. Armstrong, a pleasure." Taking her hand, he executed a firm shake. An electric jolt shot up her arm when he touched her skin. Her heart raced as he stared into her green eyes.

He nodded and replied, "Ms. Russell."

Uncomfortable with the proximity of their bodies, she moved to the opposite side of the piano, hoping to break the connection she was feeling. "Just how did you end up on the board of my dance company?"

Alan propped his arm on top of the piano. "David has mentioned your company several times over the past few months. When the vacancy on the board presented itself, he convinced me I could be of service to the community if I agreed to fill the position."

David interrupted and in a serious tone asked, "Do you have a few minutes to talk business with us?"

"I don't know, David, do you? As I recall, you're getting married in about ten days. Shouldn't your time be filled with wedding business instead of your volunteer work? And besides it's been a long day."

Putting his arm around her shoulder, he said, "You're starting to ramble and you look tired. I'm sure it has been a long day because your days are always long. Have you been resting enough during your recovery?"

"You don't have to worry about that. Barb has been watching me like a hawk, to the point of timing my afternoon naps."

"Good." He shook a finger close to her face and added, "You work too hard and play too little. But this business shouldn't wait." A frown creased his forehead as he spoke.

"I don't like the sound of this. Let's walk back to my office." She gathered her sweater and stack of papers then led them down the hallway. All she had to offer was bottled water. She should have restocked the refrigerator, but it wasn't a priority. There was always so much to be done.

"There's water in the fridge," she said, pointing to the corner of the room across from her desk. "Help yourself while I change into my street clothes. Sorry I can't offer you something else," trailed her voice as she hurried away. Within minutes she entered the office and sat down behind her desk.

"Hmm—expeditious," observed Alan. He sat down in one of the chairs facing her desk.

"Quick change, I've been doing it for years backstage. I guess you could call it an occupational talent." Leaning forward, her elbows resting on the desk, she readied herself for the newest obstacle facing the company's survival. "Okay, David, what's up?"

He cleared his throat, "As you know, the state of the economy is in a mess, has been for a while. We got a notice yesterday—federal funding for performing art groups like ours is being suspended."

"How long is the suspension?"

"Indefinite, we lose our funding at the end of the season."

She sat for a moment, staring at the large blank wall opposite her desk. She stood up. Panic edged into her voice. "But David, without federal funding our finances will be in a precarious position." The pitch of her voice rose as she continued. "Worst-case scenario I might even have to shut down the company." Jillian plopped back down in her chair, and placed her elbows on the desk. She ran her fingers through her curly, red hair, revealing the scar on her temple. Jillian massaged her temples, willing the tears welling up behind her eyes to stay put as she let the full weight of the news sink in.

"Now Jilly, why do you always focus on the worst-case scenario? Let's take this one step at a time and see what can be worked out."

"I just thought we were getting to the point where I had a shot at working on the art and not worrying about necessary things like money." The trio fell silent for several minutes. "Well, if I don't take a sleeping pill tonight, I'm going to have the cleanest home on my street by morning."

Looking at Alan, David explained, "She cleans when she's stressed."

"I suppose there are more harmful ways to de-stress, and being clean is a positive thing." He shrugged and raised his eyebrows.

Jillian sighed, "Maybe I should stay here tonight, and then we can take the cleaning crew off our budget." The men remained silent.

"Good grief, boys, I'm just kidding, and besides, I've decided in favor of a sleeping pill, so I'm going home."

Alan stood up. "Well I'm up for a challenge. Let's plan a brainstorming session, maybe in the next few days. We'll come up with some ideas to deal with the loss of funding."

With a pensive look, Jillian replied, "Sounds great, Alan, but somebody in this room is getting married, and I don't think he should be focused on anything but his wedding. However I'm willing to pick your brain." *Let's see if you're qualified to be a board member.*

"Hey," said David, "I may be getting married, but I can answer for myself. I've done everything my bride has instructed me to do, so I'm good to go."

"Terrific, but you'd better check with Ann first." Jillian stood up and massaged the back of her neck, hoping to rub away some of the tension. Turning toward Alan, she said, "I bet you didn't think you'd be jumping onto a sinking ship when you agreed to come aboard."

"No worries, I'm always looking for a chance to be a knight in shining armor for a beautiful damsel in distress," he said, bowing low with a playful grin on his face.

Jillian laughed, "You're not serious! A bit of advice—don't give up your day job for acting."

"I admit it, I've done theater. The line was from a character I portrayed—in the seventh grade. My mother was proud of my performance." He ended with a laugh. The tension in the air dissipated.

"I'm tired, so if you'll walk me to my car, I think I'll go home and take something to help me sleep. David, call me later this week with a time for our meeting."

They paused at the door to set the alarm and turn out the lights. When they reached her car, David opened the door. Touching her shoulders, he stopped her from getting inside.

"You've worked hard these past six years."

She nodded, afraid if she tried to respond the tears would come.

"Well, my friend, no one will ever be able to say you haven't suffered for your art. We'll jump this hurdle too." She responded with a weak smile as he kissed her forehead.

"Good night guys." She slid behind the wheel and, looking up at them, smiled. "Thanks for the support."

David and Alan watched as she pulled out of the parking lot onto the street. Alan's gaze remained on the street long after her car disappeared. Turning to face his friend, he said, "Beautiful, and a temper to match her red hair."

"I've known her for six years. I've seen her upset, but never seen a temper tantrum. For a while I wasn't so sure we weren't heading in that direction at the beginning of our encounter tonight."

"Things calmed down, but we'll see how the next meeting goes." They walked toward the cars.

"So, you fixed her shoulder."

"Yep, just doing my job."

"I was out of town when the explosion happened. I'm glad you were there for Jillian. You're a good doctor, and she's a good friend—so I'm glad you were there."

Alan opened the door to his SUV and paused. "So what else can you tell me about Jillian Russell?"

"Don't you think it'll be more interesting finding out on your own?" The corners of his mouth stretched into a grin. "You know, Alan, dating is not a bad thing. Sometimes it can even turn into a wonderful, permanent situation. I will clue you in on one thing. I've never known Jilly to be a damsel in distress. She's a strong woman."

Jillian pulled the covers over her shoulders, up under her chin, and closed her eyes. Even with the exhaustion from her long day, sleep did not come. Her mind wouldn't shut down. She shifted to her right side and placed a pillow between her knees. *How could all my hard work hit a dead end?* The last six years had been a struggle, but she had welcomed the work and the distraction it brought from her tragic personal life. It had consumed her energy and time, leaving nothing with which to pursue a social life. Until tonight, that had been okay.

Agitation claimed her attention, and she punched her pillow. She had met someone tonight, and it had reminded her of the deep thoughts she'd had after the explosion—about letting go of her grief and pulling down barriers. How could she make it work? For sure, they had started out on the wrong foot. After all, she had fired him as her doctor. But now that he was a board member, she could get to know him from a different perspective. A premonitory feeling gave question to how their lives might become intertwined. She shuddered.

Unable to relax, Jillian got up and went to the kitchen. She thought about taking the sleeping pill she had mentioned earlier, but instead put the kettle on the stove for tea. She stepped into the living area and focused her attention on the pictures interspersed between books and awards arranged on the bookcase.

She pulled her robe around her to keep the chilly air from sending her back to her covers. She picked up a picture frame from the shelf then sat down on the sofa as her mind drifted. Her grandmother, who had raised her from the age of ten, had died during Thanksgiving break of Jillian's last semester at The University of North Carolina at Charlotte. She had been twenty-two at the time. Agnes Russell had supported and encouraged Jillian's pursuit of ballet. And she had been Jillian's last link to family since her father's death three years prior.

Edward Russell, Jillian's father, was the reason Agnes had assumed a day-to-day role in Jillian's upbringing. He'd been a researcher absorbed in his work, and even when he'd been physically present with Jillian, he'd checked out mentally, always thinking about his work. She had often wondered if he had been thinking about his work when the car crash taking his life had occurred.

The kettle whistled. Jillian returned to the kitchen and poured water over the tea bag. She sat down, and her thoughts continued while she sipped chamomile tea from her grandmother's pretty porcelain cup.

    She had been sad when her father died, sad for him. They had never had a normal father-daughter relationship, and he had died not knowing what he had missed, but not so for her. She had listened to other girls and their stories, had watched other girls interact with their fathers, and she knew she had been cheated out of something wonderful. She had also missed out on having a mother in her life, but she wouldn't think about her tonight.

    She stood up and carried her cup to the sink then walked toward her bedroom, her thoughts turning to Alan. He had caught her eye, appearing confident, even determined, to resolve her financial debacle. Her long-term goal for her company was to be sought out, a place where talented artists could grow and thrive in their profession. David and the other board members would have to find a way to keep them funded. Failure was not an option as far as she was concerned. At the age of thirty-two, she had experienced professional disappointment and the loss of family as well. She was turning her life around, was proud of what she had accomplished since moving to Charlotte. She was not going down without a fight!

    Alan was attractive and also amusing. Smiling, she remembered how he had bantered with her. *And his lips, how delicious. Wow—why am I thinking about his lips?* She had taken a hiatus from her personal life far too long, and tonight a desire had awakened inside of her. After six years of loneliness, maybe it was time to reclaim the part of her life she had put to rest. But she didn't even know where to begin.

Four

It had been four days since David had dropped the bombshell. Since then, Jillian had been working hard to keep her anxiety at bay so she would have a clear mind to continue her work at the studio. The funding for their future might be drying up, but the expenses for the *Cinderella* production were covered, so the show must go on. She focused her thoughts to brainstorming. The ideas they compiled today could become a means to stabilize the future of the company. Only then would she be able to turn her full attention to teaching and working with the company artists.

Jillian took extra care with her hair and makeup. The pile of clothes on her bed was evidence she was having a difficult time choosing the right outfit. She decided on a mushroom-colored cashmere sweater. It hugged her body from the v-neck down to the ribbed trim around the bottom edge. She chose a brown tweed pencil skirt with brown tall boots to finish the ensemble, chiding herself for putting such effort into getting dressed for a business meeting. Even though she wasn't willing to admit it to herself, deep down she knew the reason for such attention to detail.

Concentrating on building her business the past six years, she'd had no time to think about men or feelings or desire. Meeting Alan the other night as Mr. Armstrong, the civic volunteer, not Dr. Armstrong, had stirred sensations that had been buried too deep for too long. It was as if she had been slumbering for the past six years and was given a sudden awakening by Prince Charming. Smiling at the analogy, she remembered *The Sleeping Beauty* was one of the ballets on the pick list for next fall's performance. She was certain she wanted to spend time getting to know him. But as she took a last look in the mirror, she frowned, knowing she had no spare time to put toward that endeavor.

Sighing, she pushed her arms into her coat, picked up her handbag, and stepped outside. The winter air was crisp but pleasant. There was no bothersome wind whipping about today. The sky was a gorgeous blue without a cloud to be seen. It was like looking at a blank canvas waiting for the artist's brush. During the drive to the restaurant, she listened to the first movement of Beethoven's *Pathetique Piano Sonata*, choreographing moves in her head as she drove. *I guess I'm not much different from my dad. Ballet to me is like research was to him. It's always in my thoughts. It's my life.*

Jillian walked into the restaurant, and a tingle of excitement ran up her spine as she anticipated seeing Alan. She was also eager to get started with plans to ensure the survival of her company. The raw feelings she had experienced the past few days made her determined to do whatever it would take to keep her company afloat. The hostess led her toward the back of the restaurant. It was quiet in the back, with less foot traffic, a good place for a working lunch.

Alan stood up as she walked toward him, their eyes locking on one another. She returned a smile taking in the handsome man standing before her. He appeared relaxed and comfortable in his jeans, light blue shirt open at the collar, and sports coat. He had a light growth of stubble on his face that made him look sexier than she remembered. She was glad she had put the extra time and effort into her appearance.

He pulled out her chair. "Jillian, I'm glad you're here."

Looking up at him, she said, "Thank you, Alan. I'm glad to be here." He settled in the seat across from her and she asked, "Is David running late? He's always on time."

"Didn't he send you a text? He wanted me to know he had a wedding emergency and wasn't going to make it to lunch."

Jillian frowned. "I knew he didn't need to add any extra to his plate, this week of all weeks, and now we're down by one brain. It's got to affect our work today." She began digging through her handbag for her phone and came up empty. "Great, I left my phone on the charger at home. I guess I'll see his text later."

Alan's phone rang. Looking at the screen, he said, "It's David. Please excuse me for a moment." He stood up and politely walked away from the table.

Jillian pulled a small spiral notebook and pen from her handbag. She didn't like wasting time, and she had come up with some new ideas while listening to the piano sonata. She was jotting them down when Alan returned.

Glancing up, she asked, "Everything alright?"

"Yes, but I think he'd rather be here with us than involved with wedding drama." Alan motioned to the pad. "Starting without me?"

"No, I'm just writing down some choreography I dreamed up on the drive here. If you'll excuse me, I'm going to the ladies' room. I won't be long," she said as she stood up. In a causal fashion, Jillian walked toward the ladies' room until she was out of his sight then blew out a big breath. She pushed open the bathroom door. *Why did David have to ditch on me today?*

Feeling flustered by the less-than-ideal situation, she wasn't sure if she could make it through lunch alone with this handsome stranger. She knew nothing about him, and she was so out of practice being alone with the opposite sex. If her life continued with all the stress she'd been experiencing, it was possible she'd need anti-anxiety medication. *Come on, Jillian, he's just a man, a gorgeous hunk of a man.* Looking in the mirror, she took some deep breaths. Every hair in place, no lipstick smudges. She pushed the door open and headed back to the table.

Alan stood up as she approached and held out her chair again. "Well, I say we go ahead with our meeting, but let's order first—I'm starving. I've been up most of the night."

"You couldn't sleep?" she asked, picking up her menu.

"No, I was working."

Folding her hands on the table and tilting her head she said, "Don't tell me you work twenty-four-seven."

"No, thank goodness. When I moved to Charlotte last year, the medical center had just been designated a Level Two trauma center and was hiring additional staff. I was lucky enough to land a day-shift position. I guess the timing was right. My sister, Jenny, lives here with her husband and infant son. And I was looking for a new start."

"So why were you working last night?"

"One of the docs on the night shift is on paternity leave, so I'm helping out."

"How generous of you."

"I think it's important for a man to have time with his newborn baby, if he wants it. And I want as much trauma experience as I can get in the next year or two. So we both win."

She sipped her water. "Oh? What happens after you get your experience?"

"I plan to leave Charlotte, when the time is right, and move to a remote area somewhere on the east coast to provide medical care where there's a greater need."

"I see." The tenseness in her stomach that had assaulted her in the ladies' room, and had started to recede, flared up again. She had to work at keeping the disappointment out of her voice. "So you have your whole life planned out."

"No. I just think you have to set goals, have something to aim for."

Jillian wanted to hear more about Alan's life, but she didn't want to get too personal with him. If she asked questions, he'd probably ask her personal questions. And she wasn't ready to part with any details of her past, especially to a new acquaintance. Besides, she was eager to hear his ideas for securing her company's future. She picked up her pen to initiate the business portion of their meeting. "So, Mr. Armstrong, what ideas do you have for saving my company?" she asked.

"Off the top of my head, I'd say we need more personalized community involvement. You've got good support from the business sector, but for your company to become an institution in Charlotte, you've got to capture people's hearts and their money."

"How do you propose I do that?"

"Make it tangible. Get them involved beyond just writing a check. Sign up volunteers to come in and work with the costumes, the props, et cetera."

Jillian frowned. "I'm not sure I like the idea of just anyone having access to the studio and the artists."

"Screening the applicants is a must. I've seen it done elsewhere, and the help they provide is amazing. We need to advertise, maybe something like this." He took the paper and pen out of her hand.

Get Involved
Make it Personal
Become the Heart of
THE NORTH CAROLINA BALLET COMPANY
Apply to Volunteer Today!

Tapping the pen against the table, he said, "It could use an artist's touch. Maybe some hearts or flowers and such, but you get the idea."

"Yeah, I'll get one of the volunteers right on it."

"All right—an attempt at humor. Take some time to think about it, let it grow on you. Hey, I do have some good news. I have my first official duty as board member."

Jillian picked up a piece of bread, "I love good news."

"The call from David was to ask me to make contact with a potential contributor." He pulled up a screen on his smartphone. "A Ms. Audrey Harris. She wants to meet and discuss a donation. David will be tied up for about three weeks with his wedding and honeymoon, so he asked me to step up and be the contact person."

"Alan that's great. I don't mean to be crass, but maybe she's a recent widow and wants to make a large donation."

He gave a solid laugh, "Aren't you the sensitive type." He paused while the waitress refilled his tea glass. "Since I'm new to North Carolina, sell me on why I should want to support the arts through your dance company. Give me some history I can share with Ms. Harris."

Jillian leaned forward, and pulled in a breath. "I moved to Charlotte six years ago from Dixon, North Carolina. Dixon is about two hours north of here. I wanted to start a dance company, and I felt I could be more successful in a metropolitan city." She left out personal details like she had no remaining family and wanted a fresh start in a new location. But she wasn't new to Charlotte because she had attended The University of North Carolina, receiving her bachelor's degree in dance.

Leaning back in her chair, she continued, "I began with the dance school, which was well received. My second year I started the dance company. Over the last four years, I've added additional dancers, and we're still growing. I want the *corps de ballet* to have more dancers, and we also need to build our number of soloists. Years out, I even want to have our own live orchestra."

Alan whistled. "Wow, you have some big plans running through your pretty head."

Jillian raised an eyebrow. "I've always said if you're going to dream, then dream big."

He moved his salad bowl aside. "I've been doing some thinking the last couple of days, and I've come up with an idea to help make all of what you just said come true. But I don't want you to freak out."

Jillian laid her fork down and gave Alan her undivided attention. She focused on his eyes, gleaming with excitement. "Okay, let's hear it."

"A huge, fundraising event, a black-tie affair. You need to announce to the elite of Charlotte, and hey, the whole state, you are ready to accept their generosity in helping to put North Carolina on the map as a major player in the world of ballet."

Her eyes widened. "Alan, do you know how much work would have to go into a black-tie affair?"

"As a matter of fact I do."

Jillian took a gulp of water then dabbed at her lips with her napkin. "I suppose if I had six months to plan—" Her voice tapered off.

"More like twelve weeks. You need to strike while the North Carolina Ballet Company is on everyone's mind. Right after your *Cinderella* production closes. And you should make this an annual event. It should be the same time each year. People will look forward to it and plan their calendar around it so they won't miss it."

Jillian swallowed. "Alan, I don't think I can pull it off in twelve weeks. I've no time for myself, let alone the time to put into a fundraiser of this caliber." Her face became red as she added hand motions to her words. "There are days when I struggle to accomplish everything needing to be done to keep us on track with *Cinderella*."

"A good point. You can't do it all. You have to delegate, learn to rely on others, or you'll never realize the dreams you were talking about earlier. One person alone can only do so much. There's strength in numbers, or so my grandmother says."

Her teeth sank into her lower lip. In a quiet voice she said, "I have a confession to declare."

Alan leaned forward, the trace of a smile on his face. "I'm not a priest, but I'm willing to listen."

"It's difficult for me to let go—of anything."

Alan moved back. "I see." The smile grew into laughter. "But think about this. There are benefits to letting go. It frees you to pursue other things." With an intent look, he added, "Or new relationships."

She did not respond but sat twirling the end of her red hair between two fingers. "Okay, you win. Now where am I supposed to get this extra help?"

"I have the perfect person in mind. My sister Jenny. She's been on several planning committees for this type of event. I'll talk to her about setting up a time to meet. The clock's ticking so we need to get this going."

She declined the offer of dessert, and Jillian realized her anxiety about being alone with Alan had resolved, and she had been enjoying their time together. They stood to leave, and her napkin fell to the floor from her lap. She bent her knees, retrieving it. She returned it to the table, but her hand knocked over a full water glass. The water splashed down the front of Alan's jeans. She was mortified, her hands flying to her mouth, "Oh Alan, I'm so sorry." She could feel heat move from her neck upward. She knew, even without the aid of a mirror, that a flush of red covered her face.

Alan chuckled. "It's alright, Jillian, it's just water, and I'm heading home." He patted his jeans with a napkin. "Don't worry about it."

He helped her into her coat, and they walked outside, her heart pounding in her chest. Stopping at her car, they lingered before he opened the car door. Her thoughts and emotions were conflicted. She didn't want their time together to end, yet as he touched her wrists and slid his fingers down over her hands, her stomach tensed. She was uncertain if she could commit to even such a small gesture of hand holding.

They focused on each other's gaze, and Jillian eased her hands away. "I'd better let you go so you can get some sleep. Thanks for lunch. I enjoyed the afternoon. And again, I'm so sorry about the water."

"You're welcome—we'll talk again soon," he replied as he closed her door.

Five

Jillian sat at the reception desk at the front of the studio. When the isolation closed around her in her office, she would come to share Barbara's desk. The afternoon sunshine spilled into the room, resting on her face. She was working on preliminary plans for the scenery to be used in their next production, while Barbara worked on a list of props they would need to acquire. Jillian was finding it hard to keep her focus on the task at hand, tapping her pencil against the cup sitting in front of her.

"Jillian, can you quit with the tapping?" Barbara asked as she glared at her.

"Oh, sorry," replied Jillian, looking up and noting the frown on Barbara's face. "I didn't realize—"

"Okay, let's have it."

"My pencil?"

Barbara pushed her chair away from the desk and stood up. "Cute—I want to know what's going on. You've been quiet the last couple of days, not like you. And you've been restless."

Jillian squirmed in her chair. "Barb, you know I tend to get this way before our productions go live."

"Correction, you get this way just prior to opening night. We're weeks away from opening night."

Jillian knew the determined look in her eyes would require an explanation, but she was not ready to let Barbara into her thoughts or give up her feelings. How could she, when she wasn't even sure what those feelings were? It had only been yesterday she and Alan had spent an enjoyable afternoon talking strategy. It was the most pleasant afternoon she had spent in years, and Jillian couldn't stop thinking about him. But she wasn't ready to share.

"Barb, there's nothing to spill. I'm preoccupied with the fact that maybe we're doing all this work today for nothing. There may not be a next production." She hoped her explanation was sufficient. She just wasn't ready to talk about *him* to anyone.

"Why don't you change your clothes and take some practice time. You're not accomplishing anything here, and I know how much satisfaction you get from a good practice session. This can wait for a few days. Go on, just don't overdo it."

"We do have some downtime in Studio B, and I'll be in a better frame of mind for rehearsal tonight. I'll see you later." Before walking through the door she said, "Thanks, Barb, for always having my back."

Alan heard the music before he reached the studio door. Staring through the window, he saw a lone figure in the dim light of the room, swirling around and jumping with graceful movements through the air. The music escalated with tension. She executed smooth landings back to the floor with apparent ease, as the music's tension resolved. The artist's face was subdued by the dim light, conjuring an enigmatic figure as she moved about the room. Concentrating on the elusive figure, he realized it was Jillian. She continued to dance, bewitching him with the vision of the delicate ballerina she portrayed. He could not recall having ever seen a more beautiful sight.

With a desire to be closer to her, he opened the door and stepped inside unnoticed. She was lovely to watch. He leaned against the wall, memorizing each movement she made. When the music ended, she stepped over to the barre on the mirrored wall and picked up the white towel hanging there. Jillian wrapped it around her neck. She appeared winded as she walked over to a long bench positioned on the wall adjacent to the mirrors. After several ragged breaths, she reached in her bag and pulled out an inhaler. Jillian placed it between her lips and took a puff then tossed it back into her bag. Wiping her face and neck with the towel, she turned around.

Surprised to see she was not alone, she felt a rush of adrenaline flow through her body. "Alan, what are—you doing here?" Her breathlessness hampered a smooth flow of speech.

"Are you—playing hooky from work?" Her heartbeat galloped as the excitement of seeing him took hold of her body.

He walked toward her, his dimples induced by his smile. "Just doing some volunteer work today. You see, I recently joined the board of directors of a dance company, and I'm trying to make a great impression on the owner."

His tone of voice changed from playful to serious. "I hope you don't mind my coming in while you were dancing. There was no one in the reception area. When I heard the music, I couldn't resist. So what's with the inhaler?"

Annoyed with the question, she folded her arms against her chest. "Sometimes I get a little winded after a lengthy rehearsal." Changing the subject, she asked, "And you're here because?"

He reached in his pocket and held up a piece of paper. "For the fundraiser. I wanted your opinion in case these aren't any good and I have to go back to the drawing board."

"Wow, when you said you like a challenge, you meant it." She took the paper from his hand, little jolts of electric shocks running up her arm as their fingers touched. She sat down, remembering the insecurity that had plagued her the day before at the beginning of their lunch encounter.

Walking toward her, he asked, "So is this what you do with your spare time?"

"Who has spare time? I was treating myself today to some practice time. With so many things to be done with the production, my personal practice seems to fall to the bottom of the list. In a way, this was a luxury for me today."

He sat down beside her on the bench and turned to face her. "What I saw of your dance I enjoyed."

Arching her left eyebrow, she asked, "Are you familiar with the art of ballet, Mr. Armstrong?"

"My experience is limited, but I know what I like, and I like watching you."

Listening to Alan talk, Jillian became aware of heat on her cheeks and hoped they weren't a noticeable shade of red.

"I watched my little sister change from a gangly, awkward preteen to a graceful dancer. And I dutifully attended my share of her recitals."

Jillian blew out a breath, relieved the conversation was deflected from her. "I'm impressed. How old is your sister? Does she still dance?" The questions were out of her mouth before she realized she was crossing the line into his private life. She was also aware of how close he was to crossing into her personal space, as she stood up to put some distance between them.

"Jenny is thirty and was freelancing until last year, when she became pregnant with Thomas. By the way, I talked to her last night, and she is willing to assist with the fundraiser. It seems being a stay-at-home mom to a newborn baby leaves her with the need for adult contact and conversation. I gave her the studio number. She said she'd give you a call in the next few days. Look, since we have a few more things to discuss, why don't we go somewhere for dinner, instead of staying here in this empty studio?"

Twisting the towel in her hand, she answered, "I like the way you think, but the studio won't be empty for long. There's a rehearsal tonight." She couldn't remember the last time she wanted to skip rehearsal and do something else. "Can you hit the highlights about the other things?" *Did I catch a fleeting look of disappointment in his eyes?*

"Okay, there's the matter of setting up a meeting with the potential benefactor. I thought maybe a tour of the studio and an introduction to the owner of the North Carolina Ballet Company might be a good start to opening communications with Ms. Harris. If your schedule permits, I thought we could shoot for Monday. There's no time like the present to accept her generosity."

It was so hard to turn him down when those dimples appeared with every smile. "I have some time between one and three, so set it up. Anything else?" she asked. She moved a few steps to the linen hamper and tossed the towel inside.

Alan stood up. "There is something else I was going to mention." He paused.

Jillian turned around, and as she moved toward him, she tripped over a shoe left behind by someone. She lost her balance, and with amazing timing, Alan broke her fall, catching her by the shoulders. The heat of his hands spread through her body.

His hands lingered after he pulled her upright. "Are you okay? Your head almost collided with the edge of the bench, and it wouldn't have been pretty."

Her breath caught in her chest. "Well, I guess my secret is out." She giggled to hide her embarrassment. "I'm a klutz, except, of course, when I'm dancing."

"So, Ms. Klutz, are you sure you're all right?" He guided her to sit on the bench. "You didn't twist your ankle?"

His eyes pierced through her. She was not used to such scrutiny and felt she was losing control of the situation. One more flash of those dimples and she might cave.

"No, my ankle is fine. I'm good. So, you said there was something you wanted to mention." *He must think I'm a* klutz. *First the water on his pants and now tripping over my feet.* Looking up, she saw his eyes remained fixed on her.

"Are you sure you can't skip rehearsal and go to dinner with me?" He removed his hands from her shoulders and reclaimed his seat.

"Somehow, I think it would send the wrong message about professional obligations if I decided to cut rehearsal tonight."

His head bobbed up and down. He sighed. "Well, we can't have that. So if you won't lower your professional standards and go to dinner, I was wondering if you'd allow me to escort you to David and Ann's wedding on Saturday."

The question took her by surprise, but what a wonderful surprise! She sat without moving, her stillness rendering a statuesque appearance. The silence continued.

"It's not a hard question. Just give a yes or no."

Butterflies circled in her stomach. Her heart rate galloped, and a seed of panic threatened to shut down her voice. On one hand, she wanted to go with him. On the other she knew she shouldn't.

Alan snapped his fingers in her direction. "Jillian—hello? Where'd you go?"

She focused her eyes on his handsome face. "Um, I'm sorry. My mind ran off on a little tangent about what dress I would wear. I'd love to go to the wedding with you." She flashed a big smile and wondered how she could do such a horrible thing to him.

Jillian was finding it difficult to concentrate during rehearsal. Her mind kept wandering to Alan. She made a tremendous effort to file him away in the recesses of her mind so the dancers wouldn't be aware of her distraction. There was usually no getting by with sloppy footwork or less than perfect *tendu jetés,* deep *pliés,* or *rond de jambs,* but tonight her scrutiny of their work was not up to par.

She clapped her hands to signal the end of rehearsal. "Ladies and gentlemen," she said in a crisp, clear voice. "Time is up for tonight. Antoinette and Sarah, where are you?" She acknowledged the two women and added, "A word before you leave please. Everyone check with Barbara and pick up a copy of the revised rehearsal schedule. I believe we'll be starting Thursday's rehearsal with the second appearance of the fairy godmother in Scene One. Be prepared to work long and hard." She didn't have to say it. Her dancers always worked hard.

The group is coming together well, and in two months we'll do Cinderella proud. Jillian moved across the room to the piano. As if on cue, the two women joined her.

"Ladies, let's talk about our main character. I'm having difficulty choosing the lead. It's a nice problem to have," she said, smiling at them. She paused for a moment, and pressing her hands together, she touched her chin with her joined index fingers. "I'd like you both to dance for a panel next week, and then we'll choose which of you should portray Cinderella and which of you will be her understudy. Check with me on Thursday, and I'll have the day and time set."

Dismissing the women for the night, Jillian made two observations. She saw the look of disdain on Antoinette's face as she gathered her bag and shoes and walked away in a sulk. Sarah, eyes sparkling with excitement, rushed away to share her news with other dancers. *Ah, dissension in the ranks. Not to worry, competition can be healthy.* Jillian sighed. She wished she'd given in earlier to Alan. If she had, she'd be with him right now.

Six

Alan stood at Jillian's door, his hand suspended over the doorbell. He checked his watch again. It would never do for him to be early. He knew from past experiences a woman expected to use all her allotted time to get ready for a big reveal like this formal one. He wanted things to go well tonight and didn't deny the fact he liked Jillian and wanted to spend time getting to know her. Checking his watch again, he was now a respectable three minutes past due. He rang the bell and waited. He couldn't remember being this nervous around the last two or three women he had dated, but then again, they hadn't been Jillian.

He sucked in a deep breath as the door opened. There she was, breathtaking, a vision of loveliness, wearing a champagne-colored gown. His eyes took in, with appreciation, the straight strapless neckline down to the fitted bodice that accentuated her small waist and on down to the full skirt that extended to just short of the floor. His eyes moved back up to her face. Her red hair was swept up on top of her head with a few ringlets touching her neck. Gold earrings dangled from her earlobes, and the perfect amount of makeup accentuated her beauty. "Wow!" was all he could manage to say.

She flashed a big smile his way. "Hi. Nice tux," she commented, opening the door wider. "Please, come in."

"Thanks. You look incredible. But, you do know it's bad manners to outshine the bride, right?" He watched as a flush of color moved from her neck up to the top of her head.

"Well—ah, thank you," she stammered. "I'm almost ready to go. I just need to get my evening bag and wrap." She pointed to the sofa. "Have a seat. I'll just be a minute."

Not bothering to sit, Alan glanced at his surroundings. It was a clean space but rather sterile-looking. There was no warmth or depth to it, just the necessities. He found it interesting her office was cozier than her home. As he thought about it, he came to the realization about how much time Jillian spent at the studio. Her books were housed in a built-in bookcase. Some framed photographs and various awards were displayed on the shelves. He walked to the bookcase and becoming focused on a particular picture, picked up the frame. This was his first point of reference to Jillian's past life as a dancer. A prickly sensation on the back of his neck took him by surprise.

"That's the costume I wore when I portrayed Odette in *Swan Lake*, my second summer at ECBT. I loved dancing the part of Odette." He could tell the mention of her past dancing experience made her sad.

"Nice." He placed the frame back on the shelf and helped her into her jacket.

They set out, and he was determined to make their night unforgettable.

The wedding ceremony had been beautiful. David had looked handsome as he'd focused on Ann walking down the aisle toward him. They were a perfect match for one another. It was at such times that an intense desire to experience the joy of loving someone who was meant just for her engulfed Jillian.

The reception got underway and Jillian saw couples everywhere she looked. As she watched their interactions, the desire she had been feeling was snuffed out like a flame of fire dancing on the wick of a candle that, with one swift motion, was quickly extinguished.

Who was she kidding? Her grandmother's words ran through her mind. *You get out of life what you put into it.* She had said this to Jillian more than once. *So what do I have?* She had a thriving dance school and a dance company growing in size and reputation year after year. Rebuilding a professional life had been the focus of her life the past six years, and it showed in the success she enjoyed. Even with all the success, there were times she wished for more. She was thirty-two years old with no prospect of sharing an intimate life with anyone.

And then she'd met Alan. Initially, she hadn't wanted him near her. He had caused her physical pain with his examinations. Everything after the explosion had been confusing, and coupled with the effects of the pain medication she had taken, well, it was no wonder her behavior had been erratic. When she'd spent time with him at lunch, her view of him had begun to change.

Jillian was standing near the stage where the band was playing when she felt a light touch on her shoulder.

"Hi there. Do you always migrate to a stage when you see one?"

She turned at the sound of Alan's voice. "I was just listening to the music. It's great. Live music is always so much better than recorded music."

He listened for a moment and nodded. "I never thought about it, but I think you're right. Are you ready to find our table?"

"Maybe... is everything alright?" A look of confusion crossed his face and she added, "Your phone call to the hospital. Is everything alright?"

"Oh, yes, just a little mix-up with the schedule. I'm second on call tonight, not first-call, so we're good."

She realized she was happy he wasn't being called away. "I think we're at table twelve."

He guided her through the maze of people. When they reached their table, he pulled out her chair. "Can I get you something from the bar?"

"Yes, thank you." She slid into her seat. "I'll have a glass of white wine." Jillian talked with the other guests at the table, four of whom she knew and two she did not. They recapped the beautiful ceremony they had just witnessed, which led to strolls down memory lane of their own wedding days for two of the couples. She managed to keep a smile on her face as she listened to them, feeling a twinge of jealousy that they had memories she might never have.

Alan returned with their drinks and sat her glass of wine in front of her. "What did I miss?"

"Some wedding stories from our married table mates," she replied. Introductions were made all around, and he took the empty chair next to her.

He turned toward Jillian. "I was hoping to find out tonight what it's like to dance with a real live ballerina. Would you be interested in satisfying my curiosity?" he asked with a grin.

She gazed into his brown eyes. "Well, Mr. Armstrong, you're in luck because I never pass up a chance to dance, if I can help it."

"I'm going to hold you to that statement later."

The bride's father welcomed everyone to the reception. Dinner was served, and they enjoyed the interaction with the others at their table while they dined. The twinge of jealously Jillian had experienced earlier disappeared. She ate and drank, anticipating what it would be like to dance with Alan.

They watched the traditional father-daughter and mother-son dances. David and Ann shared their first dance as husband and wife, enamored with one another and appearing oblivious to their guests. And then the guests were invited to join in.

Alan led Jillian to the dance floor. He was light on his feet, an excellent dancer, which pleased Jillian. She laughed, feeling carefree as he twirled her around on the dance floor.

They finished the third dance, and the mood changed as the band started playing a slow-tempo song. It felt so right when Alan pulled her close into his arms, so she gave no resistance. They barely moved as she laid her head against his broad chest, listening to the sound of his beating heart. Warmth flooded her entire body. She pulled her head away so she could look up into his dark, brown eyes. The music ended.

Alan relaxed his arms. "How about a break? Would you like some more wine?" he asked.

She broke eye contact, disappointed he wanted to stop dancing. Her legs tingled as she allowed him to guide her back to their table. Jillian watched Alan walk toward the bar and frowned, trying to get a handle on her emotions. She knew when he'd offered to be her escort she should have declined and had spent the last few days convincing herself it was no big deal. He was just her escort for the night. It had all changed the moment she'd answered her door and their evening together had begun.

The festivities continued, and when it was time for the couple's send-off, Jillian was sad her evening with Alan would soon come to an end. Ann positioned her back toward the single, female guests. Jillian remained at Alan's side. "Aren't you going to get in line to catch the bouquet?"

A sense of melancholy passed through her as she replied, "Alan, I'm thirty-two, so I'll leave the bouquet-catching to the twenty-somethings."

With great effort she added to the shrieks of laughter when Ann tossed her bouquet. They watched as David retrieved the garter from her leg and sent it flying through the air toward the waiting single men. They waved and clapped with the rest of the crowd, watching the newlyweds climb into the waiting limo and drive away

As she waved, Jillian surrendered to the numbness that would keep her safe from her emotions. She still had to say goodnight to Alan and attempt to keep her betraying physical reactions from emerging.

The drive to her townhouse was quiet. Alan put a CD into the player and set the volume on low. She leaned her head back, closing her eyes as they rode without talking. Arriving at the townhouse, Alan parked and walked around to Jillian's side of the SUV. It had been a long day and the effects of the wine she had consumed were taking their toll.

He opened her door, and she swung her legs out. Jillian stumbled when she stood up.

"Whoa there." He steadied her with a strong hand.

She leaned in close to his chest, taking in just one more smell of his masculine scent before righting herself. "I'm okay, but shame on you, Alan Armstrong, for contributing to my wine consumption tonight."

He laughed. "Oh, so now I'm at fault." They walked up to the front door and stopped. "I had good time tonight, Jillian. So good in fact, I want to spend more nights with you." He leaned down and brushed his lips across her mouth.

The second kiss was long and lingering. Jillian responded eagerly. She touched his arms and pulled herself closer to him. They came up for air, and she came to her senses, pulling away, angry with her loss of control. He moved forward, his face coming toward her to reclaim her lips. She turned her head away and said, "We can't do this."

Alan smiled and replied, "Sure we can. And I think we do it well."

She stared into his eyes and in a wooden voice repeated, "We can't do this."

The brightness left his eyes. His grin faded.

A lone tear rolled down her cheek as she whispered, "I'm married." The words were out of her mouth before she realized what she had said.

~

A breathless, punched-in-the-gut sensation jolted him. In the short time he'd known Jillian, he had become invested emotionally, but only now was he willing to admit that to himself. To hear she was unavailable, perhaps unattainable, was a crushing blow. *Choose your words with care* echoed over and over in his mind as they stared at each other. The warning fizzled, and agitation claimed his demeanor, showing in his voice.

"What do you mean, you're *married*? David never told me you're married!"

"David doesn't know. No one in Charlotte knows, except Barb."

His voice rose in volume as he continued. "So, did you think you would just keep it to yourself? Were you going to see how far we could build a relationship before I found out?" He saw the look of torment in her eyes as she turned her back to him. He pulled his lips together, counting to ten. He touched her on the shoulder and in a calmer voice said, "Jillian, let's go inside and talk. It's too cold to stand out here—I don't want you to be cold."

She needed to be cold—needed the cold numbness to shut down her feelings for Alan. It was the only decent thing to do. He shouldn't be involved with a married woman. Jillian handed him the key and stepped aside. He opened the door and guided her inside, his hand touching the small of her back. Despite the cold night air, her skin burned with his touch, and heat spread throughout her body. This was going to be more difficult than she had thought. She had known this day might come, but six years had dulled her good senses and left her open for the heartache about to take place.

Without speaking, Alan helped her remove her jacket then took a seat in the chair across from the sofa. She was grateful for his silence as she gathered her thoughts. Unable to look at his face, she stared at her hands lying in her lap.

In a quiet voice she said, "I've been estranged from my husband for almost seven years. He is a dancer with the Royal Danish Ballet. After he left, I fell into a state of depression for some time. When I was able to start putting my life back together, I had to put him completely out of my mind."

She stood and began to pace. "I suppose I could have, I should have divorced him. But that would have entailed dredging up all the heartache I'd gone through to get over my loss. There has been no reason to even entertain the thought of divorce—until now. Tears spilled down her cheeks. "I can't talk about this anymore tonight. Please don't ask me to continue."

Alan walked over to her and, touching her chin, lifted her face. "No more talking tonight. I'll go so you can rest, but I'll see you on Monday for our appointment with Ms. Harris." He kissed her on top of her head and walked out the door.

Jillian reclaimed her seat on the sofa. She picked up a pillow, and hugged it to her chest as the floodgates opened. How could she have become so emotionally invested in someone she had known for such a short time? It didn't make sense. This was not simply a physical attraction. It was an attraction that pulled at her soul. She crossed the room and removed a tissue from the box on the end table. She settled in the wingback chair and wiped her eyes. Why hadn't she ended her marriage when it was over? These feelings for Alan had come on fast and strong, out of nowhere, and now because of her timidity in the past, she couldn't act on them.

She picked up her phone and touched the number on her contact list. After a long pause, she drew in a deep breath and said, "I need you, Barb. Can you come over?" She burst into tears again.

The door opened. Barbara looked at her friend and immediately knew the pain she was feeling was because of a man. Jillian clung to her friend, as if she was a solid branch she had found and grabbed before going over the proverbial waterfall.

"Shhh…" She soothed her. "It's okay, I'm here."

Jillian pulled away. "Thanks for coming. I'm so messed up!"

"Maybe from the neck up, but your gown is gorgeous." She grinned at her friend, hoping to coax a smile out of her. She wasn't sure what was going on, but Jillian had been there for her in a most dark time of her life, and she would do the same for her now. "Let me unzip your gown, and while you change I'll make some tea."

While Barbara busied herself in the kitchen, she strategically lined up the facts. Jillian had no social life. She spent all her time at the studio. This person had to have made contact with her at the studio. So by the time the kettle was whistling, she assumed all the upheaval in her friend's life was due to the new board member, Alan Armstrong. Jillian walked into the small kitchen. She had removed the smeared makeup, her eyes now red around the rims. She sat down as Barbara placed a cup in front of her and joined her at the table.

"Are you ready to tell me about Alan?"

"You know?"

Barbara sipped her tea. "To be honest, I just figured it out. I'm guessing he was at the wedding. What did he do that has upset you so much? I know—he asked you out, and you won't let yourself go out with him. I'm going to preach it one more time. You should get a divorce."

"I went to the wedding *with* Alan, and I had a wonderful time."

Barbara's mouth dropped open. She was dumbfounded Jillian had stepped out of the nest of security she had padded around herself over the years. It was obvious it had been a bold decision, made without asking what anyone else thought or wavering over the pros and cons.

"Wow, you must have meant what you said about being loved and giving love. I knew something was going on with you this week." Her eyes clouded with suspicion. "If you had such a wonderful time, why are you so upset? I don't understand the problem."

"When we were saying good-night at the door, he kissed me. After the second kiss, I was feeling so guilty, not so much about Jared, but the fact Alan was kissing a married woman. So I told him." She stood up and moved aimlessly around the kitchen. "He was upset at first and then so concerned for me." She turned to face Barbara, tears gathering in her eyes. "I want to spend time with him, get to know him. Barb, what am I going to do?"

"You're going to get a divorce."

Seven

Audrey Harris stared into the mirror as she applied her makeup. She raised her mascara brush to her right eye and stopped before it touched her lashes. She pushed the brush back in its container. Closing her eyes, she recalled the day she had received the P.I.'s initial report. She had sat at her desk mesmerized by the words on the paper. Even now, just recalling that day produced jolts of prickly shocks to the back of her neck. There had been additional reports after the first, detailing pieces of the last twenty-plus years of Jillian Russell's life, and there were gaps of time missing from the reports. Audrey was glad to know she was successful and hoped, content, since fate had played with the poor girl's life with such harshness. There was no mention of a significant other, and if that were the case, it made Audrey wonder if she was maybe at least in part to blame.

She crossed into the bedroom and opened the bedside table drawer. She pulled out a framed picture of a young, redheaded girl with long, curly hair and enormous, green eyes. Audrey sat on the edge of the bed, and stared, her eyes boring into the old photograph. She allowed feelings of remorse to flood her heart for several moments. She positioned the picture frame on the bedside table, and returned to the bathroom to finish applying her makeup.

A shiver of excitement ran up her spine. She was going to see Jillian in person today. Reading reports and looking at pictures had been adequate until Audrey had moved to Charlotte six months ago. Being in such close proximity to Jillian made the desire to see and connect with her grow with each passing day. For a month, the P.I. had been tailing Jillian to make a record of her routine. Audrey had hoped to orchestrate a *spontaneous* meeting and prayed a friendship might spring from it. Week to week the report read much the same. Jillian would leave home and go to the studio where she spent the majority of her day, leaving on occasion for errands or a quick lunch. She would return home in the evening, sometimes as late as ten o'clock.

This was troubling to Audrey. Having a passion for the arts was wonderful, but what about the other things giving meaning to one's life? What about family, hobbies, and romance? Jillian seemed to have none of these, and it made Audrey sad.

After her costume company had received several requests for donations to local charities, Audrey decided to be proactive in her desire to meet Jillian. She couldn't rely on fate or the outcome of a *spontaneous* meeting. Instead, Audrey decided to approach The North Carolina Ballet Company with the prospect of a donation. She applied her signature red lipstick. After twenty-seven years, today was the day she would see Jillian again.

Alan stepped into the studio and walked toward Barbara's desk. She held the phone to her ear, gesturing with her index finger for him to wait. He was anxious to see Jillian after her mind-boggling revelation on Saturday night. *Married!* He was having a hard time wrapping his brain around that one. Barbara ended the call and sat the phone on its base.

Alan moved closer to the desk. "Hey, Barbara, is Jillian in her office?" He wanted this meeting with Audrey Harris to be a success, and he needed to know Jillian's frame of mind before Ms. Harris arrived.

"Hi Alan, she's not here."

"No? She's supposed to be here for a meeting. Maybe she forgot."

Barbara stood up, her hands resting on the desk. "She didn't forget. She was called away on business. I hope she'll be back soon. Can I get you something to drink while you wait?"

"No thanks." He checked his watch. The optimism he brought with him took a plunge. Maybe Ms. Harris would be late, giving Jillian time to make it back. He would start the tour and hoped by the time they got to her office, Jillian would be sitting behind her desk. When they had talked on the phone, she had seemed excited about meeting Jillian. He would just have to make sure he dazzled the old lady with his wit and charm so she would be compelled to write out a big check, even if she didn't get to meet her.

He closed his eyes, exhaling audibly as Jillian came to mind. The second kiss... he couldn't get it out of his mind. Everything had been headed in a positive direction. She was beautiful—a talented woman, fun to be with, charming, and a great kisser. Wouldn't you know it had to end, even before it began?

The door to the studio opened. Alan jerked his head in its direction, hoping to see Jillian. Instead he saw an impeccably dressed woman who appeared to be in her fifties with short, strawberry-blond hair and green, intelligent-looking eyes.

Alan approached her. "Hello, are you Ms. Harris?"

Smiling, she replied, "Yes I am. Mr. Armstrong?"

"Yes ma'am, but please call me Alan." Audrey held out her hand, and he responded with a quick handshake. Her grip was firm. Alan could tell just from her handshake she was a woman with a purpose. Her demeanor reminded him of his mother, not a bad thing. He admired women who knew what they wanted out of life and who felt sure of their ability to obtain it.

"Alright, Alan, and where will I find Ms. Russell?"

Time to start charming. "Jillian had planned to be here but was called away at the last minute. I'm hopeful she'll be back soon." As Alan explained the situation, he noticed the disappointment in her eyes.

He pushed ahead "Please allow me to show you around and share some facts about the North Carolina Ballet Company."

As Jillian entered her office, Alan stood up and faced her. "I can't believe you bailed on me this afternoon! What was so important you couldn't be here to meet Ms. Harris? How important is this company to you, Jillian?" He pounded his fist on her desk as he continued. The sound made her jump.

"If we don't seize every opportunity presented to us, you may just have to shut down your company. And then what a pickle." He couldn't believe he was resorting to using his grandmother's expression. He began to pace as he continued to rant. "The barrier, meaning your dance company, that's been keeping you from social obligations will be gone, and you'll be left exposed to the world, with nothing to occupy your time. But then on the upside of things you might have time to build some relationships instead of avoiding them."

Her green eyes flashed with anger, "Are you finished?"

He stopped pacing. "Yes I believe so, for now."

"I didn't think I would be gone so long, and I was sure you would be able to handle things. In order to move forward with *The Sleeping Beauty* in the fall, I had to make some decisions today to ensure the props we'll need for the production will be available." Her voice became brittle. "Your life may run smooth and on course, Mr. Armstrong, but mine does not. In this business there are detours and unexpected issues that must be dealt with in a quick manner, which is what I was doing today. I'm sorry I wasn't here this afternoon, and I hope I have the chance to meet Ms. Harris soon, but I did what needed to be done today."

He backed off. "She seemed noncommittal when she left. You may have missed out on a much-needed donation. Acquiring financial support is part of the big picture, Jillian. You may not like it, but that's why you have people like David and me. People who will cultivate the things you need—the things you don't want to deal with."

His passion was rekindled as his voice rose. "We need every dollar aimed in our direction. You can't afford to mess this up." He paused for a breath and added in a softer tone, "If I haven't heard anything from Ms. Harris in a couple of days, I'll touch base with her."

Looking down at her feet, she mumbled, "Thanks." She lifted her eyes to his face. "I'm sorry if I messed things up. I'm used to working alone, so I don't have this collaboration thing down quite yet, but I'll work on it."

"Great, if you're willing to learn, then I'm willing to teach you everything I know about collaborating." Taking her hand, he asked, "Will you have dinner with me on Thursday? An early dinner, so it won't interfere with rehearsal. We need to talk."

With a half-smile she said, "I'd like that. I should call Ms. Harris to apologize. Leave her number with Barb, and I promise I'll do it first thing tomorrow."

Eight

The competent, young woman answered the phone on the first ring. "Harris Costumes, how may I direct your call?"

"Good morning. This is Jillian Russell. I'd like to speak with Ms. Harris, if she's available."

"Please hold while I check for you." The line fell silent; then the elevator music began. Jillian inspected the polish on her fingernails and was satisfied there were no chips on the ten fingers displayed in front of her. If she hadn't promised Alan she'd apologize, this phone call wouldn't have been added to her already full list for the day.

"Good morning, Ms. Russell. This is Audrey Harris."

"Ms. Harris, thank you for taking my call. I want to apologize for missing you yesterday at the studio. I understand you had a good talk with Mr. Armstrong."

"Yes, we did. We had a fine talk, but I must say I was disappointed I missed meeting you. Would you be free for lunch today?"

Fidgeting in her chair, Jillian replied, "I'm sorry, Ms. Harris, my day is booked."

No response.

Jillian shook her head. She wasn't going to make this easy. "However, I'm free tomorrow."

"Wonderful, how about twelve-thirty at Maddie's on Lee Street?"

"Sounds great, I'll see you tomorrow at twelve-thirty. Have a good day."

"Thank you, I will."

Jillian checked her schedule for the next day to see what she could rearrange to accommodate the lunch date. The phone rang. She remained absorbed in her task as she picked up the phone. "Hey, Barb, what is it?"

"There's a Jenny Reid asking for you."

Flipping the page of her planner she replied, "I don't know any Jenny Reid. Take a message for me. I'm busy. Wait! That's Alan's sister. I'll talk to her. Thanks, Barb."

Jillian ran her free hand through her hair. She could feel the start of a headache. She made an effort to bring a bright tone to her voice. "Good morning, Jenny. Alan said you'd be calling."

"Jillian, I'd like to do this meeting in person. Are you free for lunch today?"

The question of the day. "I'm sorry, Jenny, but my day is booked. I could meet later this afternoon for a drink or coffee, if you prefer."

"Coffee sounds great. Is four o'clock good for you?"

"Sure, there's a place a few blocks from the studio called Java. It's on Mill Street."

"I'll see you there at four. Bye, Jillian."

"Goodbye." The day was going downhill. She was supposed to be checking things off her list, not adding to it. Her shoulders dropped as she let out a sigh and leaned back in her chair. Jillian looked around her office, enjoying the sense of comfort she drew from the space. Over the last few years she had decorated little by little until finally she had a cozy area where she spent the majority of her time. She stared at the blank wall across from her desk. It was bare, had been bare for six years, waiting for just the right adornment. She had tried a few paintings but they had not suited the space, so she'd removed them and waited. Her thoughts drifted to Alan. Was it symbolic that her wall was as blank as her love life? Nothing was going to change the wall or her life unless her actions became proactive to both dilemmas.

Her thoughts returned to her calendar. Normally she'd make these adjustments to her schedule without a hitch. Alan was right. She needed to start delegating tasks so she could make time for other things. And people, other than artists and students. But first she had to lose this overwhelmed feeling. *Focus Jillian. One task at a time and move on.* With a renewed spirit, she grabbed the list for the day and began prioritizing. What didn't get done today would be moved to the list for tomorrow. She made a vow to start leaving the studio at a decent hour. She might even whittle down her time at the studio to bankers hours, but she knew it wouldn't happen right away.

Jillian opened the door to the coffee shop, and her eyes swept the room. She saw a woman with a baby stroller parked beside her chair. Jenny Reid was petite compared to her brother, but she had Alan's chocolate-brown eyes. She had picked a table off to the side of the shop. Jillian moved toward the table, eager to get acquainted with Jenny, and in the process, maybe learn about her brother as well. She stopped next to the stroller and looked down at the sleeping bundle.

The brunette stood and held out her hand. "Hi, I'm Jenny Reid. It's nice to meet you, Jillian. Can I get you something to drink?"

Hospitable right from the start. "Yes, thank you. I'll have a low-fat vanilla latte." As she waited for Jenny to return, Jillian focused on the beautiful baby, and it made her heart ache with desire to hold him close.

"So, Alan tells me you're in need of some help to get this fundraiser going." She passed the cup to Jillian and claimed her seat next to her son.

"Yes, I guess I do. He has managed to convince me this is a good way to make up for the loss of federal funding we've been receiving for the last several years. To tell the truth, I'm feeling quite overwhelmed right now."

"I think this could be a good thing for both of us." The baby made soft sounds and stretched. Jenny lifted him out of the stroller and cradled him in the crook of her arm. "I love my son with all my heart, and it was my choice to retire from working. But I could use some adult companionship about now."

"Before we get into planning this event, I'd love to hear about your dancing. What have you done in the last year?"

"In the last year, nothing. I stopped taking jobs when I entered my second trimester of my pregnancy. I wanted to keep dancing a while longer, but Mark, that's my husband, was worried it might endanger my pregnancy. My last job was in the *corps de ballet* with a small ballet company in upstate New York. We performed *Swan Lake*."

Jillian listened with envy. "I love *Swan Lake*." And then in a quiet whisper she added, "I miss dancing."

"Why did you stop? I remember thinking JB Russell was somebody to watch. You were destined to have a fabulous dance career. I saw you perform both summers you were at the ECBT Summer Intensive. I guess it was about, oh, fourteen years ago. Doesn't it make us sound so old now?" She ended with a girlish giggle.

Taken by surprise about her past, she wasn't quite sure how to respond. A prickly sensation teased at the base of her neck as she asked, "How do you know about the East Coast Ballet Theater summer program?"

Jenny placed the sleeping baby back in the stroller. "I was a few years behind you in their program. A bunch of us students always attended the production performance of the advanced classes at the end of the summer. I realized when you walked in here Jillian and JB are one and the same. So when did you change from JB to Jillian?"

"Wow, I'm always amazed when the saying *'it's a small world'* has application to my life. That was a long time ago. I suppose I was going through a phase. I haven't gone by JB since I came back from New York and started filling out college admission applications, but enough about me. I can't take up your whole afternoon, and I suppose this little one will be waking up soon, wanting to be fed." She touched his soft, little hand and an ache throbbed in her heart. "So tell me everything you know about a black-tie fundraiser."

During the next hour, an outline was generated that included tasks to be performed, deadlines to be met, hors d'oeuvres and dinner menu suggestions, wine list and miscellaneous items. Jillian was amazed at how fast Jenny had everything organized on paper. They divided the master list into three smaller lists. Jillian took two of the lists, which she would share with Barbara, and left one with Jenny. They made plans to meet in ten days to monitor each other's progress.

As an afterthought, Jillian asked, "Would you happen to be free tomorrow afternoon at four o'clock? I had a last minute cancellation of one of my judges for a panel audition tomorrow. I don't want to reschedule. I need to get Cinderella and her understudy cast tomorrow to keep our rehearsal schedule moving on target. So, would you be interested in helping me out?"

"If you'll keep an eye on Thomas, I'll make a quick phone call. Excuse me." Jenny stepped away from their table and returned a few minutes later with a smile on her face. "I'd love to."

Nine

Jillian awoke the next morning with a headache behind her eyes, a grinding sensation making her nauseated. She wanted to pull the covers over her head and hide from the world. But she knew she couldn't. She had another full day ahead, with or without a headache. She showered and dressed then headed out the door to stop at Java on her way to the studio, hoping a dose of caffeine would stave off her headache before it could become full-blown.

An hour later she was at her desk, working through her list of objectives for the day, when Barbara stuck her head in the door. "Got a minute?" she asked.

"One or two, but not much more," she replied as she stood up and crossed the room to the sofa. She patted the cushion beside her and said, "Come have a seat."

Barbara sat down on the sofa. Pushing her sleeves up, she looked her friend in the eyes. Using a steady voice she spoke. "Jillian, I think we should talk about what we discussed the other night. You know, about getting a lawyer to help you with your divorce from Jared. I've been doing some research, and I've found someone who can handle this for you." She leaned in toward Jillian. "Please tell me you're going to do this."

Jillian twisted in her seat and twirled the end of her hair around her index finger. "To be honest, Barb, finding a lawyer hasn't even made it to my list. I know this is something I need to do. I want to let go of that part of my past so I can have a future." She stood up and pulled her arms to her chest. "But I also know it won't be painless."

"Jillian, I know deep down you have the strength you need to do this. You know I'll help you through the sad memories. You were so good to me when my life was falling apart. Sometimes it takes two pairs of eyes to get us where we need to go."

Jillian sighed. "Just tell me what I need to do."

To make up for missing Audrey at the studio, Jillian made sure she was at Mattie's five minutes early. By habit, she was punctual for appointments, but she was certain she didn't want to start her meeting with Audrey by showing up late. As she waited, she thought about how her social life had been expanding, without any real effort on her part. For the past fifteen months, Barb had been the total sum of her social life outside the studio, and there had been no social life at all prior to her arrival in Charlotte. In the span of two weeks, she'd had two new people pop into her life, brother and sister at that. Maybe The Man Upstairs had been listening to her thoughts those weeks after the explosion when she'd vowed to die having loved and been loved. Her contemplation was interrupted by a voice.

"Jillian Russell?"

Looking up, she saw a meticulously dressed woman with a warm smile and alert green eyes that probably didn't miss a thing.

"Yes, I'm Jillian. You must be Ms. Harris."

"Please, call me Audrey. Shall we get a table?" she asked as she guided Jillian by the elbow and walked up to the hostess. "A table for two, please."

They settled into comfortable chairs. Audrey had had to restrain herself from pulling Jillian into a big bear hug. The hostess assured them the waitress would take their order soon.

"I'm so glad you were able to have lunch with me today. Have you eaten here before? They have delicious salads."

Audrey knew she should tone down her enthusiasm, but how could she do that? She was sitting here with her daughter! She had played out this meeting many times in her mind, but her imagination had never captured the rush of feelings she was experiencing as she sat across the table from her own flesh and blood.

"No, I've not eaten here before. Salad sounds like a good choice. Do you have a favorite?"

Audrey wished they could get past the small talk and move on to more significant subjects. She knew she had to tread with care and act like a stranger. Actually she was a stranger, who knew many things about Jillian, but wanted to know everything, to ask a million questions. Her heartbeat drummed in her chest. Today would go down in her personal history as one of the best days of her life.

"My favorite is the garden salad with grilled chicken."

The waitress appeared. With her pen poised to write she asked, "Are you ladies ready to order?"

Looking up, Jillian said, "My lunch partner recommends the garden salad with grilled chicken. I'll have low-fat ranch dressing on the side and unsweetened iced tea, please."

"That sounds great, except I'd like honey-mustard dressing, *not* low fat, and *sweet* tea." She looked at Jillian. "I have no reason at this point in my life to struggle to remain a size ten. Size twelve suits me just fine."

Jillian's lips curved into a smile. "So, Audrey, Alan tells me you've been in Charlotte about a year. Where did you live before you moved here?"

Audrey's heel of her right foot thumped noiselessly on the floor. It was hard for her to contain her excitement, hoping she appeared cool and collected from the waist up.

"I moved here from Roanoke, Virginia, after living there for twenty-two years. I still have an accessory business there. I'm waiting to see how I do here before deciding the fate of Harris Accessories."

"What kind of accessories?"

"Oh, handbags, scarves, hats, jewelry—to name a few. I'm carrying one of my handbags today." She lifted it off the purse hook fastened to the table and handed it to Jillian.

She rubbed her fingers over the soft leather. "This is beautiful," she said, handing it back to her lunch partner. "So, why the change to costumes?" Conversation lulled as the waitress arrived with their salads.

Audrey took a drink of her tea and continued. "I wanted a new design challenge. I figured since the University of North Carolina has a dance school this might be a good place to start a line of costumes and dance wear. I hoped I would be able to pull them away from some of their vendors with some initial incentives. The business is going well, but at my age, I'm more interested in settling down and becoming a benevolent citizen. After looking around Charlotte over the last six months, I've decided I'd like to support The North Carolina Ballet Company in whatever fashion we decide upon. I'll be in touch with Mr. Armstrong this week and get things moving along. How's the salad?"

"It's delicious, just as you said." She paused. "Audrey, I don't know what to say. I feel like I come up a little short just saying thank you."

"Nonsense, a thank you will do just fine." She put a forkful of salad in her mouth, not wanting their lunch to end before she made some arrangement to meet Jillian again. "Tell me again how long you've lived in Charlotte."

"I moved here six years ago, but I attended the University of North Carolina and received my Bachelor of Arts in Dance and a Professional Training Certificate in Ballet Performance, let's see, nine years ago."

A surge of pride filled Audrey as she listened to Jillian's words. "Well, you should know your way around town. I've been so busy getting my business off the ground I haven't had much time to socialize. I know there are wonderful places to go and things to do, but I don't want to do it alone. Are you interested in art? I know there are several galleries in the area."

"I do like browsing through art galleries, but I'm ashamed to say I haven't been in one since my second summer in New York years ago."

"I hate to put you on the spot, but I will anyway. Would you be interested in exploring what Charlotte has to offer with me? I'd love the company."

Jillian hesitated then replied, "I wouldn't mind keeping you company. I just don't know when I would find the time. This is a busy time for us at the studio."

"I understand, but let me give you some free advice. To have a life outside your studio, you have to make the time."

"I have been meaning to leave the studio earlier in the evening, but I haven't been able to make it happen. I guess old habits are hard to break."

"That's why you need to be accountable to someone besides yourself. You need to have a scheduled activity away from the studio, say once a week. If you're meeting someone, you'll have more chance of making it happen. And it doesn't matter what it is. It could be lunch or shopping or a movie. When was the last time you went to the movies?

Jillian looked thoughtful as she replied, "You know, Audrey, I can't remember. I'm getting your point."

Audrey's excitement grew. "Or a short trip to one of the galleries, just to check things out with a promise to return later to give it a good going through." She knew she shouldn't push but couldn't stop herself. "How about next week?"

"Next week?"

"Make a commitment to start allowing time outside of the studio. Let's make plans now to check out one of the galleries next week. Do you have your appointment book with you?" Audrey found it difficult to contain her excitement.

She saw a spark in Jillian's eyes and could tell the excitement was catching.

"I keep an appointment calendar in my phone." She opened her purse and pulled out her phone. "Audrey, I'd like to give this a try. The art gallery sounds interesting, but I need to shop for a new dress. Maybe we could kill two birds with one stone and save the gallery for another time."

"You keep your calendar in your phone? I guess I'm just old-fashioned. I like pencil and paper myself. But to each his own." Audrey flipped her book open to the appropriate page. "Next Tuesday is good for me. How about you?"

Jillian spoke up as she punched the date into her phone. "One-thirty to four o'clock is open for me. I'm sorry I can't stay longer today. This has been nice. I have to get ready to audition two of our best dancers for the part of Cinderella today."

Audrey's hand shook as she wrote. So many emotions flooded her, but she managed to hide them with a smile. She was going shopping next week with her daughter.

"I have to get ready for some afternoon appointments myself. Call with details of where we should meet, and I'll see you then."

They walked outside, and Audrey resisted the impulse to hug Jillian when they parted. She climbed into her car with such joy circulating in her body she thought her heart might burst. She was going to see Jillian again!

Ten

Alan stepped out of the shower and secured a towel at his waist. He checked his reflection in the mirror as he brushed his teeth and decided the growth of stubble from the last forty-eight hours was pretty uniform and decided not to shave. He was tucking his shirt into his pants when his cell phone rang. He didn't recognize the number.

"Hello, this is Dr. Armstrong."

"Hello, Alan. This is Barbara Brooks."

Pulling on his socks, he said, "Barbara, what can I do for you?"

"Jillian asked me to call and let you know she's not going to be able to go to dinner with you. She sends her apologies."

"Wait, don't hang up. Why is she cancelling?"

"She has a headache."

Alan was speechless.

"Well, I've delivered her message. Have a good evening, Alan." She hung up.

He continued to dress while he raged to himself. *A headache! She couldn't come up with a better excuse? I'm not going to let her do this. I'm not going to let her hide from me.* He picked up his car keys, mumbling as he pulled on his jacket and headed out the front door. His anger built on the drive to the studio. If she was planning to remain married, why had she let him escort her to the wedding? Didn't she know it was sort of a date? And why did she let him kiss her? And why did she kiss him back? He was crazy about her, and even if her feelings toward him were not mutual, she should at least consider getting a divorce just to finalize her estrangement to her husband. He was going to talk some sense into her pretty, red-haired head, and he was going to do it now!

He opened the door to the studio and stepped inside. Barbara stood up as he came in.

"Alan, what are you doing here? I told you Jillian can't go to dinner with you."

"Barbara, I saw her car in the parking lot. I know she's here. Is she in her office?"

"Yes, but—"

"I'll take it from here," he said as he moved toward the hall.

"You don't understand," she said to an empty room.

Alan walked down the hall, fired up and ready to tell her what she needed to do. He stepped into the dark office. Wondering where she might have gone, he moved toward the door and then noticed someone on the sofa.

"Jillian?" he asked as he walked over to the sofa. She was lying in the dark with a cloth over her eyes and a trashcan sitting on the floor beside the sofa. He knelt beside the sofa and asked in a quiet voice, "Jillian, what's wrong?"

She moved the cloth from her eyes. "Alan, didn't you get my message? I'm sorry I had to cancel tonight, but I've had this horrible migraine for a few hours now, and it's not letting up."

"Do you get these headaches often? Are you sure it's a migraine and not a symptom of something else going on?" he asked, shifting into MD-mode.

"It's been about two years since I've had one this bad," she answered. "This has just been a stressful week. I'm hoping it will ease up soon." She placed the cloth back over her eyes.

He placed his fingers around her wrist and felt her pulse, beating steady at about seventy beats per minute. Her breathing was unlabored. "Is your vision blurred? Do you hurt anywhere other than your head?"

"No and no. I have some medication on my desk, but it expired last year, so I didn't take any."

Alan walked over to the desk and clicked on the desk lamp. He picked up the prescription bottle. "Jillian, this is old-school. There are other drugs we use now for migraines. They work better than this medication."

She swung her legs off the sofa as she sat up. "What time is it? I was waiting for dusk before I try to drive home."

Checking his watch, he said, "It's four-thirty, but I'm not going to let you drive. I'll take you myself, and we'll make a detour by a pharmacy on the way. Now, do you have any allergies to medications?"

Jillian held her head and leaned over to rest on the arm of the sofa. "No, but why—"

He interrupted her. "What's your birth date?"

"July 11, 1980."

He began jotting information down on a memo pad of paper lying on the desk. "Do you have any medical conditions I should be aware of before I call in this prescription?

"No I don't. Alan, you don't have to do this," she protested.

"Well, I have to do something. I can't leave you like this. Do you want me to take you to the ER?"

She pulled her head up, the cloth falling on her chest. "I won't go."

"Okay, no ER." Picking up the bottle again he asked, "Is this the pharmacy you want me to call?"

"Yes, I guess," she said in a small voice as she put the cloth over her eyes again.

Finished with the phone call, he squatted beside the sofa and pulled the cloth off her eyes. "Are you ready?" Resting one hand on her shoulder, he slid his other hand behind her back for support. He helped her sit up, then stand.

With one hand on her arm, he took the empty liner out of the trash can. Looking at her, he said, "Just in case."

Alan walked out of the pharmacy with the small, white bag in his hand. Well, so much for dinner plans and the talk he was anxious to have with Jillian. It would have to wait until she was feeling better. He had plenty of time to get her home and settled. He could stay a while to make sure she had no reaction to the new medication and make it home in time for his conference call. As he reached the SUV, his phone rang.

"Hey, Jen, what's up?" He tucked the bag into his pocket and gave his sister his full attention.

"Our babysitter cancelled on us. Alan, in case you don't remember, it's our anniversary," she wailed into the phone.

A smile touched Alan's lips. *Still a drama queen at her age.* "Well, that sure stinks. What are your options?"

"Only one thing I can think of, big brother. Since I don't feel comfortable leaving Thomas with anyone else, will you save my night?"

Could he juggle a sick woman, a seven-week-old baby, and a conference call?

"Now how can I refuse my little sister, especially since it's her anniversary?"

"Yes! I knew I could count on you. We have reservations at eight."

Smiling, he pictured her striking a victory pose. "Whoa! Hold on. I can babysit, but you'll have to bring Thomas to me."

"We'll be there at seven fifteen. I'm going to let you go before you change your mind."

"Just bring a loaded diaper bag. I picked up some baby equipment at a co-worker's moving sale." He opened the door and slid behind the wheel. "See you soon."

Fastening his seatbelt, he glanced over at Jillian. She was still, with her eyes closed and her eyebrows knitted together, revealing a measurable level of pain. Alan maneuvered the SUV through the late afternoon traffic with ease and remained quiet so she could rest. He hoped the new medication would give her good relief in a short period of time. Before long, the SUV came to a stop, and Alan pushed the gear into park. Jillian opened her eyes and sat forward.

"Do we have to make another stop?"

"Change of plans. I was going to stay with you for a while, but I've agreed to watch Thomas tonight, and I have a conference call at eight o'clock. It seems to me the best way to handle everything is to do it all in one place. So Thomas is coming here, and you can rest in my guest room."

"Thanks for the offer, but I'm quite capable of resting in my own bed."

He shifted in his seat to face her. "I can see you still need some work on collaboration. Jillian, it doesn't always have to be you against the world. Let me help you. Besides, I feel partly responsible for the stress you've been under this week. So, will you come inside and take your medication, please?"

She closed her eyes and rubbed her temples. "Oh, all right. I don't have the energy to argue."

She allowed Alan to guide her up the sidewalk and the three steps to his front porch. He opened the front door and ushered her inside. He led her to the living room and invited her to sit while he got a glass of water from the kitchen. When he returned, he pulled the pharmacy bag from his pocket and handed it to her.

"Thank you. I'm sorry you've had to rearrange your evening to help me out."

He sat down in a chair across from the sofa. "I didn't have to rearrange my night. I've just added to it. Jenny and Mark's babysitter cancelled at the last minute, and with it being their anniversary—well, I've always been a sucker when it comes to making my baby sister happy. I'll still be able to take my conference call, so everything's good. Let me show you to the guest room so you can rest. The medication ought to kick in soon, and you'll sleep for a while."

Jillian woke with a start. The room was dark, unfamiliar. She sat up and let her legs dangle over the side of the bed. Then she remembered—Alan's guest room. The sound of a crying babying grabbed her attention. She stood up, and walked to the door. Jillian cautiously stepped into the hallway. She followed the sound and found herself standing in front of a closed door.

She remained still for several seconds. Was she dreaming? The persistent crying urged her into action. She turned the doorknob slowly, as if she were fearful to see what was behind the door. The soft glow of a bedside lamp gave plenty of light to see the portable crib sitting on the left side of the large four-poster bed. She walked over to the crying baby and lifted him to her shoulder. She rubbed his back and made cooing sounds to soothe him. Glancing around the room, she noticed a rocking chair. It didn't fit the rest of the décor, but appeared sturdy.

She moved her precious cargo to the other side of the room and sat down with care on the cushioned seat. She pulled the quiet baby from her shoulder and cradled him in her arm. She slowly rocked back and forth. Closing her eyes, she started singing a lullaby from the collection of songs stored in her brain—the songs she had sung to Lily while she was pregnant. She opened her eyes and watched the quiet baby.

"I would have been a good mommy," she whispered.

The baby fell asleep in her arms as she continued to rock. She didn't want to let go of the awesome sensation. She had purposed not to hold a baby since she lost Lily, and now she didn't want to let go. In the silence, tears rolled down her cheeks.

Alan entered the room. He moved toward Jillian and whispered, "Why are you crying? Didn't the medication take your headache away?"

"It's much better but not gone."

Alan lowered his knees to the floor beside the rocking chair. "So why are you crying?"

"Poor, Alan. Don't you know you'd be the richest man in the world if you could figure out why women do the things we do, like cry for no good reason?" It was nice to feel his concern for her. He was a kind man, and she ached to build a relationship with him.

"Jillian, who wrote the prescription for the medication I saw on your desk this afternoon?"

"Dr. Hayes. He's been my doctor my whole life. He died about four months ago."

"But you've been living in Charlotte for six years. You've been driving two hours away when you've needed a doctor? That's crazy."

"I've needed a doctor just once. I called Dr. Hayes about my migraine, and he called in a prescription—"

"Two years ago." He finished her sentence.

"I'll be glad to help you find a doctor. When *was* the last time you had a physical?"

"Alan, if you'll take this sweet baby from my arms, I think I'd like to rest a bit longer."

"Sure, I'll take him, but we're not finished with this conversation." Alan reached for Thomas, and as he took him from her arms, he brushed Jillian's breast. A myriad of sensations jolted her body, leaving her emotions drained as she realized how much she wanted a physical relationship with Alan.

After Jared had left her, Jillian could not imagine *ever* letting a man invade her emotions again. She had kept herself sheltered for seven years and now in the period of a couple of weeks she was considering the possibility of allowing Alan into her life.

She settled onto the guest bed and thought about the dilemma she faced. Could she risk opening her heart to Alan? If she did and he broke her heart, she felt for sure she wouldn't survive. Should she take that risk?

Eleven

Franklin Witt sat at the table, sipping his morning coffee. If he wasn't pulled into a trauma right off, he liked to start his mornings in the cafeteria, people watching. He never knew what interesting conversation or interactions of hospital personnel he might hear or observe, filing those things away for later use.

He surveyed the room, his eyes landing on Alan. Franklin's mouth curled into a sneer. *The golden boy better watch his step. There's no way I'm going to let him waltz in here and take away the appointment I've been working for these last three years. There's got to be a dirty little secret in his life. If not, maybe I'll just have to make something up.*

As Alan walked by, Franklin invited him to sit. "Come on, you can spend a few minutes with a colleague before your day gets cranked up."

Alan slid into a chair and laid some papers on the table, but immediately his phone rang. Standing up, he excused himself and stepped away to talk.

Franklin eyed the top page of the papers. He turned it around and skimmed through the article. He laid the page back as Alan walked up.

"A unique way to do a job search."

"Excuse me?"

He pointed to the papers. "Looking up physician obituaries. Thinking about a new job?"

"Dr. Hayes? Someone mentioned to me he had died and I was curious, so I found a copy of the obituary. I'm not planning on going anywhere, except to check on my patients." He scooped up the papers and walked away.

No plans to share my goals with a small-minded skunk like you. I hope you think you've got some competition in me. Alan caught up to Ron Compton as he exited the cafeteria. "Morning, Ron."

"Good morning, Alan. I've been meaning to talk with you, if you've got a few minutes."

"Sure, what's up?"

"I've heard from a few people you've set up some pretty cool goals for the future."

"Maybe, what have you heard?"

"You want to use your trauma skills in a remote area somewhere on the eastern seaboard. Did I hear right?"

"You heard right. Nothing's in concrete. It's not even on paper—still working out the details up here," he said, pointing to his head.

"When you get to putting something on paper, give me a call. I think what you want to do is awesome. I might even consider the possibility of joining you, if you're interested."

"Thanks, Ron. You've just given me a couple of pros for my project I didn't know existed."

"Good, talk to you later."

His day had shifted into a better direction. Realizing he was whistling, he smiled. "You Are My Sunshine" was the tune his dad had hummed or whistled when he was happy.

Walking toward her car in the deserted parking lot, Jillian shivered as the chill of the night engulfed her. Although spring had made its entrance the week before, the weather had not adjusted. There was also an inkling of rain in the air. Pleased with herself for leaving the studio early several nights in the last few weeks, she was determined to make it happen more often. And she accepted the fact there would be some nights, like tonight, when she would be the last person out. She was even more pleased with the realization the production was showing no detrimental signs from her taking personal time for herself. It had been nice to come home and prepare a home-cooked meal or relax in a bubble bath, sipping wine and listening to classical music. It had even been nice to come home and have time to perform household chores that had been left unattended due to the combination of time constraints and lack of energy.

She touched the door handle, and glanced forward, squinting in the shallow cover of dusk. Moving closer to the front of her car, she groaned as she confirmed the front tire was flat. A light mist kissed her face as she pulled the jack and spare tire from the trunk of her car. It had been about five years since she had changed a tire, so speed was not on her side. While she worked, the heavens opened, sending a heavy downpour, and it didn't take long for Jillian to become drenched from head to toe. She deposited the flat tire and equipment into the trunk and dashed into the car. Shaking her head, the loose water scattered in all directions. She ran her hands over her face to push the rain away. Her clothes were plastered to her skin. She shivered as she started the car's engine and headed home.

The hot water of the shower warmed her from skin to bone. She stood under the waterfall for an extended period of time, thinking about her schedule for the rest of the week. And then she realized the first day of April was just three days away. She had been so preoccupied with her business problems it had slipped up on her this year. Since moving to Charlotte, she had never missed traveling back to Dixon on Lily's birthday. She always left flowers at her grave site, to mark her visit. Even though it was a two-hour drive, no way would she miss visiting this year. She would figure something out.

She stepped out of the shower. After donning her favorite terry cloth robe and some slippers, she wrapped her wet hair in a towel and picked up her phone. She made several phone calls then dialed Barbara's number. The phone rang so many times she knew it was going to voicemail, and she'd have to leave a message.

And then she heard "Hey, this better be important. I'm watching *Titanic*."

"Barb, I didn't realize it until tonight—Friday is April first."

After a pause Barb replied. "Oh, you're right. Does that mean you're going to Dixon on Friday?"

"Yes, I've arranged for Anna and Sandra to teach the two morning classes, but I haven't been able to get anyone for the three o'clock, so I'll plan to be back by then."

"Do you want some company for the trip?"

Jillian paced in the small area beside her bed. "I appreciate your offer, but I need you to take care of things at the studio, though I could use another favor."

"Name it."

"Would you order some flowers? I've got a booked day tomorrow, and I'm afraid I'll forget. A pretty arrangement, lots of purple for Grandma, a nice arrangement of masculine colors for Dad, and—"

"And pink lilies for Lily," finished Barbara. "I've got this. Good night, Jillian. See you tomorrow."

She hung up and formulated her plan. She'd have to be back by three o'clock, and Dixon was a two-hour drive from Charlotte. She could drive to Dixon after rehearsal Thursday night, get a hotel room, and go to the cemetery Friday morning, leaving in plenty of time to teach class in the afternoon.

Without bothering to dry her hair, she set the alarm, pulled down the covers on the bed, and slid underneath, seeking warmth and comfort. A lump lodged in the back of her throat. She closed her eyes and saw it happening again...

The nurse strapped on the monitor and then moved it all over her belly, searching but never finding Lily's heartbeat. Thirteen hours of labor with her heart breaking a little more as each hour passed. And then the delivery—she didn't want to push. In her drug induced state she reasoned if she didn't push, she could keep Lily with her. But the baby came out. She cried when the nurse laid the blanketed baby girl in her arms. As she opened the blanket, her breath caught in her chest. She was perfect but so still. Her eyes were closed as if she were asleep. The pink dress, provided by the hospital, made her look like the real baby she was. She pulled off the white crocheted cap and touched the dark hair she had inherited from Jared. It wasn't fair he was creeping into her thoughts. He hadn't wanted Lily, he had left them. She continued to look and touch, memorizing every feature. Her fingers were long, but dainty. She picked up her hand, cradling it between her fingers and thumb, her skin felt so soft. Next, she pulled off the white crocheted booties with pink edging around the top. She counted all her toes. Wasn't that the normal thing to do? There were ten. Her legs were long. The tears came in a torrent. She picked up her baby and held her against her chest as the tears flowed. She breathed in the baby powder scent and cried harder...

Jillian got out of bed and opened her closet door. She pulled down the square, purple box from the dark recesses of the back of the closet shelf. She settled down on the bed and opened it with caution, like she was waiting with apprehension for a jack-in-the-box to pop out. She handled the contents with care, pulling them out and lining them side-by-side on top of the comforter. The last sonogram picture taken before Lily died. Her heartbeat had been strong in the doctor's office the day the sonogram was performed. She studied the footprint and handprint cards, looking at the pattern in the print, knowing this was part of her proof that Lily had indeed been a person and unique.

She picked up the small, clear rectangle bag that held a lock of the dark hair. How long would her hair be now? A sympathy card from the nurses who had taken care of her during the two shifts she had been in labor. The sensation started. It was becoming a chore to pull air into her lungs. She opened the bedside table drawer and pulled out her inhaler. Taking two puffs, she closed her eyes, waiting for the struggle to ease. When it did, she put the items back in the box, and tied the satin ribbon to secure them. She returned the box to the closet shelf and climbed back into bed. The emotional and physical exhaustion caused her to fall asleep right away.

The next morning Jillian woke with a headache and was coughing. She had only had snatches of sleep during the night and was awake when the alarm clock had sounded. Achy joints made her groan as she dragged herself out of bed. *This is not the right time of year to get sick, but when is there a good time?* She was always busy, no time to slow down. She would have to get better at delegating more responsibility to others. Having no appetite, she skipped breakfast and headed to the studio.

Twelve

Alan sat at the bar, nursing his scotch on the rocks to make it last. He watched as the woman seated at the end of the bar was approached by a man at least five years older than she, drink in hand, trying to set himself up with her company for the evening. Good grief, he'd hated doing the bar scene when he was younger. Nothing ever played out past spending the evening drinking and talking because that was the way he had wanted it. After being dumped by Reagan, he had decided to make his career the top priority in his life. He had endured periodic blind dates and evenings out with the guys just often enough to keep them off his back.

Alan watched David make his way through The Pub's happy-hour crowd to the bar. He sat down and raised his hand at the bartender. "Bourbon on the rocks."

The bartender pointed to Alan's half-empty glass. "You want another?"

Alan covered the top of his glass with his hand. "No thanks."

"Just one?" David asked, crossing his right ankle over his left knee.

"One's my usual limit. I never know when I might be called in for a trauma."

The bartender sat David's glass on the bar. "Thanks," he murmured as he loosened his tie. He settled his attention on Alan. "So how are things with Jillian?"

Alan's lips twisted into a bitter smile. *"Harrumph."* Wearing a stony expression, he answered in a quiet voice. "Boy, I sure can pick 'em. He turned his glass up and took a drink. "But, I didn't ask you here to talk about Jillian. Well, maybe in reference to the fundraiser."

David rubbed his chin and waited for Alan to continue.

"The arrangements for the fundraiser are falling into place, but I have a couple of additional ideas that may help to boost the profits. I was telling Jillian we should make this personal to the community so they will feel they have an investment in the company. Be a sounding board and listen to my ideas."

David took a sip of his drink. "Okay, let's hear it."

Alan's voice picked up with enthusiasm. "We'll call it something like Dancing for Dollars. The first six people who donate one thousand dollars or more by a specified deadline will get to choose a dance from a scene that's been performed in the last four years of the company's existence. If we keep the choices specific to what's been done in the past, there should be costumes and props in storage we can be use, so no expenses for the entertainment. And the deadline we set should give the artists time to prepare."

David's phone rang. Looking at the caller ID he said, "It's Jilly. Hey, how are you?"

"I'm just calling to remind you Audrey wants to meet with you tomorrow."

"Yes, I remember."

"Please don't forget. I'm not sure what it's about, but it sounded important to her."

"Jilly, you know I'm a reliable guy. If I say I'm going to do something, I do it. By the way, you sound awful. Are you taking anything for the croaking noise you're making?"

"Yes, but I ran out. I might have some more at home."

David frowned. "Do you need me to go by the drugstore and bring something to the studio?"

"No need. I can stop on my way out of town tonight."

"Where are you going? You don't sound like you need to be going anywhere except to bed, much less out of town."

"David, it's just overnight. I'll be back tomorrow afternoon." She finished her comment with a sneeze.

"Okay, I'll talk to you tomorrow. Safe driving."

Hanging up he said, "She sounds worse than yesterday, and she's going out of town tonight. I don't think she ought to go, but she's going. Once she sets her mind to something, there's little chance anyone can change it."

Alan finished his drink and said, "Sounds like a challenge to me. Do you think I need to check on her?"

"That might not be such a bad idea."

"I do have my ideas to share with her. She doesn't have to know I heard your half of the conversation .But first tell me what you think of the idea."

"I don't know. A thousand dollars is a pretty steep price tag."

"Yes, for the average person, but remember we're trying to attract people who won't miss a thousand dollars. Look at it this way, some people like the idea of giving but also getting a little something in return. We can call it an Artistic Thank You. The first six donors will have the privilege of selecting the six dances for the entertainment. Another idea is to have our company dancers reserved to dine with our patrons. We'll seat one or two dancers at a table, and then for an extra fifty dollars added to the price of the admission ticket, our patrons can dine with their favorite dancer. We can call it First Come, First Reserved. Hmm, I just thought that one up."

"I wouldn't quit your day job to work in advertising, if I were you. But I like the second idea because people who can't afford to donate a thousand dollars can have a chance to dine with the dancers as well. The sooner Jillian hears your ideas, the sooner we can start planning. I think tonight would be a great time to talk to her about them. Rehearsal's over at eight."

※

Jillian put an overnight bag into the back seat of her silver sedan as Alan swung his '67 sports car in the driveway beside it. He jerked to a stop, counting to five, hoping to slow his emotions before talking to her. Smiling, he approached her. She looked tired, and he could tell it took effort for her to return even a small smile.

"Hi, new car?" she questioned.

"Not new, I've had it since residency. My dad gave it to me when I moved to Boston."

She nodded. "Nice."

"I stopped by the studio with a couple of new ideas for the fundraiser. Barbara told me you left a little early tonight." He pointed in the direction of the overnight bag. "Are you going somewhere?"

In a hoarse voice she answered, "Just an overnight trip to Dixon. I'll be back tomorrow afternoon."

"Wow, where'd you get the hoarse voice?"

She closed the door of her car. "I got caught in a downpour changing a flat tire Tuesday evening. It'll be gone before I know it," she said as she erupted into a coughing fit.

"Impressive cough. Let's go inside." He put his arm around her waist and guided her toward the townhouse. "So what are you taking to get rid of your cough?"

She lowered her head to her chest and mumbled, "I used all the cough medicine I had, but I think I have some cough drops in my purse."

He shook his head. He knew all about her independent streak, but now he knew she had weaknesses too. He was impressed by what she had done with the company, but it had come with a price. Not only had she given up her social life, but she was ignoring her health, and he wasn't going to let that happen.

He led her to the kitchen table and settled her into the nearest chair. "Jillian, do you have to go to Dixon, tonight? I'm not going for points here, just telling the truth. You look *awful*."

"Alan, this is a personal matter. I've done this every year since I moved to Charlotte, and I will not skip it this year because of a cold." She punctuated her words with more coughing. Alan frowned as he pulled on the refrigerator door handle and took out a bottle of water. With a twisting motion, he pulled off the cap. As he handed the bottle to Jillian, he could see the determination in her eyes.

He sat down in the chair next to her. "I can see this trip means a lot to you, but I'm concerned for your safety. Let me drive you to Dixon, and I promise not to ask questions. I'll stay out of your way. I want you to be safe, and I don't want you to be alone."

Jillian touched Alan's hand as she made eye contact. "I'm tired of being alone, so I'd appreciate the company. Thank you."

He could see the anguish in her eyes through the pained stare she gave him. He wanted so much to remove the anguish for good. He had thought she would protest his offer. At times like this, he was sure he would never understand women. He knew he needed to take things at a slow pace. He had made mistakes in the past with disastrous results. He decided resolving her physical malady and supporting her with her emotional challenges, whatever they were, were the best ways to approach her tonight.

Alan patted her hand then stood up. "Now, how long has it been since you've eaten? Don't try to fool me."

Jillian rested her elbows on the table and massaged her temples. "I don't know. I haven't been hungry."

Alan searched through cabinets and pulled out a can of chicken and rice soup. "Just what the doctor ordered. You may not be hungry, but you need something in your stomach. You eat this, and we'll stop by the pharmacy to get a supply of cough medicine as we head out. Sound good?"

"I just don't think I can eat anything."
"You have to try. For me?"
She gave a toneless response. "I'll try."

※

The midnight blue sports car glided along I-85. The traffic was thinning out as they progressed north, away from Charlotte. Alan had stopped at the outset of their trip and purchased cough medicine. She had taken a dose and then allowed Alan to recline the passenger seat so she could rest while he drove. Not long after they turned onto I-85 he could tell she was asleep by her steady breathing.

He hoped he had not seemed too shocked when Jillian had opened her trunk and asked him to transfer three arrangements of flowers to his car. Going home to visit the family grave sites—it had taken him by surprise. Why was she so determined to go tonight? Why not next week when she was feeling better?

Alan placed a CD into the player and set the volume to low. Debussy's "Prelude to The Afternoon of a Faun" produced a soothing sound as the miles went by. What was it about her that made him want to come to her rescue, to make everything better for her? He noticed after a while Jillian's body seemed more relaxed than when they'd started their trip.

Alan focused on the highway stretching in front of him. The soft sounds of the piano playing Debussy's "Clair de Lune" tugged at memories he thought had been buried so deep he would never again recall them. He remembered a time when he had spent hour upon hour in the practice hall at the famed Juilliard School of Music. He had studied while Reagan practiced, perfecting her God-given talent at the piano. He especially enjoyed her interpretations of the Chopin pieces she played. He didn't listen to Chopin anymore.

They had met during intermission at a performance of the New York Philharmonic, and a budding relationship began. She'd been devoted to her art and most of their time together had been spent in the practice hall in preparation for her future. He had fallen in love with her, fallen hard, but things had not worked out. He'd begun his residency program at Boston Medical Center and she'd begun touring. She had said she couldn't take the chance. A long distance relationship might stress her career. She'd needed to give everything she had to grow her career and he'd needed to give total dedication toward his residency program. She had summed it up by saying the timing wasn't right and she would always love him. So she had broken it off and had left him devastated. He had sworn off women and buried himself in his studies, becoming proficient at handling emergent situations in a calm and decisive manner. This discovery led to his choice of becoming a trauma surgeon, at which he now excelled.

He had not thought about Reagan in years. Well, if he didn't count last year when he'd considered calling her after learning her parents had been killed in a car accident. Why now? Pain seared the back of his throat, he struggled to swallow. He beat his fist on the steering wheel. Why was she coming to his mind now? Was it because he had such strong feelings for Jillian?

Jillian coughed and stirred awake. Alan took his eyes off the road for a moment to glance at her and then focused on his driving. He was glad for the darkness, covering any telltale signs on his face that might prompt questions from her.

She faced Alan. "Have I been asleep long?" she asked.

"Close to two hours. We'll be in Dixon soon." He tried to relax his voice.

Jillian pulled her seat into an upright position. Looking straight ahead, she said, "I come here this same time every year to visit my family. I know it may sound strange since they're all gone. But I'm the only one left to do this, and I think it's important.

"I'm just the chauffeur. Don't feel like you have to explain your actions to me." He softened his voice. "Unless you want to."

"My grandmother passed away during my last semester at the University of North Carolina. She had been taking care of me since I was ten. My mother left us, my dad and me, when I was six years old." She sighed deeply and closed her eyes. "By the time I turned ten, my grandmother felt she needed to step in and help raise me. My father was absorbed in his work. He was a researcher. He didn't neglect me, but as my grandmother put it, '*He didn't have a clue how to help me bloom into a fine, young woman'*." She was silent for a few minutes. "We lost my dad my senior year in high school. He was killed in a car crash."

"I'm so sorry, Jillian. I know what it's like to lose your dad. Mine passed away three years ago."

"Well, this conversation is turning dark. Please, let's talk about something else."

"Sure, you choose the subject."

"You said something earlier in my driveway about some new ideas for the fundraiser. Let's talk about your ideas." She settled sideways in her seat, pulled her knees up toward her chest, and wrapped her arms around them. The sound of Alan's voice lulled her into a light slumber.

༄

The parking lot of the hotel was packed. Alan found a space and pulled the car to a stop. They exited the car, and Alan pulled out the overnight bag he had picked up before the stop at the pharmacy, along with Jillian's bag.

"Do you want to leave the flowers in the car?"

"I think they'll be fine. The low tonight will be in the fifties."

"Well, I think we're set. Let's head inside."

A few people mingled about in the sitting area of the lobby. The attendant at the desk smiled as they approached her. "Welcome. How may I help you?"

"I have a reservation for Jillian Russell." She rubbed her hands up and down her arms, feeling a sudden chill.

"All right, let's take a look. Here you are. Two adults?"

Alan spoke up. "No, I'll need a room as well."

"Oh, I'm sorry. We're booked, no rooms left. We're hosting a writer's convention and two weddings this weekend with out-of-town guests already here."

They looked at one another. Alan spoke first. "I guess we could go somewhere else."

Jillian bit her lower lip. "There's a smaller hotel about three miles on up the interstate."

"Sorry," the attendant interjected. "They had a fire two weeks ago and sustained a lot of damage. They're not open for business at the present time."

Jillian began coughing. She stepped away from the desk and in as quiet a voice as she could manage, she said, "Alan, I'm sorry. I never in a million years thought you wouldn't be able to get a room. I guess we could drive around and look for another place." Jillian shifted her head toward the desk. "Maybe she can recommend another hotel."

Alan put a hand on her shoulder, and with his other hand, tilted her chin upward and made eye contact. "Jillian, you're worn out. We can be adult about this and stay in the same room. It'll be fine."

Jillian moved to the desk and handed the attendant her credit card. She closed her tired eyes and rubbed the back of her neck as she waited. It wasn't long before the clerk returned her credit card with a keycard.

"You're all set. Enjoy your stay."

An awkward silence lingered in the elevator as they rode to the tenth floor. The silence followed them to Room 1028. They stopped in front of the hotel door.

Looking up at Alan, her face red, she reiterated, "I'm sorry about the accommodations, about you not being able to get a room."

"Jillian, would you stop apologizing? Like I said, we're adults, not a big deal. And you, my dear, need to get some rest, so it's silly to ride around looking for two available hotel rooms." He took the keycard and opened the door. They stood in the doorway looking at the king-size bed that filled the majority of the room. Jillian let out a groan. They moved inside and closed the door.

"It's okay, Jillian. I'll sleep in the chair over there." He walked to the corner of the room and sat down. "See, this works. I'll let you change first so you can get settled and go to sleep."

"Thank you," she murmured as she lifted her overnight bag to her shoulder and walked into the bathroom. *What have I gotten myself into now? If I didn't feel so bad, I would have insisted we keep driving.* Jillian opened her bag and took out pajamas, slippers, and a robe. She was glad she had packed pajamas and not one of her favorite satin gowns. She knotted the tie around her robe then opened the door. Jillian sat her bag on the luggage table and pulled out her outfit for the next day to hang it in the closet. "Your turn," she said, concentrating on her chore.

Alan stood up and reached for his bag. "What time are you planning to get up in the morning?"

"Seven o'clock. That will give me plenty of time at the cemetery and not be rushed getting back to the studio. I have to teach a class at three."

"Sounds like you have it all planned out." He stepped inside the bathroom and closed the door. A few minutes later, he emerged from the bathroom wearing pajama pants and a tee shirt, the material straining against his wide chest. He reached up to the closet shelf and pulled down a blanket and pillow.

Jillian's fingers ached with the desire to touch him, to feel his firm, muscled form.

"I left the bathroom light on so you can see if you have to get up during the night. You don't want to stub your toe on the furniture in an unfamiliar room."

"No, I don't want to do that. Thanks." She watched him trying to settle his too-long frame in the chair without success. How could she expect him to get any rest in a chair? And he had been so nice to drive her. The real issue here was she would like to have him in her bed. She wanted his kisses and she wanted him. But she knew it would never happen as long as she remained married. And certainly not tonight. She was sick.

"Alan, this is a big bed. There's no reason you can't sleep on the other side. You're not going to get any rest in a chair, and then I'll feel guilty."

He shifted in the chair and fell on the floor.

Jillian laughed, which led to more coughing.

Alan pulled himself up into a sitting position. "Are you sure? I think I've grown about a foot and a half since the last time I tried to sleep in a hotel chair. I recall being ten years old at the time."

Jillian giggled and relaxed back against her pillow. "Yes, I'm sure. Come to bed and get some rest, if you can. I believe the medicine is wearing off. It could be a noisy night."

Alan checked his watch. "Time for another dose." He approached the bed with the bottle of medicine, and she slid over so he could sit down. He poured the liquid into the measured med cup and handed it to her.

She drank it, and handing the cup back to him, she whispered, "Thank you, for everything." Their eyes connected and held.

Alan leaned down and kissed her forehead. "Good night, Jillian." He turned off the bedside lamp and moved to the other side of the bed.

⁂

Alan peeled off his tee shirt and slipped underneath the covers. He was used to sleeping topless, and the shirt he had tossed in his overnight bag was just too constricting for a comfortable night's sleep. He punched his pillow to help vent his frustration and placed it under his head. This was not what he had envisioned when he had had thoughts about sleeping with Jillian. Thoughts that had come to his mind, even after he'd found out about her marriage and deemed her unattainable.

Alan studied her back. He could tell she was not relaxed, holding herself in a stiff, set position as far as possible on her side of the bed without falling on the floor. After a bit, her breathing slowed, and he could see her body relax. He turned off the bedside lamp. Jillian coughed and stirred about then settled again.

Alan drifted off to sleep. He awakened to sounds coming from Jillian's side of the bed. Looking in her direction, he turned on the bedside lamp. Her eyes were closed, but she appeared agitated, her head moving about. It was difficult to understand the words mingled with crying.

Alan sat up and shifted to the center of the bed. He touched her arm as she cried out "Lily." He took her shoulders in his hands, noting her feverish skin, and shook her.

"Jillian, wake up." She did not respond to his words but continued fretting. He pushed her hair off her forehead. Her hot skin brought him concern. He stroked the side of her face. "Jillian, wake up for me."

Her eyes opened, framed with wet lashes from her tears. Her breaths came in ragged, short spurts, and he could hear wheezing. *I could use my stethoscope about now.*

"Jillian, it's okay. I've got you. Bad dream?"

She leaned her head against his bare chest, her choppy breaths continued. She wiped the tears off the left side of her face but didn't answer.

"Can you try to take some long, deep breaths for me?" He leaned her back against a pillow. *Is the wheezing more pronounced?* "Jillian, do you have your inhaler with you?"

"My bag."

Alan jumped off the bed to dig through her overnight bag. Keeping his voice calm, he said, "I'm not seeing it. Are you sure you brought it?"

"My handbag... on the chair." She sat up and swung her legs on the edge of the bed.

"Stay there. I'll bring it to you." He sat down beside her and placed the handbag on her lap.

She leaned on his arm. "You find it." Her breaths remained shallow and choppy.

The heat from her face escalated his concern, as he quickly dug through the contents of her bag, pulling out the inhaler. He set her upright and supported her as she inserted the inhaler and squeezed it then laid it on the nightstand. Alan stood up and scooped her into his arms. He placed her toward the middle of the bed then disappeared into the bathroom. He returned quickly with some cold cloths and a small bottle of complimentary water from beside the coffee maker. He crawled behind her and propped her up against his chest.

Her breathing had already improved, becoming even and unlabored.

"Here, drink this." He pressed a cloth across the back of her neck and then one across her forehead. He talked as he worked. "So I see you're letting this cold get the best of you. You're running a fever."

She shivered. "I'm cold."

"Let's pull the sheet up over you, but no blanket for now." Wanting to distract her from the chills she was feeling, he asked, "Do you remember what you were dreaming about? It might help to talk about it."

Jillian shifted on her side. "I was dreaming about my baby. She died. I'll visit her grave in the morning."

Alan was quiet. *Is she lucid? She's talking about a baby.* "Your baby's name is Lily?" he asked.

Jillian sat up. The cloth fell from her head. "How did you know?"

"You called out her name when you were crying in your sleep."

Her eyes became dark. "What else did I say?"

Alan pulled her back down against him. "I couldn't make out anything else you said because you were crying."

Jillian sat up and moved away from Alan. "And just how long did you lie there listening to me talk about my life, before you decided to wake me up?"

"Jillian, it wasn't like that. I woke up and you were talking in your sleep. I couldn't understand you, and I tried to wake you up right away." She didn't answer but he could see her body relax. "I'd like to know all about you, and I'm sure I will when you're ready to tell me about your life. Same with me, you'll find out things about my life as we go."

She lay on her side with her back to Alan. She shivered, and he pulled the sheet up over her shoulders. She coughed and said, "I don't think I want to go back to sleep now."

"You need to sleep. Do you have any aspirin with you?"

Jillian sat up. "Do you have a headache?"

"Not for me, for you. You're hot. You need some aspirin."

"I have aspirin in my handbag."

Alan searched until he found a small travel-sized bottle and shook out two tablets. He handed her the unfinished bottle of water with the pill. She drank until the bottle was empty.

"Good, now let's try something else. Roll on you right side." He slid a pillow under her back then leaned her against the pillow. "Feel better?"

"Yes." She sighed and closed her eyes.

"I'm going to move back over to the other side of the bed. Let's both try to get some rest."

"Alan, don't go. It's nice to have you close by. Will you sleep here beside me, please?"

"I can do that." He shifted to a more comfortable position, leaving space between their bodies. *Now, to convince myself I can lie beside her and sleep.*

"Earlier tonight you said you didn't want me to be alone, so don't leave me."

He stroked the side of her face. "Okay, I won't," He kissed her cheek and turned off the bedside lamp.

The room was quiet. They could hear late-nighters' muffled sounds out in the hall followed by doors nearby opening and closing.

In a whisper, Jillian asked, "Alan, are you asleep?"

"No," he whispered back. "Do you need something?"

"For a while now, I've wanted to ask you about something."

He rose on one elbow and rested the side of his face on his fist. "Okay, shoot."

"About the explosion."

They had not discussed it since their first meeting at the studio. He touched the scar on her shoulder. "What about the explosion?"

Jillian sat up. Even in the dark, Alan detected a change in her demeanor. He sat up beside her and turned on the light. Her breaths became short. He knew, without feeling her pulse, her heart rate was increasing.

"I need to know—what happened to Cathy. I know she died, but why did she die?"

"Jillian, I'm not supposed to talk about my patients."

He saw the disappointment in her eyes. He knew he should abide by HIPAA laws. He recalled a newspaper interview in which Mr. Strickland had given the cause of death. He had made it public knowledge in the interview, but it was obvious Jillian had missed it. He was just as concerned for the patient beside him as the one who had died in the ambulance. *Screw HIPAA this one time.*

"She died from an amniotic embolus."

"In English, please."

Cathy had some abdominal trauma from the explosion. Because of those injuries, when her water broke, some of the amniotic fluid invaded the maternal bloodstream, causing her death. I tried but there wasn't anything I could do."

Jillian hugged her pillow and cried for the woman she had known for less than an hour.

"Poor Mr. Strickland, to lose his wife and his baby—"

Alan pulled her into his arms. "No, Jillian. We were able to save her baby."

"How is that possible? I heard people talking while I was in the hospital. Cathy died in the ambulance."

"She went into cardiac arrest, and we couldn't revive her. But I was able to deliver her baby girl by C-section in the ambulance."

"Oh, Alan. You saved her baby?"

"Yes, we did."

She wiped the tears from her eyes. "Thank you for telling me." She settled down with Alan's arms around her and closed her eyes.

Thirteen

The air was crisp and cool. Although Alan realized it wouldn't take long for the warmth of the sun to dry the dew from the grass and push the coolness away, he was glad Jillian had donned her jacket when they had left the hotel. He followed her as she walked over to two headstones and stopped. She took the flowers Alan held and placed them against the headstones.

He walked away to give her some privacy while she *visited* her family. He leaned against the car, watching the movement of her hands and arms as she talked.

A baby – Jillian was here to visit her baby's grave. What kind of man would leave his wife because their baby died? Did Jillian still love him? Is that why she'd never divorced him? He was becoming more and more drawn to her, but what kind of future could they share if she remained married?

After a lengthy visit, Jillian walked toward the car. Alan was quiet as she picked up the arrangement of pink lilies. He moved to her side, and she looked up at him. He saw tears pooling in her eyes, producing the gorgeous green color he remembered from their first encounter in the ambulance.

"Walk with me?" she asked.

"Sure," he replied as he fell in step beside her. They followed a path to a large tree. Its branches were so wide it offered shade to the surrounding graves when the sun was high in the sky.

Jillian paused for a moment then continued on to the small grave site of Lily Russell. She knelt on the ground and with great care, placed the arrangement of flowers against the headstone. She sat without speaking for a while with Alan at her side.

"Each year when I come here, I think about how old she would be and what her life would be like, the activities she'd be involved in. I think about what she would look like, the color of her hair, her eyes. I wonder what kind of personality she might have."

Alan remained by her side, quiet, letting her talk.

"April Fool's Day. What a joke on me, thinking I was going to have this great life raising my daughter, only to have it snatched away in a heartbeat. Or, more accurately, the lack of a heartbeat." Tears rolled down her red cheeks.

Alan put his arm around her shoulder.

She rested her head against his chest and in a soft voice said, "This is the first time in seven years I have felt comfort in my grief for Lily."

He squeezed her shoulder. "I guess grief plays out in different ways for people. I don't think I could ever abandon someone I loved, just because I was hurting." Jillian's back stiffened against him. Looking at her face, he saw her lips pinched together.

"Jared didn't leave because we lost a baby. He left because I was pregnant. He wanted me to have an abortion so our professional lives could continue uninterrupted." Her shoulders shook as she coughed. Her voice was raspy now, and Alan thought he could hear wheezing when she breathed.

"I decided to change the course of my life for this baby, and I ended up losing her too." Tears flowed unchecked down her face. "I'll never risk losing another baby. I don't plan to ever get pregnant again." She turned and leaned into Alan's chest and cried full force.

Alan held her close and let her cry. *She must have felt so alone when she went through the worst tragedy of her life.* He knew without a doubt he wanted to help her find the happiness she deserved. At that moment, he knew he loved her. His phone rang, interrupting his thoughts. He stroked her hair. "Jillian, it's the hospital. I need to check in."

He stood up. "I'll just be a few minutes," he said as he walked away.

Alan had his back to Jillian while he talked to his coworker. Finished with his call, he tucked his phone in his pocket and turned around. Immediately he could tell Jillian was in respiratory distress. She was struggling to pull air into her lungs. He ran to the car and, digging through her handbag, found the inhaler. As he raced up the incline to Jillian, a sense of panic took over, something he typically didn't experience during an emergency. *Get it together.* He sat down beside her and pulled her upright. Shaking the inhaler, he said, "Alright, blow out a breath." He placed the inhaler to her mouth, and as he squeezed he instructed, "Now take a breath." He waited ten seconds and repeated the sequence. He put his arms around her, feeling her relax as her respiratory distress resolved.

Alan held her for a while and then said, "This has been some trip. Are you ready to go home?"

She nodded in the affirmative and allowed him to help her up. They walked at a slow pace to the car, holding hands without speaking. Alan helped her settle into her seat, realizing he would have to formulate an action plan to make her see they belonged together because he had fallen totally and completely in love with Jillian Russell.

⁕

Alan had been driving for about two hours, and they were close to Charlotte. He kept his hands on the steering wheel, but at intervals, glanced over at Jillian. She was quiet, in her reclined seat with her eyes closed, her face flushed. She had been sleeping for the last hour. The quietness was interrupted by her intermittent coughing. She coughed again, shifting around in her seat. The seat belt held her in check, so she didn't have much room to maneuver. She opened her eyes and focused on Alan.

"How are you doing?" Alan asked.

"I'm cold," she replied as she pulled his jacket tighter around her.

"We're almost home. Would you like to stop and get something hot to drink?" he asked.

"Hot tea sounds good," she replied.

"Alright then, let's find some tea." Alan took the next exit off the interstate and pulled into a parking space at the front of a coffee shop. He got out and walked around to the passenger side then opened the door.

Jillian swung her legs out of the car and as she stood up, her knees buckled, and Alan caught her in his arms. He eased her back into the car and squatted beside her seat. Looking at her face, he was becoming concerned and wished they were closer to Charlotte. Her glazed eyes led him to touch her hot face. "You said something earlier about teaching a class this afternoon. Maybe you could cancel. You look tired, and I know you won't want to be coughing around your students."

"Your concern is appreciated, Alan, but I can't cancel. In six years, I've never cancelled a class, and I'm not planning to start today." She raised her tissue to her face as she began coughing.

"You stay put and I'll be right back with the tea." Jillian nodded. Alan closed the door and disappeared inside. He returned with their drinks, and they started off again.

"You should let it cool a little," he said.

After a bit, she sipped her tea and then fell asleep. The rest of the ride into Charlotte was quiet except for sporadic coughs from the passenger side of the car.

Pulling onto the ER ramp, he sat for a moment to rethink his actions before cutting the engine. He would deal with Jillian's independent streak later. As he got out and walked around to the passenger side, a transporter came out with a wheelchair.

"Eric, I'll take that wheelchair. After I get my friend settled into the chair, would you park my car for me?"

"Sure, Dr. Armstrong. Whatever you need." Alan tossed the keys at the transporter. He opened the passenger door and crouched down beside the seat. "Jillian," he said in a soft voice, touching her shoulder.

She opened her eyes and after coughing asked, "Are we home?"

"Well, almost there," he answered.

"Why have we stopped?" she asked as she struggled with the seat belt to straighten up.

"I decided we needed to make a detour first. Here, let me help you up." He took her hands and pulled her up from her seat. "Now turn around and sit down. Thanks, George. I've got it from here." George nodded then walked inside. Alan placed his hands on the back of the wheelchair and, turning toward the entrance, began wheeling toward the door.

"Alan, what are you doing? I need to go to the studio. What time is it? I have a class." Her words were interrupted with coughing.

He stopped pushing the wheelchair. "Look, you're in no shape to teach a class today, so here's what you're going to do." He fought to keep the anger out of his voice. It frustrated him when people didn't pay attention to their health. "Since you haven't bothered in six years' time to find a doctor, you're going into the ER with me. I'm going to start an IV, draw some blood for labs and do a chest x-ray. After I get the results, we'll talk some more."

She closed her mouth as he pushed the wheelchair inside the door.

Fourteen

Alan stretched out on the sofa in the doctors' lounge. Tucking one arm behind his head, he pointed the remote at the television, looking for something to watch.

The door burst open. "Sorry I'm running late. I had to listen to Franklin's daily lecture on how I can improve myself as a physician. I'm glad you waited for me."

"No problem, Ron. You sounded pretty excited on your phone message." Alan pressed the power button on the remote, and the screen went blank.

"I've worked up some demographic information on two possible locations for a rural clinic operation. One is Climbing Rock in the northeastern part of the state, and the other is Hartman, Virginia. The demographics include a one-hundred-mile radius around each town. I was hoping we could go scope out the locations in person."

"Give me some time to look over the information, and we'll talk soon about scouting locations."

"Great. Here's a copy for you to keep. Sorry we can't go over it together, but I have to run. I'm hyped-up about all this, Alan. I hope we can make it work."

"Me too."

Having a lull in his schedule, Alan remained on the sofa. He hadn't lost interest in the goal he had set two years ago. But the appeal of being the one to provide the care to the patients was losing its luster. He still wanted to be a part of the project, to help plan it and even help with financial support, but to leave Charlotte now that his heart was taken—he just didn't think it would happen.

Jillian sat at her desk, examining the revision of the proof for the *Cinderella* program. She sighed with relief. It looked good this time around, making this another item she could check off her list as completed. Opening night was three weeks away and the black-tie fundraiser was scheduled a week after. Smiling, she realized everything was falling into place. A small voice reminded her to stay alert for any red flags, suggesting possible complications to a successful ending of the company's fifth season. Since the ER visit she'd felt better than she had in the past several weeks and knew she was at the top of her game. She wouldn't miss any red flags.

Checking her watch, she was glad to see she had time to do a few more things before meeting with Audrey for their weekly rendezvous. Jillian was happy to steal away from the studio for a few hours each week. As opening night loomed closer, she found it invigorating to take a break from all the production hoopla. When she returned to focus on her work, she found her head was clear, and she was ready to jump back into action.

She enjoyed the time she spent with Audrey, whose engaging personality pulled Jillian out of her introversion. She found herself expressing her feelings and telling Audrey things about her past she had never put into words, even to Barb. There was a connection between them. Their friendship thrived because Audrey accepted her unconditionally.

At one o'clock, Jillian drove out of the studio parking lot, heading to the art gallery district in NoDa. Audrey was waiting for her at the entrance of the Pierce Grady Gallery As they walked through the doors, Jillian took Audrey by the arm and led her to the gallery's permanent collection. They enjoyed a slow walk through the European Art Collection section, admiring works by Renaissance and Baroque artists and nineteenth-century French impressionism.

"So, how are things looking for opening night?"

"Everything seems to be falling into place, but I'm cautious with my thoughts. I'm seasoned enough to realize anything can go wrong at any time. I have no doubt the professionalism of the group will carry us through any obstacles we meet." They strolled to the end of the collection.

"I believe you're ready and that's good. Oh—here's the section of new artists. I always check out the new ones. I like to predict who will have a successful future. I've hit the nail on the head a few times."

Jillian stared at the cool, green eyes looking back at her. *What would it have been like to have had Audrey's guidance when I was growing up?* They perused the area and as they came to the last artist's works, Audrey paused. She took her time looking at each piece, moving about and looking from different angles.

"This is the one. Take my advice—keep your eyes and ears open about Serena Morgan's work."

Jillian had always been a fan of impressionism, but something about the clean lines and sharp details caught her attention. No softness around the edges, the artist's feelings announced on the canvas for all to see, holding nothing back.

They moved on to the area housing current exhibitions of pieces on loan to the gallery. A Degas piece, entitled *Ballet Rehearsal,* hung prominently on the wall. Jillian kept circling back to admire it. "I've always like his *Blue Dancers* but this one—I'm drawn to it."

"It's no mystery to me, Jillian. Your art is in your soul, and it's reflected in your taste of style, music, and even artwork. I don't connect to this piece like you do, but that's okay."

Feeling happy and not wanting their afternoon to end, Jillian asked, "Do you have time to make a stop at Java before I head back to the studio?"

Jillian entered the studio thirty-five minutes before rehearsal was to start. She sat down on the floor and wrapped and secured the ribbons of her ballet slippers around her ankles. She winced, her left ankle feeling a little tender today. But she was used to the aches and pains of a dancer's life. She began to stretch, preparing her body for rehearsal. As she moved to the barre, dancers began invading the space, replicating the things she had already done. At three o'clock, she motioned to the practice pianist and said, "Let's begin."

The dancers moved to the barre as Jillian recited, "*Battement tendu, tendu jet é, frapp é, fondue, rond de jambes*. She moved among the dancers, extending a leg, pulling out an arm. The cadence of the piano continued as Barbara crossed the studio floor and spoke in a confidential manner to Jillian. The silencing of her voice broke the concentration of the dancers. She held up an arm, signaling the pianist to stop then faced the dancers. "Constance, please take over. I'll be back soon."

The sound of the piano resumed as Jillian followed Barbara to the reception area. Upon seeing the stranger, she stopped abruptly. He was a man of great stature with dark, searching eyes. Her stomach rolled. In a defensive move, she joined Barbara behind her desk. A feeling of dread engulfed her. Her heart raced, but decided in that second she was not going to let him intimidate her. She relaxed her muscles. "I understand you need to speak with me. Can I help you with something?"

"Are you Jillian Bailey Russell?" His voice resonated with depth and power.

"Yes, I am," she replied.

"I have some documents for you, and I need your signature to verify receipt of said documents."

She glanced at the upper left-hand corner and saw *McKenzie, Woodard & Donaldson, LLC* imprinted on the envelope. She took the clipboard the man offered and signed her name.

He exchanged the envelope for the clipboard, tipped his hat, and said, "You ladies have a fine day." And then he was gone.

Jillian licked her dry lips. "Barb, let's go to my office."

Barbara pulled a chair beside the desk. Jillian handed her a letter opener.

"Open it for me, please."

She sliced through the top of the envelope, and passed the contents to Jillian. The papers trembled in her hands. She glanced over the words, not taking in what was written on the page. Her eyes were pulled to Jared's signature at the bottom. She experienced a lag in processing the information before her. She had tucked her brief time with Jared in a far corner of her mind and had not let it emerge for seven years. She sat without moving or talking.

Barbara touched her shoulder. "Hey, are you okay?"

"Just a little shell-shocked, even though I knew it was coming. I initiated the divorce."

"This is good, Jillian. Now you can have a real relationship with Alan, if that's what you want."

Jillian's breath caught in her chest. Her shoulders slumped as she gazed down at the floor.

"Oh, I get it. As long as you were married, you were safe. Now your safety zone is gone. The real test starts now. Can you and Alan make it as a couple? Remember, Jillian, you were the one telling me after the explosion you didn't want to die not having had a man in your life to love, and who would love you back. You need to think hard about this, but not for long. You've got this gorgeous man who wants you. The question is what are you going to do about it?" She squeezed her hand. "Lecture over."

Jillian stood up and moved toward the door. "Good, you're giving me a headache. I'm going back to rehearsal, and then I plan to get out of here at a decent hour tonight." She turned to leave, but Barbara's words stopped her.

"Sounds like a terrific idea, and I have just the plans for your night. My tickets to the Reagan Whitmore concert are yours."

Jillian whirled around. "I can't take your tickets. You've been talking nonstop about this concert since you won those tickets last week. And what about your date with Roger?"

Barbara's eyes sparkled with excitement. "I'll keep my date with Roger. We'll just do something else." She took a step toward Jillian and poked her shoulder with her finger. "*You will take my tickets.* Think of it as a divorce gift. Call Alan and ask him out but don't tell him where you're going. Tell him it's a mystery date. At some point tonight, you can give him the news about your divorce. Oh, and the best part about the ticket package is backstage passes to meet Reagan."

Jillian closed her eyes and for the first time in years felt lighthearted. "All right, I'll do it." Her eyes grew large with panic. "Barb, what am I going to wear?"

"You'll figure it out." She passed by Jillian and stepped into the hallway. "Now call, before you go back to rehearsal. Call him."

Jillian watched the muscles in her forearm twitch as she reached for her phone for the third time. Her sweaty hand made contact with the pink-trimmed rectangle. She touched the screen to scroll down her contact list and selected Alan's name. Sitting back in her chair, she crossed her legs, waiting for him to answer. Taking a calming breath, she waited as the call went to voicemail. This might be her only chance so she took it.

"Hey, Alan, it's Jillian. I'll be leaving the studio early tonight, and I'd like to spend the evening with you. I have everything planned. Meet me at Brookhaven Grille at six-thirty. I'd appreciate a call back if you can't make it, so I can alter my plans. Otherwise, I'll see you at six-thirty. Oh, and wear a suit. Bye." Pressing the end button and closing her eyes, she blew out a breath. "Done—and I can't take it back."

Fifteen

Jillian sat at the table, sipping white wine, as she twirled the end of a red curl around her finger. She had not heard anything back from Alan, so she assumed he would show up soon. But what if he hadn't gotten her message? Plan B—she could attend the concert alone. An evening of a first-rate performance would be a good way to spend her new-found leisure time. A tingle of excitement had raced through her while she dressed for her evening with Alan. The green cocktail dress accentuated her eyes and fit her to perfection. She reveled in lightheartedness. Her marriage, dissolved on paper, gave her future a clean slate. She knew she wanted to spend time, lots of time, with Alan. And now she could do it with a clear conscience.

Feeling a light touch on her shoulder, she tilted her head upward. Alan bent down and kissed her on the cheek then took the seat across from her. Her pulse quickened in anticipation of what the night might bring.

"I'm sure glad I checked my messages between surgery and rounds today. I would have been disappointed if I had missed out on your offer tonight. I'm curious about our itinerary since you told me to wear a suit. Do I get a hint?"

Her lips curved into a smile. "Let's order dinner and I'll think about it."

After a satisfying dinner of salad and pasta, combined with small talk, Alan relaxed back in his chair and said, "Okay, give it up."

She fluttered her eyelashes and asked in her best southern accent, "Why, sir, whatever do you mean?"

Alan threw his head back and laughed. "A new side of Jillian Russell I didn't know existed. Do you do other accents as well?"

"As a matter of fact, I do." And then her voice became serious. "Here's the thing. I have some news I'd like to share with you." She paused for a moment, wondering what he would think about her announcement. And then in a rush of words, she blurted out, "Jared signed the divorce papers I sent to him."

Alan sat for a moment then took her hand and kissed it. Staring into her eyes, he said, "His loss is my gain."

If she had been standing, she would have melted to the ground on quivering legs. Mesmerized by his eyes, the short, simple statement he had just spoken told her everything she longed to hear. They were finally on the same page about where they wanted to take their relationship.

She pulled her hand back. Clearing her throat she said, "We should be leaving so we'll be on time for the next stop on our itinerary."

Holding hands, they walked the short distance to the concert hall.

"Are we going to hear the Charlotte Philharmonic perform? This will be my first time to hear them play."

"I'm sorry to disappoint you, but Barbara won tickets to hear this pianist, and she gave them to me."

Alan frowned "A pianist—okay."

"Not only are we going to hear her play, but the package includes backstage passes to meet Reagan Whitmore."

Stopping and pulling back on her hand, Alan echoed, "Reagan Whitmore?"

"Yes. Is something wrong?"

"No, I've heard her play. She's a fine artist."

Jillian glanced at her watch then stepped away, taking Alan with her. "We should find our seats. Her performance starts in ten minutes."

※

Alan tuned out Jillian's lighthearted chatter and focused on the grand piano on the stage. *Reagan was here in Charlotte! And I will see her backstage after the concert.* He had had such high hopes for the night when he had heard Jillian's news. But now to have his past collide with his future was almost comical. The house lights dimmed and a hush fell over the audience.

Reagan walked onto the stage amid the applause of the excited audience. She bowed at her waist, a graceful bow, before taking her seat at the piano. Alan's breath caught in his throat. She was stunning in a muted, turquoise-lace mermaid gown. The neckline was sheer with beautiful beading. The skirt flowed to the ground. As usual, her long, dark brown hair was swept in an updo.

She opened with Beethoven's "Sonata No. 8 in C minor." It was executed with a flawless precision, no surprise to Alan. He watched her body move in the familiar rhythm to the sounds she produced, movement that he remembered as clearly as if he had watched her play yesterday. Her fingers flew over the keys and twenty minutes after she'd begun, she ended the piece with a stellar finish. Reagan stood, bowed, and left the stage. The house lights remained dimmed.

Jillian lightly touched Alan's arm. "She's magnificent. I can't wait to meet her. I'll have to get Barb a nice thank you gift for the tickets."

Alan nodded. If the lights had been up, Jillian might have seen his trans-like state when he replied, "She's just as I remember her."

Reagan returned and resumed the first portion of the program. Schubert's "Impromptu in G flat major" was followed by Rachmaninoff's "Prelude Op. 23 No. 5." As Reagan bowed, Alan glanced at the program. *She's ending the first half with Chopin.* The polonaise was short, but had a powerful ending. Reagan exited the stage amid a thunder of applause as the house lights came up. People began leaving their seats to move about during the intermission.

Alan and Jillian walked through the noisy lobby without attempting to talk. He took a place in line for two glasses of wine while Jillian went in search of the ladies' room. How was he going to handle seeing Reagan after all these years, after all the pain he had endured? He didn't know any way to convince Jillian to skip the backstage meeting. Should he tell her about knowing Reagan, about loving Reagan?

When Jillian caught up with Alan, he was still at a loss as to what he should do. Handing her a glass of wine, he decided to leave it up to fate. She looked beautiful this evening in the green dress that accented her eyes. He like the way her red hair flowed over her shoulders. She wore her hair up most of the time, and he liked the change.

Alan had been encouraged by the news of her divorce. As they had moved toward the concert hall, he had felt a charge of electricity passing between them, excited that maybe now they had a shot at a future together. He had been walking on air until he heard Reagan's name, and then he plummeted to reality.

"Good evening, Dr. Armstrong."

Alan shifted his head toward the sound of his boss's voice. Shaking hands, he replied, "Dr. Schuster, it's nice to see you."

"I'd like you to meet Mrs. Schuster. Annabelle, this is Alan Armstrong, one of our trauma surgeons at Bradley."

Alan nodded. "Mrs. Schuster, it's so nice to meet you. Let me introduce my friend, Jillian Russell."

"Ms. Russell, how do you do? Russell, I've heard that name somewhere," drawled Annabelle in a genuine southern accent.

"Jillian is the owner and artistic director of the North Carolina Ballet Company. Perhaps you've seen some of our recent advertising for their upcoming production of *Cinderella*."

"Now I remember, we received an invitation to a black-tie fundraiser. We've not been invited in the past. It's our first invitation."

She sounds a little irritated. Ready with service recovery, Alan spoke up. "Please be assured, you've not been overlooked for past fundraisers. This is the company's first black-tie affair. So we hope you and Dr. Schuster will come and enjoy the evening with us."

Appearing to have been soothed, she answered, "We'll have to see about putting it on our calendar. John, I think it's time we return to our seats. Good night." Dr. Schuster nodded and followed his wife.

"Thanks for taking the lead. I felt tongue-tied, which makes me wonder if I'll survive the fundraiser. My comfort zone is limited to small group activity."

"I don't believe you. I've seen you running rehearsals with a crowd of dancers."

"That's being in charge, taking the lead. I'm talking about social situations." The lights blinked, signaling the end of intermission.

"No problem, I have your back, and so do Jenny and Audrey and Barbara. It'll be fine," he answered as he touched the small of Jillian's back, guiding her through the crowd of people as they returned to their seats.

The second portion of the program was as wonderful as the first. But as the conclusion of each piece brought them closer to the end of the concert and the meeting backstage, Alan found himself wishing he could run away. *Why did Reagan have to come out of my past on the same night I feel my relationship with Jillian is going to make a huge leap into the future?* He didn't know if he would have ever told Jillian about Reagan. But now the past relationship was staring them in the face, and the decision had been made for him. Within the next hour, Jillian would know about Reagan. The applause broke into his thoughts, and he joined the rest of the audience in a standing ovation for the acclaimed artist.

Alan eyed the exits, envious of the crowd of people heading toward the back of the concert hall. Jillian gave a light tug on his arm.

"Let's go meet Reagan Whitmore. I'm so excited."

Alan's limbs tingled as he followed her toward the steps leading to the stage. Jillian presented their passes, and they were ushered to a back area where a controlled line of a dozen or so people stood in front of them, waiting at Reagan's dressing room door.

He couldn't let this revelation smack her in the face. He had to prepare her. "Jillian, there's something I want to tell you—"

"Oh look. There she is," said Jillian, pointing toward the front of the line.

Alan froze as he stared at the woman with whom he had once planned to spend a lifetime. Moving down the line, Reagan's pace was slow, taking the time to chat with each person as she signed programs. He was gazing at her beautiful face when she made contact with his eyes. Her arms fell to her sides.

She murmured, "Excuse me," pushing past the waiting fans. She walked up to Alan and asked, "Is it really you?"

The blood rushed to Alan's head, and his temples throbbed as he replied, "It's me."

Reagan, being a bit shorter than Alan, wrapped her arms around his waist and hugged him close. Alan was pulled into his memories from their past and hugged her back, remembering what their embraces had felt like so many years ago. He pushed her back but didn't release her. Not knowing what to say, he uttered the first thought that came to his mind.

"I'm sorry about your mom and dad. I should have called."

In an instant, he saw the pain register in her eyes and was sorry for saying something so personal to her amid the strangers around them. She stepped back.

"I should continue meeting everyone." Returning to the front of the line, she resumed the meet-and-greet process.

Jillian had been quiet, still as a statue, taking in the exchange. Before Alan could say a word, she turned and retreated down the steps of the stage. He lost no time in running after her, calling her name. Alan heard Reagan's name shouted and looked back at the stage. He saw her crumpled form on the floor. Glancing to the back of the concert hall, he saw no sign of Jillian. He felt pull from both directions, but the physician side of him won out, and he ran on stage and knelt by Reagan's limp form.

His assessment skills kicked into action. She had a pulse and was breathing, but her color was not good. Someone had taken over and was moving the small crowd of people away from their space. He picked her up and carried her toward the dressing room. The same take-charge person appeared beside them. She opened the door and after they stepped inside, closed it, leaving the curious onlookers on the other side of the door. Alan laid her on the sofa. Her skin was pale and clammy. The helper handed Alan a wet cloth. He wiped Reagan's face and neck. She began to stir.

"Reagan, it's Alan, open your eyes." Her eyelids fluttered and then opened, revealing the hazel eyes he remembered so well. Her eyes rested on Alan's face.

"What happened?"

"I'm not sure. I left the stage, and I heard someone shout your name. When I turned around, you were on the floor. What do you remember?"

"I remember seeing you leave. I was curious, as well as a few other people, so we followed you onto the stage. I started to feel dizzy and needed to sit down, so I moved toward my piano bench, but I don't remember anything more."

"Excuse me. I'm Stella, Reagan's assistant." She sat a glass of juice on the round, cocktail table. "Reagan, you should drink this. You still have some diehard fans waiting outside. Do you feel up to finishing your meet-and-greet?"

"Yes, of course. Just let me sit for a few minutes. Do we have any CDs handy we can give them, since they're being patient about my situation?"

"I'll see what I can find while your drink your juice."

Reagan moved to a sitting position and reached for the glass of juice. Alan sat down beside her. He picked up her wrist and held it until he felt a steady pulse. He studied her face, noting the dark circles under her eyes, concealed by makeup, until he had wiped her face with the cloth. He was relieved to see some color returning to her face.

"Your situation—has this happened before? Maybe you should go back to your hotel and rest."

"Thank you for your concern, Alan, but I'll be fine." She raised her glass. "A little juice to bring up my blood sugar and I'll be good to go.

Allen studied her face as he listened to her speech.

"I was through half of the crowd before all this excitement stirred things up. It won't take long to meet the others. So how long are you going to keep me in suspense? Who was the young lady you were running after?"

Stella interrupted, "Reagan, you should finish your meet-and-greet. It's getting late."

"You're right, Stella." She stood up on wobbly legs and proceeded to the door. Turning to Alan, she asked, "Will you be here when I get back?"

"No, I have some fence mending to do. Where are you staying? Maybe we could meet tomorrow."

"I'm staying at the Windom Hotel." She moved toward her assistant. "Stella—lunch?"

"We have to leave by one o'clock for DC."

"Well then, maybe next time. Goodbye, Alan," she said as she walked out the door.

Jillian rushed down the street toward the parking garage. How could Alan be so insensitive? Why had he not said anything about knowing Reagan before they went backstage?

This was a new side of Alan, and she was sure she didn't like it. What should she do now? She had glanced over her shoulder twice since leaving the concert hall, but he had not followed her out of the building. She stopped short as she realized this was the woman Jenny had once mentioned. A pianist to whom Alan had given his heart, only to have it shattered. But not just any pianist, it had been Reagan Whitmore! The realization she had met a woman from Alan's past in the flesh made Jillian's heart race. She was flooded with insecurity at the possibility of Alan rejecting her after seeing and holding his past love.

Arriving at her parked car, she fumbled with the key then managed to unlock the door. She slid into the driver's seat, shaking as a jumble of emotions attacked her. Nausea bubbled up from her stomach into her throat. The desire to vent her frustration and hurt consumed her. She pulled out her cell phone, scrolled down her contact list, and touched the screen. She licked her dry lips and waited.

"Hi. I know it's late, but would you mind if I came over?" A tear rolled down her right cheek. "Thanks, I'll see you soon." Jillian turned the key in the ignition and started the engine. She pulled out of the parking garage and drove with the radio on to distract her from thinking. It was a short drive to her destination. She parked beside the curb. She could feel her legs shake as she made her way to the house. The door opened before she could press the doorbell. Jillian hesitated before stepping over the threshold into the foyer. Should she bother Audrey with her problems?

"Thanks for seeing me. Something happened tonight that upset me, and I need to talk to someone. But if it's too late or you don't want to listen, I'll understand."

Audrey put her arm around Jillian and gave her shoulder a squeeze. "Of course I'll listen. I put some water on for tea after you called. It should be ready." She guided Jillian to the kitchen.

Her eyes widened. "Oh my," was all Jillian could say as her eyes moved around the spacious, gourmet kitchen. A centralized island dominated the room. Taking in the space, she noted a freestanding workstation with a butcher-block surface that included a utility sink with a long neck faucet. Off to one side was a walk-in pantry. The appliances were all high-end.

"You must like to cook."

A smile brightened Audrey's face. "The kitchen came with the house, but before my husband, Benjamin, died, I did enjoy cooking." Her smile faded, and she stared into the air. "It's no fun to cook for one."

"I know how you feel, but what a waste of such a wonderful kitchen." She ran her hand over the granite top of the island.

Audrey poured hot water into two teacups and added a teabag to each one. "You should come over sometime and cook. If you want, we could fix a meal here instead of going out."

"I'd love to prepare a dinner in this kitchen." Her mood seemed to lighten as they took their teacups and walked into the family room, adjacent to the kitchen. Audrey had that effect on her.

After they were seated, Audrey said, "Now tell me, what's bothering you."

Jillian twisted the end of her hair between her index and middle finger. "It has to do with my date tonight with Alan, but I should explain something to you first." She paused then pulled in a big breath of air. "Seven years ago I married a dancer named Jared. We became estranged when he moved away to take a job with the Royal Danish Ballet. I didn't divorce him. I just wanted to put the whole ugly mess behind me and get on with my life. Then I met Alan, and because of the feelings I have for him, I decided I wanted the divorce. The finalized papers arrived earlier today by messenger. Barb convinced me to ask Alan out tonight so I could tell him about the divorce." She paused to sip her tea.

"Did Alan know about your marriage?"

"Yes. After our second kiss, I felt so guilty the words were out of mouth before I realized what I had said."

"So he knew you were married, and then you gave him the news about your divorce. How did he respond?"

Jillian stood and began pacing in front of the large coffee table. "He was wonderful. While we were walking from the restaurant to the concert hall, I felt this renewed excitement about our future. And in truth, I was looking forward to the end of our date." Jillian's eyes darted to the floor. "I wanted him to kiss me again."

"But it didn't happen?"

Jillian raised her head, her eyes meeting Audrey's as she sat down again. "We never finished our date. Barb had given me tickets to the Reagan Whitmore piano concert she had won last week. The package included backstage passes to meet Reagan. So after the concert we were waiting in line to meet her. She was signing autographs and then she saw Alan. She stopped what she was doing, and as simple as anything, walked back to him and put her arms around him. He held her and then said something about her parents, which seemed to upset her. She retreated away from him and returned to signing programs. I freaked out and left. I heard Alan call my name, but I didn't stop. After I got outside, I headed to the parking garage, but he didn't follow me. I'm so mixed up! I'm angry—I'm sad. I know I handled this badly but I was so surprised—"

"Darling, life is full of pitfalls. These situations should make us look hard at who we are and what we want out of life. It you do, maybe you can stay away from the pitfalls. So, you have feelings for Alan?"

"Yes, strong feelings."

"And you're certain you want him in your future?"

"Yes."

"Let's think about Alan for a moment. How did he react to Reagan hugging him?"

"Well, he hugged her back."

"A natural response. Now the work begins. Relationships just don't happen. I know at first there's the smitten factor drawing two people together, but beyond that, it takes work. Communication is important. It can reduce the number of pitfalls along the way. So if you don't talk to Alan about tonight, your tender, budding relationship may experience a pitfall it might not survive."

Audrey patted Jillian's hand. "Talk to Alan—and this is really important—listen to him when he talks to you about what happened tonight."

Jillian covered her mouth to hide a yawn. "I'm sorry—it's been a long day. I need to go home. Thank you for letting me talk everything out. I might be able to sleep now." They walked toward the front door.

"I was glad to listen. Anytime you need anything, all you have to do is call. Hmm... I think those are some of the lyrics from a 1970s' James Taylor song."

Audrey's quirkiness brought a smile to Jillian's face. "Good night, Audrey, and thanks."

"Careful driving."

Sixteen

The knock on the hotel door brought Reagan to her feet. Looking through the peep hole, she groaned when she saw Alan standing on the other side of the door. She had not been up long enough to put on her makeup and didn't want him to see her without it. The insomnia she had been experiencing the past few months had left her looking tired and gaunt. The circles under her eyes were becoming more difficult to cover with makeup. The overwhelming sadness over her parents' deaths was taking its toll on her. And then last night, a bright light had appeared in the form of Alan Armstrong, giving her dark existence a reason to remember the past and smile.

Reagan's sigh was heavy. Was this a mistake? She knew she wasn't the same person she'd been eleven years ago. She didn't have the energy to be that young woman again, even for Alan. She pulled the door open. "What are you doing here?" she asked. Her words come out with a harshness she had not intended.

Smiling, he held up a bag. "I brought bagels." He stepped inside and walked across the suite. Placing the bag and two cups of coffee on the table, he asked, "How are you feeling this morning?"

"So, this isn't a social call?" She eyed him suspiciously.

"Sure it is. I'm just being polite."

"Alan, it's eight o'clock in the morning."

"Sounds like a good time for breakfast. And to tell the truth, I wanted to check on you before you left town."

She looked down at the floor and remained silent.

"Reagan, please talk to me. I want to help if I can."

"I'll admit it. I'm tired." She raised her head. "We're at the end of the tour, and I'm tired."

Alan pointed to a chair, and she sat down. He pushed the bag of bagels and a coffee in front of her. Crossing his arms, he said, "Tell me about this low-blood-sugar business."

"I'd rather you tell me about your mystery lady. Did you straighten everything out with her?"

Alan sat down in the chair opposite Reagan. "I'm sorry to say I haven't. I tried calling her a few times last night, but she didn't answer. It's a shame things turned out the way they did. Jillian was so excited about meeting you."

"I'm flattered. Maybe I'll get to meet her someday."

"I'll try to talk to her today. Now, stop changing the subject. While you answer my question, I expect you to eat a bagel."

She pulled a bagel out of the bag and smeared some strawberry-flavored cream cheese on top. "I don't know why you're getting so worked up over this."

He stared her down. "I'm not leaving until you tell me what's going on."

"I still have to pack for DC."

Alan crossed his right ankle over his left knee and leaned toward Reagan. "Then you should probably start talking."

She took her time chewing the piece of bagel that was in her mouth. Finally, she admitted, "I've had two episodes. The first was two cities ago, and the last one, well, you saw the last one. I just need some rest."

Alan sipped his coffee then reached in the bag for a bagel. "When does your tour end?"

"I have DC and New York then a three-week break before my next tour begins."

"Will you be going home to San Francisco?"

Reagan closed her eyes for brief seconds. "No, I don't have any plans to go to San Francisco." "Stella has booked a beach condo for two weeks in the Caribbean. She's been trying to talk me into spending my third week on a singles' cruise. She said it would be good for me to get out and mingle. I think the beach sounds good, but I'm not up to a cruise. If I like the location in Barbados, I might spend my third week there as well."

"Or you could come back here and spend a week with a friend."

"Stay here—with you?"

"Why not? I'm your friend."

Reagan stood up and moved away from the table. She turned around and looked at Alan. "You're serious."

"Yes, I am. Aren't you tired of hotel rooms and hotel food?" I can guarantee some delicious home-cooked meals while you're here."

A grin spread across her lips. "You learned to cook?"

Alan laughed. "I do all right, but I was talking about Jenny. She lives here in Charlotte with her husband, and they have a newborn son. Jenny's the cook I was referring to."

"Jenny has a husband—and a baby!"

"Please say you'll spend your last week with us. I can schedule a physical for you while you're in town."

"It's not necessary."

Alan walked over to her and placed his hands on her shoulders. "What can it hurt? If nothing else, it'll confirm for me that you're okay."

"I haven't even agreed to come back."

"You owe me."

She stepped back. Her nostrils flared as she pulled in a noisy breath. "I owe you?"

Alan laughed. "I can see it still doesn't take much to rouse your ire. All I meant was I stopped to check on you when I should have run after Jillian. So now you have to help me fix things with her. It might soothe her to hear you're coming back, and she'll get to meet you."

"I've got to pack. Here's the deal. I'll call you from Barbados and give you my decision. How much notice do you need?"

"Call me at the end of your first week. We'll make the week as busy or restful as you want."

"Sounds wonderful."

"We aim to please."

Traffic was light for a Saturday morning. Alan drove the two miles from downtown Charlotte to the studio in less than ten minutes. He parked beside Jillian's car and sat for a few minutes, thinking about how to tell her about Reagan. Taking a deep breath, he moved from his car to the studio door. It was locked. He pulled again, just to make sure. Yep, locked. He reached in his pocket for his cell phone and scrolled down to Jillian's number.

On the fourth ring, he contemplated leaving a message, when he heard, "Good morning, Alan."

He strained to read the tone of her voice. "Hi, Jillian. I'm at the studio door. May I please come in, so we can talk about last night?"

After a long pause, she whispered, "I'll be right there."

As they walked through the dark reception area and hallway, she explained, "Barb's not coming in today. I don't like to be here alone without locking the door."

"A good move, I completely agree." They entered her lighted office, and seeing her red-rimmed, puffy eyes, remorse filled him, that he had caused her distress. He touched her shoulders. "Jillian, I'm so sorry about last night."

She moved away and settled into her seat behind the desk, putting distance between them. "Alan, I'm sorry I didn't give you a chance to talk last night. I'm ready to listen now, if you have anything you want to say."

He sat down on the sofa. "I was taken off-guard when you announced we'd be meeting Reagan. I met her eleven years ago. She was a student at Juilliard, finishing her degree." He paused, knowing his words were going to hurt her. "We fell in love. Six months later, she left on her first tour, and I headed to Boston to start my residency program at Boston Medical. Six months after that, she broke off our relationship. She said the timing wasn't right." He ran his hand through his hair. "I didn't know what to say to you last night. I'm sorry I screwed things up."

Jillian spoke in a soft voice. "How did you feel last night when you saw her?"

"During the concert, I was mesmerized by her performance. Backstage it was—surreal. She hugged. I hugged back. After you left the stage I followed *you*, so I'd like you to take that as my feelings for you being stronger than my feelings for Reagan."

"When I got outside, I looked back twice, and you weren't there."

"While I was following you, I heard someone shout Reagan's name. She had fainted on the stage. I looked at the back of the concert hall, and you were gone. So I went to Reagan. She needed my help."

"Is she okay?"

"I'm not convinced she is. I'm trying to talk her into coming back for a week before her next tour begins."

"I see." She closed her eyes and rubbed the scar on her right temple.

"I don't think you do, Jillian." He stood up and walked behind the desk. He pulled her out of the chair against him and kissed her. A long, intense kiss. Cupping her face between his hands, he followed the first kiss with a gentler one. Her arms encircled his neck, and he kissed her cheek. With his mouth close to her ear, he whispered, "I'm in love with you, not Reagan." He pushed her backward, so he was looking into her eyes. "And somehow I'm going to prove to you we belong together. Be sure you lock the door behind me."

His footsteps echoed in the empty studio as he walked away."

It took a moment for his words to register in her brain, and by then he was gone. *He loves me!* Jillian's knees began shaking, and she eased back down into her chair. Audrey was right. She needed to decide what she wanted out of life. Barb was right. She had to make a decision about Alan soon. *He loves me! What am I going to do about that?*

Seventeen

Jillian walked into Studio A with Barbara and Jenny at the conclusion of their black-tie affair meeting. She drew in a breath, taking in the smell of leather mixed with sweat lingering in the air. It was a familiar scent, one that was not displeasing to her. Looking around, a smile of satisfaction appeared on her face. Some of the company dancers were on the floor stretching, while others were working at the barre. Jasmine was repairing her shoe with a needle and thread. Their professionalism was evident, putting their downtime to good use, as the studio was restaged for the next scene.

The trio sat down as the new scene began. Alan opened the studio door and, slipping in quietly, joined the women. Sitting down beside Jenny on the long bench, he held out his hand and deposited a blue, stuffed puppy in Jenny's lap.

"Thanks for bringing Puppy back. I think Thomas has missed him."

"No problem," he whispered. "What are we watching?"

"Cinderella and the Prince are dancing at the ball."

The group was quiet as they watched the couple dance with ease around the floor. The scene was going well until Cinderella stumbled, breaking their rhythm. Antoinette bent over at her waist and grabbed her partner's arm then sank to the floor, guarding her right side. Alan and Jillian reached her at the same time.

Jillian knelt beside the dancer. "Antoinette, what's wrong?"

"Pain—my right side."

"Let's take her to your office." As he talked, Alan picked up the dancer and carried her out of the studio. He laid her down as Jillian pushed a chair beside the sofa for him.

He sat down and explained, "Antoinette, my name is Alan, and I'm a doctor. Would you let me examine you and see if I can help? Jillian will stay right here with us."

Her hand remained on her right side. "Please, just make the pain go away so I can get back to rehearsal."

He glanced up at Jillian, his lips pressed together. "I'll do my best. Now, I'm going to press on your abdomen, and you tell me when you feel pain. Here we go." Alan pressed above her umbilicus, and as he moved his skilled hands across the lower right quadrant of her abdomen, she cried out in pain. He pulled his hands away.

Jillian pushed stray hair from Antoinette's forehead. "Alan, her head is hot."

Alan laid a hand on her cheek. "Antoinette, how long have you had this pain?"

Antoinette looked up at Jillian with questioning eyes.

Jillian nodded.

"I haven't felt well today. The pain wasn't bad at first, but it hurts now."

"We're going to take you to Bradley Medical Center, where I work. We'll take care of your pain."

Antoinette grabbed her hand. "Are you coming with me? I've never been hospitalized."

She patted her arm. "Of course, Antoinette, I'll come with you. Let me take care of a few things here while Alan helps you to the car."

Jillian returned to the studio. She spent a few minutes talking with Barbara and Jenny then, moving to the front of the group, clapped her hands together.

"Okay, everyone, listen up." She shifted to her right. "Sarah, we'll need you to assume the role of Cinderella." Motioning for Jenny to join her, she added, "Jenny Reid will be taking over for me while I'm at the hospital. Check with Barbara before you leave for any changes to our schedule. People, our show opens in two weeks, and *we will be ready*. I'll try to give you an update before the end of rehearsal." She rushed out the door.

Two hours later, Jillian was seated in the deserted waiting area, her elbows resting on her knees with her hands folded over the back of her neck. A pair of shoes, covered by blue paper covers, moved into her line of vision. She jerked her head upright. There was no need to speak; the question was stated in her expression. Alan pulled off his surgical cap and sat down beside her. "She's being moved to the recovery room. We were lucky. We got to her appendix before it ruptured. She'll have a much easier recovery because of that, but I'm sorry to say, not in time for opening night."

"I had a feeling—Sarah will do a fine job portraying Cinderella. But now I've got to figure out how to cover Sarah's parts in the *corps de ballet*." She closed her eyes and rubbed her right temple.

Alan placed his hands on her shoulders and started to massage away the knot at the base of her neck. "What would be the normal thing to do in a situation like this?"

Jillian stood up and started pacing. "In our five year history, I've never been faced with this problem. I suppose I'll contact an agency and hire someone to fill in."

"Why would you call an agency when you already have a fill in?"

Jillian stopped pacing. "What are you talking about?"

"Well, Jenny, of course. This is her thing. She's good at freelance work, remember?"

Jillian eased herself down into a chair. "I feel bad she didn't come to mind. What makes you think Jenny would be interested? She stopped performing to stay home with Thomas."

"One, she won't have to leave Thomas, and two, I think she misses dancing more than she thought she would. You won't know unless you ask. Let's check on Antoinette, then we'll stop by Jenny's on the way to pick up your car."

Jillian kissed him on the cheek. "You're a natural at making everything better."

He laughed as they stood up. "Maybe I should include that on my resume."

She faced him and, resting her hands on his arms, looked into his eyes. "I'm serious, my life isn't any smoother since I met you, but you sure make the bumps easier to tolerate."

He tilted her head upward and lowered his lips to hers. She raised her arms to his shoulders, and he pulled her close then lifted her off the ground. After several kisses, he allowed her feet to drift back to the floor. Before he released her, he whispered in her ear, "If you'd let me, I'd do whatever it takes to make your life run as smooth as silk."

Jillian finished tying the ribbons of her pointe shoe around her ankle as Jenny entered the studio.

"Hey, JB, I'm ready to get to work."

Smiling, relief flooded Jillian's body. *She's here. We can move on with the production, so quit worrying.* Closing her eyes, she pinched the bridge of her nose with her thumb and index finger to push away the tears that threatened.

"Are you okay?"

"Yes, I'm just so excited you're here. Let's warm up, and then I'll take you through the *corps de ballet* parts in Act One."

"Sounds like a plan. I'll be ready in a few. How is Sarah handling her new role?"

Jillian began stretching her limbs. "She's doing a great job. I have no regrets about having chosen her for the understudy."

She moved to the barre, and within minutes Jenny joined her. They worked for over an hour. Stopping for a short break, Jillian sat down, winded from the workout. Taking some time to recover, she finally spoke.

"I've got several of the corps members coming in to— run through what we've been working on. They're due to be here in about ten—minutes. After we finish rehearsing with them, I've penciled in a two-hour break to talk through Act Two. Then we'll work about three more hours, same setup as now. We'll work together on the dances, take a short break, and then go through what we've worked on with some of the corps members."

"Okay, sounds great." Jenny wiped her face and neck with a white, fluffy towel.

"So, Alan's been looking pretty happy these days. Would you happen to know anything about it?"

A blush of color burst on Jillian's cheeks, and her lips captured a smile. "Things are good between us, Jen. I'm happy too."

Jenny put her arm around her shoulder and gave her a squeeze. "Good. You both deserve to be happy."

A frown appeared on Jillian's face. "I'm a little anxious about Reagan's visit next week. Alan says he loves her as a friend, but I just don't know if his feelings will change while she's here. I guess I'm confused. He loves *me*, but he's invited *her* to stay in his guest room?"

"About that—"

The dancers filed into the studio. Jillian stood up. "We'll finish this later."

Rehearsal resumed, and Jillian once again became a director instead of a performer. It dampened her mood. The group worked at a steady pace for an hour, stopping when necessary to correct missed steps or cues. Then she called for a break. Audrey took the opportunity to step into the studio.

"Can I borrow Jenny for a quick fitting?"

"Sure. You can use my office."

"Why don't you come with us? I want your opinion."

The trio walked into the office and Jenny stepped behind the changing screen to put on her costume.

"We might as well sit while we can," offered Audrey, unable to hide a mischievous grin.

Jillian sat down behind her desk, and her face froze as she stared straight ahead. On the wall opposite her desk was a large Degas reproduction of *The Rehearsal*.

Audrey watched her expression. Unable to stand her silence, she asked, "Do you like it?"

"Audrey, you shouldn't have—"

The smile left Audrey's face. "Did I do something wrong?"

"No—"

"You don't like it?"

"I do like it – I love it."

"I don't understand. I watched you circle back around the original more than once at the gallery. I thought you liked it, and I wanted you to have something that would bring you joy. And maybe remind you of the time we've spent together."

"I didn't mean to hurt your feelings or disappoint you, but you caught me off guard. It's like you're paying me to spend time with you."

"Jillian, it's nothing of the sort. I watched you admire something beautiful, and I wanted you to have a piece of something beautiful. That's all there is to it."

Audrey groaned. Boy, she had botched this up. She couldn't tell her as her mother, she wanted to give her something tangible to make up for all the birthdays and Christmases she had missed. She couldn't tell her she was the woman who left her so many years ago. Not yet. She wasn't ready to risk losing the relationship they were building.

"Why don't you leave it on the wall for a few days and then see how you feel about it. You can let me know what you decide when you come over on Saturday to cook. Oh look—Jenny, it fits just right, and with little altering."

Jenny turned in a circle. "So, JB, what do you think?"

Jillian shifted her eyes from the large painting to her friend. "You look lovely, Jen."

Eighteen

Why had she let Audrey talk her into this dinner party? A big sigh slipped out as she stood alone in the palatial kitchen, slicing strawberries and adding them to the spinach leaves. Audrey had suggested she spend time with Reagan and get a feel for her intentions toward Alan. She had been gracious enough to offer her home for a neutral meeting place, and the dinner party had grown from the idea.

Audrey swept into the kitchen, bringing an air of excitement with her. "It's time to slide the stuffed mushrooms into the oven. I put the merlot beside the wine glasses in the sitting room."

"Good." Her terse reply was followed by her exit from the kitchen into the family room. She stared out the windows into the massive, wooded scenery with her arms folded across her chest. It would be a spectacular sight this fall when the leaves turned to beautiful shades of red, gold, and orange.

"Having trouble with your decision to spend the evening with Reagan?" Audrey asked in a soft tone, moving into the room to stand close by. Jillian spun around with confusion in her eyes.

"I'm bringing enough baggage into this relationship without adding problems that may not be real, just in my own mind."

She led Jillian to the sofa. "Why don't you try approaching tonight from a different angle? Look at this evening as an opportunity to get to know Reagan. I've read a few things about her over the past few years, and it's all been positive."

"I'd like to, but my perspective on the matter is jaded. I see her as a contender for the man I love."

"I don't think that's fair, Jillian. So, shift gears. Make it your goal tonight to give Reagan a nice evening with old friends and new acquaintances. I know the food will be good. Dinner parties are my forte. She must be tired from all the traveling she does, the majority of her interactions being on a superficial level. She could use this time with all of us."

How does Audrey do it? Always gives me the shove I need to try something out of my comfort zone. Am I willing to try because it's Audrey asking?

"I'll give it my best shot."

"Great, now let's go see to the rest of our culinary delights." As they entered the kitchen, the doorbell rang.

"Someone's anxious." Jillian removed her apron. "We still have fifteen minutes before they're supposed to be here."

Audrey sat a pot of water on the stove. "It's Alan. I asked him to come a little early. Would you get the door for me, please?"

Jillian smoothed the folds of her dress as she walked to the foyer. She opened the door, and her breath caught in her throat. These new feelings took her by surprise at times. He was so handsome and ever the gentleman with a bottle of wine in hand. Alan stepped across the threshold. He set the bottle on the foyer table and pulled her close. It always amazed her how she could get so lost in his eyes. As he kissed her, she could smell the scent of aftershave mixed with the pure maleness of him. She didn't want to leave his arms but pulled herself away.

"Good evening, Mr. Armstrong."

"Hello there, Ms. Russell." His voice was low and sexy.

She had to put a stop to his playfulness, wrong place and wrong time. She patted her hair in place. "Where's our guest of honor?"

She'll be along with Jenny, Mark, and Thomas. She's staying with them this week, a change of pace for her, even more so with a baby in the house."

"I don't understand. I thought she was staying with you."

"Well, let's just say sometimes I act or speak before I think."

"Yes, I know from personal experience."

"I'm sorry I wasn't thinking about your feelings when I suggested to Reagan she come back to town and spend the week here. When I saw her after the concert, she appeared so fragile. Then I talked to her the next day and found out she wasn't planning to go home to San Francisco during her break, so I just spoke up."

She put her arm through his, and they strolled into the sitting room. "You're worried about her. I didn't mean to make this hard for you. I just didn't understand—I don't understand—"

Alan touched his fingers to her lips. "Reagan needs rest, which she's had for the past two weeks. And I think she may need some medical attention as well. I do know she needs her friends, old and new. That's what I hope she gets out of this week in Charlotte."

Leaning against him on the sofa, Jillian reached up and stroked the side of his face, her eyes bright with threatened tears. "You're so good to me, Mr. Armstrong. I'm not sure I deserve it."

Alan cradled her face in his hands and kissed her. The gentle approach did it—it roped her in. Jillian wrapped her arms around his neck and returned a fervent kiss to his lips.

Audrey walked in. "Well, kids, I see your night is getting off to a great start."

Jillian pulled herself away from their embrace, a sense of embarrassment ensuing. Alan stood up and approached Audrey.

"I want to thank you again for your gracious offer to welcome my friend to town with a home-cooked meal. You've gone to so much trouble. I don't know how to thank you."

"You're welcome, Alan. I've enjoyed every minute of the preparations. Besides, I think dining at a restaurant would have been too impersonal, knowing the focus of tonight is to get everyone acquainted."

"You're a smart woman, and I'm lucky to know you." He gave her a quick peck on the cheek. The doorbell rang.

"Let me get the door for you." As he moved toward the door, Audrey joined Jillian in the sitting room. Suddenly, the room was full with people and sound. A flutter danced in her stomach. Her gaze darted to Jenny, looking for a sign of encouragement for a good night.

Alan followed Jenny into the kitchen to retrieve the stuffed mushrooms. He had wanted to have a few minutes alone with her to check on Reagan. The opportunity presented itself as soon as Audrey, with reluctance, attempted to excuse herself to the kitchen.

Surveying the scene, Alan jumped in. "No need to give up holding my sweet nephew, Audrey."

This brought an immediate smile to her face.

"Jenny and I will see to the appetizers." He took his sister by the hand, pulling her toward the kitchen.

"Thank you, Alan—and Jenny. The serving plate is on the counter next to the stove," she called out while they made their way to the kitchen.

As soon as their feet hit the kitchen floor, he pounced. "Okay, tell me—how's she doing?"

"Why are you so uptight about Reagan's visit? After all, you're the one who invited her to Charlotte." Jenny began transferring the appetizers from the baking sheet to the serving plate.

"I just want everything to go well. Does she look rested to you? Do you think I should push her to see someone for a physical?"

Jenny laid the spatula on the counter and turned to face him. "Alan, chill! She's been with me all of six hours today. She appears rested, a little anxious about being around a baby. Other than that, I don't have much to report, as if I knew I was going to have to spy on her and report back to you. And another thing, why did you ever think it would be okay for her to stay with you when you have obvious feelings for Jillian? I just don't understand you sometimes."

Alan began pacing, his eyes focused on the floor. "Okay, I admit it. I'm great at being a trauma surgeon, but when it comes to my personal life, I stink. I just wanted to do whatever I could for Reagan. At the time, I wasn't thinking about how it might make Jillian feel."

"So, how strong are your feelings for Jillian?

The pacing came to a halt. "What do you mean?"

"Do you hear "Wedding March" playing in your subconscious when you think of her? If you do, then you need to take into account her feelings when you make big decisions. Like inviting a female friend to stay with you for a week. Or moving to some remote place to practice medicine when you have a perfect job here. So it bears repeating… Sometimes I just don't understand you."

"How did my little sister get so smart? I'm the big brother here. I'm supposed to have all the answers." Alan's shoulders drooped as he slid his hands into his pockets.

"I don't have all the answers. You just don't have any insight on being a woman. Lucky for you—you have me. And you have memories of Dad, how he loved and treated Mom. Use those memories to guide you, when I'm not around."

"Hey, did you guys have to grow those mushrooms?" Mark walked into the kitchen. "We've got people starving out there."

"By people, do you mean you? We got a little tied up in conversation, but they're all set to go." Jenny handed him the platter, and they moved toward the sitting room.

※

Jillian wandered into the family room, looking for the jacket she had brought with her. Retrieving it from the back of the sofa, she walked into the kitchen as Reagan stepped into the kitchen from the deck. They looked at each other simultaneously and stopped. Jillian felt trapped. Now she would have to interact with her alone. She rubbed the back of her neck, feeling the earlier tension flaring up again.

Reagan was the first to speak. "Hey, need any help?"

"No, just claiming my jacket. Audrey likes her house a little on the cool side, but I came prepared." Holding up her jacket, she said, "I hope I didn't disturb you."

Smiling, Reagan waved her phone. "Just checking in with my assistant, at her request. She does enough worrying for the both of us, but she's good at her job."

Jillian pulled on her jacket and picked up a cup. "Coffee?"

"I'd better not, or I won't get to sleep for hours. And then Stella will worry about my not sleeping." A grin settled on her face.

"Touring must be the most amazing thing." A surprising peacefulness settled over Jillian as her posture relaxed. She sat down with her cup and pointed to a chair with her hand.

Reagan joined her at the table. "It was, at first—I mean, it is. But I've been touring for eleven years, and I'm beginning to feel worn down. There's a definite down-side to touring."

"I almost had a performance career, but it didn't work out."

"What happened?"

Jillian's face became expressionless. "I was diagnosed with exercise-induced asthma, and my doctor advised me to stop performing. He suggested teaching as an alternative." She turned her head in Reagan's direction. "And now I have my ballet company, too."

An ache throbbed deep in Jillian's chest as she longed to voice her grief over her lost career to someone who would understand. She moved her gaze from Reagan and stared into the space in front of her, pulling in a deep breath. "Sometimes I lay awake at night trying to imagine how successful I might have been—where my dancing would have taken me."

"My dad used to say, 'Reagan baby, the grass always looks greener on the other side'. As a successful artist, I can tell you all about the negatives of an artist's life."

"I'm sure you can. But there must be positives that have kept you touring for eleven years. I think not knowing how far I could have gone is one of my frustrations."

Reagan moved to the kitchen sink and helped herself to a glass of water. "I believe things happen for a reason. Or, if they don't happen, the timing isn't right." She took a drink of the cool water and reclaimed her seat at the table. "I can see you have feelings for Alan. Your lives have intersected at this place and time. There is a reason you are here and not somewhere else pursuing your dancing career. Maybe this is where you are meant to be, and Alan is the person you're supposed to be with."

"Maybe so." Jillian shifted in her chair. "Reagan, how would you feel if you injured your hand, and you couldn't play anymore?"

"I suppose I could give you a brave answer about coping with a bad situation, but I guess I'll never know, unless something like that happens."

"It has taken me six years of hard work to create a new life, different from the one I had planned as a performer. I cherish the relationship I'm building with Alan, but—since I've been rehearsing with Jenny, to get her ready for opening night, I've felt like my old self when I dance. The asthma doesn't seem to be an issue like it was when I moved to Charlotte. In a way I'm mourning again, because I don't see a barrier to my dancing. Of course if I were on a rigorous schedule of rehearsals and performances, I might have the asthma attacks again. Who knows? I don't have the time to practice to test my theory." She gave a forced smile. "I'm sorry, I've been bending your ear, and you'd probably rather be with the others." Jillian stood up and placed her cup in the sink.

"I'm happy you've used me for a sounding board. Isn't that what friends are for, even new ones? I have few friends, one of the disadvantages of a touring career. I hope we keep in touch when I get back out on the road."

"I'd like that. And I wish you could stay for opening night, but again, a disadvantage to your touring career."

"I'd love to see the performance, in particular Jenny, but I'm due to fly out Friday morning. I've never had great timing."

Nineteen

Opening night—there was nothing like it. The smell of leather mixed with polish, the dazzling lights coupled with the colorful costumes, the rush of adrenaline. Jillian stood backstage and watched the last-minute scurrying ignite a sizzle of excitement in the air. She wavered between a sense of déjà vu and novice emotions as the night began to unfold. She had new friends and Alan to share in her passion of her company, as she hoped for another night of success.

The past week had been a time of revelation. At the dinner party, she had noticed a new dimension to Audrey's personality. She had beamed as she fed the small crowd of people and took time to cuddle Thomas. A look of satisfaction had played on her face the entire evening. Jillian knew she had topped off her night when, while they were loading the dishwasher, she'd thanked Audrey for the Degas painting and said she would treasure it as much as she treasured their friendship.

Reagan's visit had given Jillian the opportunity to embark on a new relationship. She had had lunch twice that week with Jenny and Reagan. It had been a delightful time until Jenny had mentioned Alan's rural clinic project. From her description, he seemed to be deep into the planning stage. The thing that hurt the most was Alan had never talked about it with her.

On Thursday, he had brought Reagan by the studio to watch the dress rehearsal. She had wanted to ask him about it, ask him why he had never mentioned something so important to him. But she'd let it go and concentrated on Reagan's visit to her studio. Jillian had been touched close to tears when Reagan had handed her the autographed program she had missed at the concert and a CD of one of her live recordings. Ashamed of her initial reaction, she now was able to see Alan had been true to his word. He was in love with *her*, but also a good friend to Reagan. Her emotions had been stirred again when Reagan had called the studio the next day to say she wanted to alter her plans to leave later if a ticket was available for the opening night performance.

Jillian's habit was to watch the company performances alongside the stage manager. Tonight would be different. She would be in the audience, surrounded by her friends.

Approaching the stage manager in her three-inch heels and Jovani designer gown, her face lit up with a smile. "Hey, Walt, any problems to report?"

He gave a soft whistle. "Aren't you something!"

"You like this old gown?" She smiled at the older man.

"I may be old, but I can still see. I like it better than the sweat pants and tee shirt you usually wear during the performances. So I guess you're going to see things from a different perspective tonight."

"That's the plan." She stared in the direction of the stage but didn't move.

"Everything's fine here. You should head out to your seat in the audience. It'll be *curtain up* before you know it."

"Jillian—"

She turned around at the sound of her name. "Audrey, what are you doing back here?"

"It's getting late. We weren't sure if your plans to watch from the audience had changed, so I volunteered to check on you. And look at you—you look amazing."

Jillian approached her and gave her a hug.

"What was that for?"

"Thank you for the beautiful flower arrangement. And how clever to arrange it in a glass slipper!"

"My idea. I'm just lucky to have people who can accommodate my requests."

Audrey started for the stairs, but Jillian took hold of her arm.

"Is something wrong?"

She pulled her deeper into the wings of the stage. "There's something I want to say before we join the others." Jillian could feel her eyes tearing up. She placed a hand on her chest. "Audrey, I'm so grateful you've become a part of my life. As I told you the other night, I treasure your friendship. But more than that, I want you to know how much I appreciate the advice and guidance you've given me over the last few months. You're the closest thing to a mother I've ever known—" Moving closer, her voice became a whisper. "I just wanted you to know."

Audrey could feel her heart racing as she squeezed her eyes shut. From the beginning of the charade, she had dreaded this moment because of the potential risk it held. She opened her eyes and took a moment to focus on the face that had her same green eyes. Knowing it had to end, she let the words tumble out of her mouth, and there was no way to take them back.

"I'm your mother."

"That's funny, Audrey—"

"I'm the woman who left you and your father twenty-seven years ago." Realizing the impact her confession would have on her daughter, Audrey turned and hurried away. She couldn't watch the pain play out on her beautiful face.

Jillian stood anchored in place. She sucked in a breath of air. Her forehead wrinkled in disbelief as she shook her head. "No, it's not true." Her chest tingled. A flash of dizziness engulfed her.

"There you are." Alan moved toward her. "It's almost time for David to give the opening remarks before the—" She grabbed his arm for support.

"Jillian, what's wrong? And where's Audrey?"

"Can we sit for a moment before we join the others?" He led her toward a row of chairs against a wall.

He sat down beside her and shifted her to face him. "What's wrong?" He squeezed her upper arms. "Tell me what has you so upset."

She pulled her hair off her neck with one hand and fanned herself with the other. Letting her hair flow down around her shoulders, she dropped both hands to grab the sides of her chair. She looked up into Alan's eyes. "She's my mother."

"Who's your mother?"

"Audrey—she says she's my mother." She shook her head. "I can't believe it. All these years—wondering about her, and she's been right under my nose these last few months."

The orchestra began warming up. Alan stood up. "Let me take you home."

"No! I can't leave. Just give me a few minutes to pull myself together."

"Where is Audrey now?"

"I have no idea, but I hope she has enough good sense to stay away from me." Jillian's lips trembled as her eyes watered. "Do you think she's telling the truth?"

He pulled a handkerchief from his pocket and handed it to her. "I don't know what she would gain from it being a lie. Are you sure you don't want to go home? We can say you're not feeling well, and we wouldn't be stretching the truth."

"I don't have a choice. I can't walk out on my company's performance. Let me detour by the ladies' room and fix my face. Will you check our seats and give me a heads-up if she's there?"

"Sure, but we should hurry."

There was no sign of Audrey anywhere as they took their seats. The night seemed to inch by in slow motion, a blurred rendition of the production Jillian knew from beginning to end, inside and out. At one point, a lucid thought came to her mind. *Thank goodness we videotape so I can see this later.*

The production ended, but the evening wasn't over. While the cast celebration revved up, Jillian returned to the ladies' room and collapsed on the sofa. She was once again at a crossroads in her life. The woes of her company took second place to the struggle stirring in her personal life. Would she, could she, accept Audrey as her mother? The events of the evening weighed heavy on her emotions, producing the physical symptoms of a migraine.

Jillian was lying on the sofa when Jenny entered the ladies' room. "Alan asked me to check in here for you. He said he hadn't seen you for a while. You don't look so good. Maybe I should get him."

"Yes, please" was all she could manage to say, as she closed her eyes.

෴

She moved her fingers away from her temples and opened her eyes as Alan sat down beside her. He presented his public persona, calm and reassuring, while he scolded himself silently for not taking her home earlier in the evening.

"Migraine?" he asked in a quiet voice.

"Yes, and I don't have my medication with me because I'm carrying a small evening bag.

"Then I guess it's time to go home. Jenny, can you find David and let him know I'm taking Jillian home?"

"Sure. Feel better, JB."

"Thanks."

He watched her face. The smile didn't quite make it. "All right, let's get you home."

He helped her up, and she stumbled in her three-inch heels. "I think it might be safer for me to walk barefoot to the car."

"You may be right about that. Here, let me unfasten them for you. Sit down." He put one knee on the floor as he unfastened the first shoe.

A weak smile formed on her lips. Alan looked up at her "What?"

"Who knew someday I would have my own Prince Charming? How do you do it?"

He finished with the second shoe and slid up onto the sofa beside her. "Do what?"

She stared into his eyes. "Just look at the train wreck my life has become tonight, and you can still make me smile."

"What can I say? I'm just what the doctor ordered." He kissed her on the cheek. "Are you okay to walk?" He helped her off the sofa.

"I'm fine, but I know if I fall, you'll be there to pick me up. I love you, Alan—you've become my knight in shining armor."

She reached up and pulled his head down, meeting his lips in a fervent kiss.

Alan retrieved her shoes off the floor then guided her to the door. "Let's take this conversation out of the public arena and move it to a more private setting." *She said it—she loves me!*

The drive home was harsh. Between the motion of the car and the lights on the highway, Jillian's body had had enough. "I feel sick, please pull over. I have to get out."

Alan checked in his rearview mirror and pulled the car to a smooth stop along the shoulder of the road. Moving with urgency, Jillian left her seat and made it across the asphalt shoulder just in time. She bent over the guard rail and vomited. Feeling Alan's hands on her shoulders, she reached back and took the handkerchief he offered.

"I'm sorry this migraine is so rough." He put his arm around her waist. "Ready to go back?"

"Yes, I think so."

He helped her to the car and she slid into her seat. He closed the door as gentle as was possible.

Once they were inside her townhouse, Jillian headed to her bedroom, and Alan moved toward the kitchen to bring her a glass of water. While she changed, he pulled down the covers on the bed. He could hear her vomiting again. He knocked on the bathroom door.

"Can I help?"

The door opened. She was wiping her face with a washcloth. "Please turn off the light." She left the bathroom light on and the door ajar, casting a small sliver of light into the bedroom.

"Where's your medication?" he asked while she crawled into bed.

Pointing to the bedside table, she remained quiet as she placed the cloth over her eyes.

"Here, lean up on your elbow and take this."

She swallowed the pill without difficulty and he settled her back in bed then moved toward the door.

"Please don't leave—will you stay a while?"

"Sure." He moved onto the bed beside her. Propping his cheek on his hand, he used his free hand to massage her temples with gentle movements.

"How's that feel?"

"Good, thank you." They rested without talking for a while.

Jillian broke the silence. "Do you think my life will ever get to the point where it won't suck?"

He kissed her on the side of the face. "Stick with me, and you'll see how great it can be." Fifteen minutes later, she was asleep, and he left the room.

Alan removed his shoes and reclined on the sofa. Tucking an arm behind his head, he listened out for any sound from the bedroom. *She's seen only one doctor most of her life. Did he just not keep up with research and medical technology, making it impossible to give best practice care?*

He recalled the conversation with Reagan as he'd driven her to the airport. She'd been concerned for Jillian. She'd thought she would never be happy unless Jillian could know for sure if she could or couldn't dance and perform. *How am I going to help her with that? Was it possible she had been misdiagnosed?* The first time he'd seen her dance, she'd been winded but stable. He wouldn't even have thought about asthma, if he hadn't seen her use the inhaler that day. The asthma attacks he had witnessed had been brought on by anxiety and grieving over Lily. She had been calm and able to help Antoinette when she'd needed it, no anxiety then. *So, what's going on? Is it possible she could have a performance career?*

The sun streamed in through the sheers covering the windows in Audrey's bedroom. She turned over on her left side, and her face was assaulted by the early morning sun. She shielded her eyes with her hands, not wanting to get up and start her day. Last night had been horrible, her masquerade ending with the truth coming out to Jillian that she was her mother. She knew it couldn't go on forever, but she had wanted a little more time. And she didn't know what to do about it now. Should she give Jillian time to process the news and then approach her? Should she wait for Jillian to come to her?

Audrey pulled on her robe and, once in the kitchen, drank two cups of coffee. Now that she was awake, anger overshadowed her disposition, taking her back to remember how she had struggled with the anger after leaving Ed and Jillian. Staring at her hands, she cracked her knuckles. A bad habit she had acquired years ago when anger had surfaced, when her life had seemed so out of control.

She began a rhythmic rocking in her chair, and an overpowering sense of dread engulfed her. Audrey knew after she dealt with the anger, putting it in its proper place, the loneliness would come. Would she survive it this time? She had no desire to find another Benjamin to save her and make her feel safe like her second husband had done.

"Audrey?"

Jumping at the sound of her name, she moved out of the kitchen and found Alan at the foot of the stairs. "What are you doing here?"

"I'm here to make sure you're okay. You didn't answer the doorbell or my knocking. Your door was unlocked, and I was worried, so I came in."

"Thank you—I'm fine, dear." He followed her into the sitting room. "I'm not so sure."

"What did Jillian say about everything?"

"Not much, just that you had told her you are her mother. She was pretty freaked out."

"After I told her, I left—like a coward. I never intended to tell her in such a public setting. But the things she was saying were so powerful and endearing. It just seemed like the right time. As soon as I heard the words coming out of my mouth, I knew I couldn't face her reaction. I ran away. Is she all right?"

"I think she's still processing everything. I know once that's done, she'll have a lot of questions, but I don't know when she'll be ready to hear the answers."

"I didn't mean to hurt her. I just wanted my daughter back." The tears came.

Alan moved beside her and gave her a literal shoulder to cry on.

She pulled a tissue out of her pocket and straightened up. "Thank you for checking on me. I don't feel so alone."

He stood up to leave. "Call me if you need anything."

She accompanied him to the door. He turned toward her. "Just give her some time, Audrey."

She closed the door behind him, wondering if she would go to her grave with a broken heart.

Twenty

Jenny gave a quick knock on the open office door as she stepped inside. "Hey, JB, I need the check for the caterer—and I finalized the head count for dinner. Would you sign off on this so I can take it with the check by their office on my way home?"

Jenny noticed the dark smudges under Jillian's eyes.

Looking up from her paperwork, she managed a half-smile. "Sure, where do you need me to sign?"

Jenny moved around to Jillian's side of the desk and slid the paper in front of her. Looking up, the blank wall across the room stared back at her. "What happened to your Degas reproduction?"

"I put it away. I can't work in here if all I do is think of Audrey. And I thought of her every time I saw the painting—so I took it down."

"That makes sense, I guess."

"I sent it back to her." Jillian looked up at her friend. "I shouldn't have done it, but when I took it down, I was so mad. I knew it would hurt her when I returned it." Her cheeks became red as she admitted to her shameful behavior.

"Our friendship is new, and I don't want to pry—but if you want to talk about Audrey, I'll be glad to listen."

"I don't know what to say. A little over two months ago, a woman entered my life. I liked her, liked being around her.

We connected, and the next thing I know she says she is the mother who deserted me twenty-seven years ago. What am I supposed to say? How am I supposed to feel?"

"Have you been able to verify she is telling the truth?"

Jillian pushed her palms against her forehead, squeezing her eyes shut. "The only thing I've done is try to push her out of my mind, and I haven't been successful."

"If I were in your shoes, I'd have to know. As unpleasant as it might be, I'd go to her and demand to hear her story. Why she left and why she came back. But that's me."

"Part of me wants to know. I just can't deal with her now. The fundraiser is less than a week away, and I have to focus on it. The future of my company is too important to too many people. If I decide to see Audrey, it will have to wait until after the fundraiser."

"Good, you've made a decision. It's a start. Just take things a step at a time, and there will be less chance of this thing snowballing on you."

Jillian leaned over and hugged her friend. "Thanks, Jen. It's nice to know I have support when I need it."

"You know it. I'd better go. I told the sitter I wouldn't be gone long today. Bye, JB."

"Bye, and thanks for the advice."

༄

Alan pulled the front door open before his sister had a chance to ring the doorbell. He seized the opportunity to take Thomas in his arms, while Jenny struggled with the diaper bag.

"Thanks, it's been one of those days. You're a lifesaver, in more ways than one." They moved inside and settled Thomas into the playpen Alan had set up in the living room.

"How long does a dress fitting take, anyway?" he asked.

"I can't say for sure. I just know I want this dress to wow my husband at the fundraiser. It's looking a little baggy since I've lost my baby weight Do you have somewhere you need to be this afternoon?"

Alan took the diaper bag and set it on the coffee table. "No, I just like to ask questions you can't answer."

She made a face at her brother. "For a thirty-six year old grown man, you're such a dork sometimes."

"Well, here's a question you might be able to answer for me."

Jenny sank into the sofa. "Answer my question first. Have you seen Jillian today?"

"Not today—I tried spending a little time with her last night, but she was exhausted, so I didn't stay long. Why do you want to know?"

"I just wanted to make sure she's doing okay. I talked with her a little while yesterday. I know she's not resting well. The dark circles under her eyes were a dead giveaway." She reached over the side of the playpen and moved a few toys closer to her baby boy. When Alan gave no response, she looked up. "Is something wrong?"

Alan sat down on the chair across from the sofa. With his elbows on his knees, he leaned forward. "I'm not sure. The days you spent practicing with Jillian—did she seem to have difficulty handling the practice?"

"How do you mean?"

"I'm talking physical, was her breathing labored? Did she tire after little exertion?"

Jenny rubbed the side of her face. "Let's see—the first few days she seemed to wear down before me, but the more we practiced, she seemed to be holding her own better. And the first day her breathing was a bit ragged, but that improved too. Why do you ask?"

"Just trying to convince Jillian maybe she should find a new physician here in Charlotte. The physician she has used most of her life died a few months ago."

"No other reason?"

Alan stood up and kissed her on top of the head. "Don't you have some place to be?"

He led her to the door, sending her on her way. Returning to the living room, he sat next to the playpen. Picking up a soft bat, he squeezed the end of it. The squeaking sound made the baby laugh. "Well, Thomas, I think it's time to have a talk with Jillian."

Jillian rolled over in bed with a groan and hit the snooze button on the alarm. Three seconds later, she bolted upright in bed, realizing it was Saturday, and tonight would seal her fate. The uncertainty of what was to come made her stomach tense up. She hurried toward the kitchen to the coffee maker, her recent coffee habit having been influenced by Audrey. She refused to think about her today.

Jillian's mind raced through the two possibilities of tonight's outcome. She rubbed the back of her neck as she thought about how many lives would be affected by a poor result. Opening her notebook, she reviewed her to-do list for the day. She was leaving nothing to chance.

She carried her coffee cup into the bedroom and paused at the closet door to stare at the purple gown hanging there. Audrey came to her mind. This was the dress they had bought on their first outing together. She had made the decision to buy it after Audrey had insisted she try it on. Jillian's color choices were limited because of her copper red hair. She had to avoid many colors she would like to have worn. She had tried on two dresses and had opted for yet another champagne-colored gown, when Audrey had spoken up about the purple color called regency. Once she had it on and stood in front of the mirror, she'd also known it was the right choice.

It was an ankle-length gown made of chiffon and charmeuse. An A-line gown with a princess scoop neck and a showering of beading over the bodice. It was different from the gown she had worn to the wedding. Appropriate for tonight's occasion. Staring at the dress, Jillian was glad she had listened to Audrey. She had not realized until now, how intertwined into her life the woman had become. The process had been so natural. It was going to be difficult not to think about her. She had not wanted to see her. Confusion claimed her mind as she admitted to herself she felt hurt Audrey had not attempted to make contact with her this past week.

The doorbell rang, sounding louder than normal. Would everything have an exaggerated sound and feel today? She wiggled into her robe and headed to the door, wondering who would be calling this early in the morning.

Pulling open the door, she found her old and new friends, smiling at her. They were dressed in sweatpants and tee shirts.

"Great. You're up," said Barbara as the duo stepped into the living room. "We're here to keep you on course today."

Jenny headed toward the kitchen. "Good, I see the coffee's ready." She pulled a cup out of the cabinet. Holding the cup in the air, she motioned to Barbara. Receiving an affirmative nod, she pulled a second cup off the shelf.

"We have the whole day planned. Get dressed because we have an appointment in twenty minutes at the spa. Then hair and makeup later this afternoon."

Jillian's feet remained still, her mouth open in surprise. "Barb, I don't understand."

"You're wasting time. We don't want to be late. Throw on some clothes and we'll talk on the way."

After settling into the car for the short ride to the spa, Jenny spoke up. "Jillian, we know this hasn't been an easy week for you. We've given you space to work things out on your own, but we're here for you if you want to talk. Even if you don't want to talk, we're here for you. If it's distractions you need today, we can keep you busy. Just tell us what you need."

Jillian squirmed in her seat. "At this point, I don't know. I was so comfortable around Audrey, and the rapport between us was awesome. I know I have to handle this *thing* between us, but I'm just not ready. And besides, tonight may be a game changer for me and the company, so I think it best if I set thoughts of Audrey aside, for today at least.

Barbara stared at the road as she drove. "Okay, that's settled. No talk about Audrey—today."

They rode in silence the rest of the way to the spa. Twenty minutes later, Jillian rested face down on the masseur's table, feeling the tension dissolve as her shoulders and neck were massaged. She realized how lucky she was to have friends who cared about her wellbeing. After a shower and change of clothes, they walked into Orchards Restaurant. They dined on the luscious brunch set before them.

"Not fair, Jillian, you're not eating your share. We put a lot of thought into making this a good day for you."

"I appreciate all the trouble you've gone to. It's just—my stomach is a little nervous. I just can't eat."

"Maybe a few small snacks spaced throughout the day will be better for you. I'll make sure we have some fruit and other things to nibble on packed in our bags when we head to the salon for makeup and hair."

"Thanks, Jen."

Even with the support of her friends, she couldn't stop the old feelings from creeping back in. The same feelings she had experienced when her life began crumbling around her six and a half years ago.

Jillian answered the door. Alan looked at her beautiful face, moved closer and, taking her face in his hands, kissed her lips and hoped his kiss conveyed the promise of a wonderful evening. He stepped back, and his eyes moved down her exquisite frame then traveled back to rest on her face.

The royal purple material swirled around her as Jillian turned in a circle. A sense of déjà vu washed over him, as he remembered their first date starting in a similar manner. The difference being this time his fingers ached with the desire to touch.

"You look stunning."

"Thank you. I'm glad you like the dress. I've never worn this color before. Please, come in. I just need to put on my jewelry, and I'll be ready to go."

He stepped inside and closed the door. "Before you do, I have something I want to give you."

"I like what you just gave me. In fact, I hope you have a few of those left."

Do I see a wicked spark in her eye? He pulled a long blue box from his jacket pocket. "I hope you like it."

"What's the occasion? We both know it's not my birthday."

"This is a special night for you, and I wanted you to have something special to wear. And I'm hoping this would lift your spirits a little. It's been a hard week for you."

She opened the box. Nestled in a blue-velvet lining was a diamond circle-link bracelet in a platinum setting. Her mouth fell open. "Oh, Alan—it's gorgeous! I don't know what to say."

Heat spread through his body. Elation claimed his spirits. His gift had the effect he'd hoped it would. "When I was looking for the right gift, I was thinking diamonds—so you would sparkle tonight. But you do that all by yourself."

She held her arm out, and they watched the light bounced off the stones. He put his arm around her, and pulled her close. She smelled so good he didn't want to let her go.

"Let me get the rest of my jewelry. I'll just be a minute."

Looking around, he remembered the first night he had come to her townhouse. The night of David and Ann's wedding had started out so well and had ended in a nightmare. Tonight had to end better.

"Alan—I want you to know how much I appreciate everything you've done to make tonight happen."

He turned around to face her. "This has been a big group effort."

"Yes it has, but it was your idea, and because of it, I have hope my company will survive. Thank you." She reached up and kissed him on the cheek.

The look in her eyes made his breath quicken. If they didn't leave now, he wasn't sure he could control the urge to pull her into his arms. She grabbed a tissue and wiped the lipstick from his face.

"I need to make a good impression tonight, and being late is not the way to do it. We should go."

Alan could feel his hand shake as he pulled his fingers through his hair. "We probably should."

Jillian knew how to appear calm and collected on the outside to the guests at the fundraiser. She had this skill down pat, but she was amazed she was not freaking out on the inside. Alan sat to her left at the table during dinner, and his presence provided a calming effect. She was pleased to have his support and somehow, with him by her side, she knew she would weather whatever the outcome of tonight might be. All the seats at the tables in the ballroom were filled.

The third dance of the evening's entertainment was underway when Alan leaned over and whispered, "I just got a page from the hospital. I need to check in."

The main course was being served when he returned. His expression was grave as he reclaimed his seat next to Jillian. "I'm sorry, but I have to leave. There's been an accident involving three cars. We've got several patients coming in. I have to go."

"Oh, Alan, I'm sorry. Will you please try to call me later?"

"I can't make any promises, but yes, I'll try. I love you." He gave her a quick kiss on her lips. "I have to tell you one more time how beautiful you look tonight. You should wear that color more often." And then he was gone.

The security his presence had brought seemed to leave with him. A chill made her rub her arms as a feeling of dread passed through her body. The evening began to drag and Jillian found herself repeatedly checking her phone for a message from Alan. The inability to identify the source of her restlessness increased her impatience for the night to come to an end. She struggled to subdue her rising anxiety by assessing her surroundings. They had a full house, and everyone seemed to be enjoying themselves. When people were happy, they became cheerful givers. She had received a whispered report the proceeds from the silent auction had surpassed the amount they had hoped to garner from the venture. So with everything moving in a positive direction for the North Carolina Ballet Company, why couldn't she shake this feeling of impending doom?

The festivities ended around 10:00 p.m. Jillian stood at the back of the ballroom along with members of the board. She echoed their thanks as the guests departed. Jenny approached her, touching her arm.

"I just got the strangest text from Alan. He asked me to bring you to the hospital now, without any explanation. Do you have any idea why?"

"No, I don't. That is strange. Do you want me to help you find Mark?"

"The text said for me to bring you to the hospital. If we're going to be a while, maybe he thought Mark should go home and relieve the sitter."

"But if we take your car, how is Mark going to get home?"

"No problem. Barbara offered to take him home."

"Okay, let's go see what your brother wants."

Twenty-One

They were walking into the hospital when Jenny's phone signaled an incoming text. She read the message out loud. *Wait for me in the surgical waiting area.*

As they continued to walk to their destination, the anxiousness Jillian had experienced earlier in the evening increased. Her stomach churned, each step taking them closer to the waiting area and why they had been summoned. The room was busy for this time of night, with an atmosphere of sadness permeating the space. And then she remembered—the car accident. Several groups of people talked among themselves, some crying. They scanned the entire room, but Alan was not there.

Jenny pulled her over to a corner where there were several empty seats. Jillian attempted to sit then stood up and began pacing. And then he walked in, a somber look on his handsome face. He took her hands and led her back to the empty seat. Jenny moved over to the next chair so Alan could sit between them.

After a few minutes of silence, Jenny spoke up. "So, why did you ask us to come, Alan?"

He continued to hold Jillian's hands as he faced her. "There's something I need to tell you, and I thought it might be a good idea for Jenny to be here with you, in case I'm called away."

"Alan, you're scaring me. Just tell me—what is it?" She tightened her grip on his hands.

"I told you earlier I was called away because of several people being injured in a three-car accident."

"Yes, I remember."

"I'm sorry Jillian—Audrey was in the accident. She has serious injuries."

Jenny gasped. "Jillian, I'm so sorry."

"She's just hurt—right? She's not dead?" Jillian made a whimpering sound.

Alan pulled her close. "I promise you she's not dead. I just spent the last three hours with her in surgery."

"Please, you have to take me to her."

"You can't see her right now. She's in the recovery room, but once she's settled in ICU, I'll take you there myself. But it could be a while. It depends on how long it takes for her to stabilize from the surgery she's been through. I want Jenny to take you to the cafeteria for coffee. It's going to be a long night. Jenny. I'll text you when she's settled in ICU."

"You just take care of Audrey, and I'll take care of Jillian."

Jillian stood up and watched as Alan hurried away. "I suppose most of these people are here waiting for news about the others involved in the accident. Let's go to the cafeteria." *I don't want to overhear any details.*

Plenty of seats were available in the deserted cafeteria. They sat down and placed their foam cups of coffee on the faux-wood tabletop. Jillian propped her elbows on the table, placing her hands on the sides of her head.

Jenny sipped her coffee, giving Jillian time to process the fact that before the end of the day she would have to decide if she was in or out. *I don't skirt issues, but she's not like me.* She touched her wrist. Jillian's head came up as her hands dropped on the table.

She looks so sad, but it's time for the hard sell. Her voice was quiet but authoritative in its delivery. "This is it, JB. I know the timing stinks, but you have to decide tonight. Do you want to have Audrey in your life, or do you walk away? You can't string her along until she gets better or stronger, for you to dump her later because your past hurts too much."

Jenny watched Jillian struggle to control her crying and handed her some tissues.

She wiped her face, taking in deep breaths to settle her breathing. "We haven't heard from Alan. For all we know, she's dead."

"Oh, so you want the easy way out. Audrey's dead. Problem solved. Not gonna happen. First of all, my brother is an awesome surgeon, and he *will not* let her die. Second, Audrey has too much to live for. She's found you, and she's been so happy, she just couldn't die."

"How am I going to decide? You just said I can't walk away later."

"Well, you analyze it. List the pros and cons of the relationship—without factoring in the accident. You have to put it aside, like it didn't happen. Size up Audrey, the woman. Not Audrey, the accident victim." *Come on already, Alan. I can't keep this up.*

The silence was thick between them, and after a bit in a timid voice, Jillian offered, "We have an undeniable connection, everything just clicks between us."

"That's good. What else?"

"She always gives me the best advice." Jillian's voice gave way as tears rolled down her face.

Jenny covered her hand. "I think it's interesting you started with the positive things about your relationship instead of the obvious negative that pulled you away from her last week."

Jillian grabbed the sides of her head. "I don't know if I'll be able to forgive her—maybe you're right. I shouldn't see her if I'm going to walk away from her."

"Listen to yourself, JB. You're thinking about walking away now because you don't want to hurt her later, not because you want to get even."

Jillian jumped when the phone signaled the incoming text.

Jenny looked up from reading the message. "She's settled. He'll meet us in the waiting room." Walking to the door, they tossed their cups of cold coffee as they passed by the trashcan.

Shaking with trepidation, Jillian followed Alan into ICU428. His presence did little to calm her anxiety as noises in the ICU brought the gravity of Audrey's situation to reality for Jillian. Her stomach churned as she held her lips together to keep from crying out.

Audrey's still, white form was hard to distinguish among the sheets that covered her. *Where is the warmth and color that is always present on her face?* Jillian knew the cheek color was artificial, but she just didn't look right without it. She moved toward the bed and laid her hand on Audrey's arm, feeling her cold skin. The tube of the respirator was taped to the side of her mouth. The rhythmic sound coming from the machine gave evidence that Audrey needed help to breathe. A cuff fastened around her arm inflated every ten minutes to provide blood pressure readings. A red-dotted sensor on the tip of her index finger monitored the level of oxygen in her blood. The chirping, beeping sounds seemed magnified to Jillian's ears. She closed her eyes, hoping that when she opened them, she would see the Audrey she had become so attached to. Alan's voice jolted her from her thoughts.

"Jillian, I want you to sit down over here." He placed a chair beside the bed. "It's not as bad as it looks."

She licked her dry lips and swallowed. In a quiet voice she replied, "It looks pretty bad to me."

Alan pulled another chair to the bedside and sat down. "Let me tell you about some of this equipment we're using and what we're doing for Audrey."

Jillian reached for Alan's hand as he spoke.

"She has a closed head injury. We're concerned about swelling around the brain, which can cause the pressure in her skull to build up. We're monitoring the pressure so we can take the necessary steps to relieve it, if it becomes too high. We had to remove her spleen because there was so much internal bleeding, so we're observing for any signs and symptoms of infection. Her right ankle is broken, but the hope is she'll recover eighty to one hundred percent function with physical therapy. We're going to keep her on the ventilator for now. Her body has been pretty stressed and can use all the help we can give it."

Alan continued to talk, his voice blending in with the sounds of the ICU as Jillian's thoughts took over, spilling into the memories she had stored from the last two months. Their excursions and talks, her advice about everything imaginable, opening her home for the dinner party, the connection they shared. And then she knew—she couldn't imagine her life without Audrey. But the past was still an issue, to be dealt with later.

Jillian's grip on Alan's hand tightened, and in a whisper she asked, "Is she going to make it? Is my mother going to live?"

⁂

Jillian drew in a breath and yawned. Opening her eyes, she looked at the bedrail that fell in her line of vision. She focused on the noises that reached her ears, and memories of last night returned. She sat up and stared at Audrey, looking for any signs of change from the night before. Her eyes remained closed, the ventilator continuing to breathe for her. Looking around the room, she saw her royal purple evening gown spread across a chair. She looked down at the green scrubs she was wearing, and more memories from the night before surfaced.

A nurse stepped into the cubicle. "Ms. Russell, I'm going to have to ask you to leave. We'll be changing shifts soon, and all family members have to leave while we give report to the oncoming shift."

"How's she—how's my mother doing?" She tested the word *mother* on her lips. It was foreign to her.

"There's been no change in her level of consciousness, but her vital signs have been stable my whole shift. It's a good thing." The nurse placed her hand on Jillian's arm. "You can come back in an hour. We'll be finished with report by then. Take this time for yourself. Try to eat something or at least get some coffee. I hope Ms. Harris has a good day."

Jillian walked out of the cubicle turning to take a last look. "Thank you for the clothes and for all your help." She moved into the family waiting area outside the doors that held the visitors at bay so the ICU patients could rest and their bodies work at healing.

The coffee was dark-looking, like it had been sitting for several hours. She decided to try her luck at the cafeteria. On the way, she stopped by the gift shop and purchased a combo package of toothbrush and toothpaste. After washing her face and brushing her teeth, she came out of the ladies' room feeling less disheveled than when she'd entered.

She stepped into the cafeteria, surprised to see Alan sitting at a table, going over paperwork. "Good morning. Have you been here all night?"

He stood up. "I was coming to check on you after I finished going over my census for the day."

"They kicked me out—time for shift change or something like that."

"I see. Let me get you some breakfast."

"I'm not hungry. Maybe just some coffee?"

He returned with coffee, juice, and a muffin. "Please try to eat something. I can't stand the idea of you getting sick."

"Thank you." The words sounded hollow to her ears. She concentrated on eating and was surprised to realize she was hungry.

"I'm going to check on Audrey, and then I'll come out to the waiting area to give you an update. Maybe by then, you can go back in and sit with her. Please finish your breakfast. It may sound silly to you, but it takes energy to sit at someone's bedside. I'll see you soon." He kissed her on the cheek.

When she returned to the family waiting area, Barbara and Jenny were there. They hugged her and handed her a floral bag with a change of clothes and some necessities.

"Thanks, I don't know how long I'm going to be here." She wasn't in the mood to talk, so she was grateful her friends sat by her side without asking questions as they waited to hear Alan's report.

Joining them, he didn't have much to add to what the night shift nurse had told her earlier. "When someone sustains a head injury like Audrey has, the brain needs to rest. The pressure in her skull hasn't increased—good news. We hope she'll wake up soon, but when it might happen is unpredictable."

Jillian hugged her friends and thanked them for coming by. "I don't think it makes much sense for you to sit out here when I'll be with my mother. Thomas needs you at home, Jen."

Jillian could tell they were reluctant to leave her, but she was glad when they were gone so she could return to Audrey's side.

The nurse came in to hang a new bag of IV fluids. "Your mother might benefit from you talking to her. We can't say for sure she can't hear you. It's worth a try."

"I wouldn't know what to say."

"Talk about your memories of her. Talk about the past or what you plan to do with your future. Just talk." With a smile of encouragement, she said, "Let me know if you need anything."

How was she supposed to talk about the past when they didn't have one? A lone tear rolled down her cheek. Jillian sat up straight, an idea forming in her mind. She'd tell her mother about all the things that had been important to her while she was growing up. Jillian talked non-stop for several hours. The nurse supplied her with water and juice to keep her throat from drying out while she talked. As she opened her heart, she held Audrey's hand or stroked her cheek. Standing up to stretch, she wondered about the time. With no windows in the ICU, she had become disoriented about the time of day. When she looked up, Alan was standing inside the door.

"I think they're about to kick you out for shift change again. You are coming with me to the cafeteria, so I can make sure you have some dinner. What do you think about going home tonight?"

"Oh no! I can't do that. I can't leave her. I wouldn't leave her for dinner, if they allowed me to stay."

"The only way I'll agree to let you stay tonight is if you eat something."

She could tell by the tone of his voice he would send her home if she didn't comply. They shared a meal, and when Alan was satisfied she had eaten enough, they returned to the ICU. He wrote an order for the nurse to take Audrey off the ventilator and monitor her oxygenation and respirations through the night. Jillian was determined to continue the storytelling. She talked off and on through the night, dozing for short periods of time.

Shift change brought a new nurse, but the routine was the same. They made her leave during report. After she returned from breakfast, she sat down by Audrey's bed. The many hours of recitation was not getting the results Jillian had hoped for, and she was becoming discouraged. She rested her voice for a few hours then resumed talking. Audrey moved her head, and Jillian pressed the call light. The nurse stepped into the cubicle. "She moved her head. I saw her."

The nurse stepped over to the bedside. "Ms. Harris, can you hear me?" Audrey moaned. "Can you open your eyes for me?"

Jillian moved to her beside and observed Audrey's face. Her eyes blinked open and closed again. "Look, she opened her eyes! We have to tell Alan."

"Ms. Russell, it's a wonderful sign that she opened her eyes, and I will update Dr. Armstrong, but don't get too excited. Her body has been through a lot. She may not open her eyes again for some time. We have to be patient."

Jillian's elation over Audrey's progress fizzled as the nurse walked out the door. She moved away from the bed and sat down. She was feeling overwhelmed again when she heard a weak, raspy voice say, "Patience is—overrated—I think—I'll talk now."

Relief flooded her entire body. She jumped out of her chair and grasped Audrey's hand. "You're awake!"

Alan hurried into the room. "I hear we've got some action going on in here." He moved to the bedside. "Audrey, you're awake." Pulling a penlight from his pocket, he asked, "Can you follow my light with your eyes?" Her pupils moved with the light. He smiled. "Very good."

"Audrey, you're in the hospital. You were in a car accident. We're taking good care of you. Jillian's here. She's been waiting for you to wake up."

Audrey turned her head and looked at Jillian then reached for her hand.

"I'm here—Audrey." She couldn't call her *Mom*. The word stuck in her throat.

"Audrey, you're going to be in the hospital for a while. Jillian has been here for almost forty-eight hours. I want her to go home tonight so she can get some proper rest. Are you okay with that?" She shook her head and closed her eyes, ending the discussion.

"She'll be back tomorrow. I promise. I'm going to send the nurse in now to check on you. I'll be back later."

Before he walked away, Audrey touched his hand. "Thank you."

Twenty-Two

Alan watched through the window of the studio as Jillian practiced solo. He was glad she was taking time for herself. For weeks she had been going to the hospital every day to be with Audrey. Alan didn't know the intricacies of their pasts, but he was glad for both of them—glad the lines of communication were open.

Music from Stravinsky's "Firebird Suite" filled the air. It was an exciting sound. Jillian's dancing was energetic and wonderful to watch. She made graceful lines with her arms as she extended them upward and outward. Pointing her chin toward the ceiling accentuated her lovely, long neck. The muscles of her back flexed with movement. Alan focused on the scar on her left scapula, the result of their lives having intersected on the day of the explosion.

Today would be a test. Today he would tell Jillian what he suspected about her asthma diagnosis, and that information would test their relationship. Waiting until she stopped, Alan opened the door and clapped as he walked over to her.

"Your dancing was wonderful."

She wrapped a towel around her neck. Smiling, she executed a series of *pirouettes,* landing in front of him.

"Thank you, but to be honest, the time I've been spending in the studio has been to help blow off my anxiety over

Audrey, rather than for the sake of practice. I don't feel like I'm doing anything for her."

"Not true, I happen to know she looks forward to your daily visits. I believe your support has made all the difference in her recovery. She's going to be discharged from the hospital soon, and it wouldn't have happened this quickly without you." He took hold of the ends of the towel and pulled her close. He kissed her with vigor and wondered if this might be their last kiss. "But I don't want to talk about Audrey. I have a surprise for you." He guided her toward the door.

"Where are we going? I'll need a minute to change my clothes."

"No need, we're here," he replied as they stepped into her office. Her desk had been cleared of its usual contents and replaced with a blue gingham tablecloth. A picnic-style dinner of croissant club sandwiches, apple bacon coleslaw, tea, and peach cake was set out and waiting.

"Alan, this is so sweet. How did you know I'd be starving?" She stretched upward to kiss him on the cheek.

With a gallant gesture he pulled a chair away from the desk. "Your chair, miss."

"Why thank you, sir."

As they enjoyed the picnic meal, Alan gave an update on Audrey's condition. Finally, he came to the matter at hand. "I thought this would be a good place for our dinner, rather than a restaurant. I have something to discuss with you in private."

Jillian swiped at her mouth with a napkin and, turning her chair toward Alan, she said, "You look so serious. It's not about Audrey—"

"Jillian, I just spent the last ten minutes telling you how well she's doing. This is about you—and me." He reached out and stroked the side of her face. We've known each other for about ten months now. And during that time, we've learned things about each other. Being a physician, I've been tuned into your medical history, because it's my professional focus and because I care about you—I love you."

"Where is all this leading?"

He stood up and started pacing, sliding his hands in his pockets. "Be patient, I'm getting there. I've been concerned about the medical advice and treatment you received from your old doctor."

"Dr. Hayes."

"Yes, Dr. Hayes. How was it he convinced you to give up performing and when was that?"

"It was soon after I lost Lily. I was spending a lot of time at the studio. I guess I was dancing to distract myself from everything. But it didn't work. It seemed the harder I practiced, the more I thought about my baby. Barb was my rock during all of it. She was at the studio the first time I had trouble breathing. When it happened again the next day, she took me right over to Dr. Hayes. He said my symptoms pointed to exercise-induced asthma. He gave me an inhaler and told me I needed to give up dancing as a career."

"You didn't get a second opinion?" He snapped his fingers. "So, just like that—you gave it all up?"

"Well, yes. I wasn't functioning well on my own. I let other people tell me what I needed, but then I realized I needed to get away, to stop leaning on everyone for answers to my problems. That's when I came to Charlotte—to start over. Why are you bringing all this up now?"

"I'm bringing it up because I'm convinced you were misdiagnosed. Wouldn't you say in the last month you've been dancing a lot more than you used to?"

"Yes, I guess so."

"So how's it been going for you? Have you been using your inhaler?"

"I'd have to say I haven't used it in about six weeks. What are you saying?"

Alan took her hands and guided her to the sofa. "For a while I've been observing you, and then I started putting the pieces together. I've come up with a much different picture of your medical issues than what you've shared with me."

Jillian stood up. "I don't understand."

"Your asthma symptoms started after you lost Lily. And now you tell me you were focused on your loss when the attacks occurred. I watched you have an asthma attack when you visited Lily's grave site. When I was piecing things together, I thought perhaps the attacks were brought on from anxiety, rather than exercise. But when Antoinette became ill with acute appendicitis, you were fine—no asthma attack. Even when you saw Audrey for the first time in ICU, you managed your anxiety over the situation without an attack. So I concluded the anxiety and grief you have over the loss of your baby is what precipitates your asthma attacks."

Her teeth sunk into her bottom lip, and then she spoke. "You have to say it out loud."

Alan's clenched jaw was so tight, the vein on the side of his neck stood out. Mental anguish caused nausea to rise into his throat. Taking a deep breath, he tried to relax as he spoke.

"Jillian, if you want a dancing career, there's no reason from a medical perspective to keep you from having one." *There, I said it. I put it out there.* It had taken him several days to reconcile the fact he couldn't keep this information from her. He wanted Jillian for his wife, but not at the high price of deception and its consequences.

Sitting down, she touched her fingertips to her lips. Alan sat down next to her. "You don't have to say anything right now. Just think about your options, and we'll talk later."

With calmness, Jillian sat on the sofa while Alan packed up the remains of their picnic dinner. He walked over and, touching her elbow, leaned down and pressed a light kiss on her head. "I'll call you later."

She wasn't sure how long she sat on the sofa after he left, her thoughts scrambling as she replayed Alan's words in her mind. *Well, Fate. It's about time.* She had always hoped at some point the pendulum of her life would shift and swing in a different direction, especially where her personal life was concerned. The last several months had proved to her it could happen. She tallied the score—deserted by her mother at the tender age of six, the deaths of her father and grandmother. And then a repeat of scenarios, deserted by her husband, delivery of her stillborn baby girl. And if that wasn't enough, her career taken from her. Then the pendulum had shifted. She'd built a new career, met Alan and regained her mother, all such wonderful things. And now a miracle—the possible restoration of her career. She stood up, unable to sit still any longer. She bounced up and down on her tiptoes, eager to be moving about. It wouldn't have happened without Alan, without his love for her. She hugged her arms, twirling around the small space. A floating sensation engulfed her as her past burdens were lifted.

Realizing she had said nothing to Alan before he left, she reached for her phone. When he answered, she chimed in, "What would I ever do without you? You make everything in my world so right. I love you."

Jillian's breathing accelerated when there was no response.

"Alan, are you there?"

"Yes, I'm here. I love you, too. I wanted to give you some time for everything to sink in before I tell you what I have to say." He paused.

A chill scurried up her back "You know you can tell me anything, right?"

"I know I can. But sometimes there are things we have to say we don't want to, because we know they will be hard to hear."

An oppressive weight pushed down on her chest. "Please, just tell me."

"I want you to be happy. If it means resuming your dance career, then I want that for you—because I love you. But I need to be happy too, I deserve to be happy. I don't think I can be happy if you have a career that takes you away from me, so you have a choice to make. A dance career—or me." The phone beeped, signaling the broken connection.

A sudden coldness hit at her core as her heart pounded in her chest. A sense of disorientation made her move toward the sofa and sit down. *Choose between Alan and dancing? I can't do it. But he said I have to choose.* The initial shock dissipated, and she fell into the arm of the sofa.

As the tears emptied from her eyes and her heart rate slowed, she sat up. She needed to talk. Jenny had become a good friend, but she felt strange asking her to listen to an ultimatum posed by her brother. Barb was always there for her, a personal sounding board, but tonight she needed more than the chance to bounce an idea around. She needed Audrey, a woman full of life experiences. She had always given her good, sound advice. By the time she changed and washed her face, visiting hours at the hospital would be over. This was the loneliest she could ever remember feeling. Her emotions drained, she walked out of the studio to go home. Maybe things would look less harsh in the morning, but she doubted it.

Twenty-Three

Jillian's eyes popped open. The sun streamed through the windows, making her jump out of bed, a state of confusion engulfing her. She hadn't heard the alarm go off, and now she was late. She rubbed the base of her neck as she realized she had nowhere to be. She sat down on the bed, the fog lifting from her brain. She clenched her jaw in anguish, remembering the phone conversation from last night.

How could he do that to her—to them? To give her a promising outlook about dancing and then tell her she had to choose.

She stood under the shower. Her chin began to tremble and the tears followed. Would she ever be cried out? She made herself stop, not wanting to show up at the hospital with puffy, red eyes. Jillian turned the water off and stepped out of the shower. She grabbed a towel and wrapped it around her.

An hour later she walked into the hospital. She stopped at the gift shop and decided to pick up a few things for her mother. Jillian walked into Audrey's hospital room with a small arrangement of fresh-cut flowers, a copy of Audrey's favorite magazine, and a forced smile on her face. "Good morning, Audrey, how is the patient today?"

Audrey looked up from the book she'd been reading. "The patient is wonderful. The orthopedist said I might be able to go home day after tomorrow. It's the best news I've had since I was moved out of ICU."

Jillian settled into the chair next to the bed. "It's great news. Will you be doing outpatient physical therapy?"

"Not at first. The therapist will come to my house. Then I'll have PT in an outpatient setting. When I'm finished with my course of therapy, I hope to be functioning under my own steam. I never wanted to be an old lady with a walker or cane."

"Well, if you do what they tell you to do, maybe you'll be standing on your own when it's all said and done."

Audrey picked up on Jillian's excessive bright affect and wondered what was bothering her daughter. Mother's intuition told her something had happened since yesterday. Never one to beat around the bush, she got right to it. "So, what's going on Jillian? I can feel it—something's bothering you. I'll always have time to listen, even when I'm not a captive audience."

Jillian sighed. "I got some wonderful news last night. Without going into the how and why right now, I'll tell you Alan figured out I was misdiagnosed with exercise-induced asthma, which is what shut down my dancing career. So now it looks like I have a second chance at performing."

"That *is* wonderful news!" The sadness on Jillian's face, along with the sudden brightness of her eyes threatening tears, confirmed Audrey's suspicions. "But there's more, isn't there?"

"Alan said if I choose to resume my performance career, he will be happy for me. But he won't be happy if my dancing takes me away from him. So I have to choose between dancing or Alan." Audrey passed a box of tissues her way as tears spilled from her eyes.

"Oh, honey, I'm so sorry. I'm certain this is no pitfall. You're at a crossroad. And according to Alan, you have to choose. Do you know what you want to do?"

Jillian stared at Audrey, her eyes turning red. "I want both."

"But it's not an option. So what are you going to do?" Audrey grimaced as she shifted her body to the side of the bed.

"I know what having Alan in my life feels like. It's wonderful, and I had hoped it would continue forever. But I don't know what it's like to be a professional dancer. I had a small taste of it once, but I didn't get the chance to see where I could go with it."

Audrey stared into her eyes to get her point across. "I don't know if *you* realize it, but I heard an answer in the words you just said."

A fresh pool of tears poured down Jillian's face, her shoulders shaking as she sobbed. Audrey's heart broke for her child. She patted the bed bedside her. Jillian moved onto the bed and wrapped her arms around her, crying into her neck.

"Oh, Mom, how am I going to tell him?"

The tears welled up in Audrey's eyes and trickled down the sides of her face. *She called me Mom!* Audrey hugged her close, making cooing, shushing sounds.

"You called me Mom." Her voice cracked with emotion as she spoke.

"That's who—you've become to me."

Audrey rubbed her back in a soothing motion.

"I know we still have—struggles ahead about—the past, but I made a decision the night—you were in the accident. I decided I wanted you in my life. Our personal baggage doesn't have to be sorted out now. We'll get around to it."

Audrey reached for Jillian's hand. "I have one thing to say about Alan. Give him space and the time he needs to figure out what he wants."

Jillian touched the doorbell and stepped backward one step. She took in a deep breath when the door opened. She could tell he was caught off guard, not expecting to see her.

He lifted his chin. "Jillian, I wasn't expecting to see you until tonight, but this isn't a bad way to start my day. Please, come in."

She hesitated a moment before crossing the threshold in front of Alan. Her decision was made, and it would serve no purpose to wait. It was best for her to share it with him now. After they were settled in the living room, she looked into the eyes that had drawn her to him the first time they had met in her studio.

"I've made my decision, and I don't see any reason to wait until tonight, so—here I am."

He was quiet and still, so she continued.

"Alan, I love you. But if I don't take this chance to dance, I'll always question if I would have been successful. And then this question running around in my head might turn into bitterness at not having tried." She stood up and began to pace. "And then I might look to lay blame for missing my chance." She stopped short. "I have to do this—for my peace of mind, if for no other reason." Covering her face with her hands, she choked out her words. "Please don't hate me," she said then ran out the front door.

~

He had sat in silence, the constriction in his throat not allowing him to speak. He swallowed hard now, hoping to relieve the sensation he was feeling. He swiped at his eyes as they began to water. "I can't believe it happened again. She chose the career." He shook his head, disbelief engulfing him. *How could she do it? I thought she was different from Reagan. I thought she was going to choose a life with me.*

Without warning, he kicked the bottom edge of the sofa but received little satisfaction for his effort. He wanted to push his fist through a wall, but his good sense of self-preservation kicked in and saved him from following through. He didn't need to screw up his career by injuring his hand. Stomping past the table in the foyer, he grabbed his keys on the way out.

He swung the SUV into Jenny's driveway, not remembering the drive from his own home. He could tell his anger was easing as he slammed the car door with less force than he had used earlier. He started walking toward the porch and stopped, not sure if he could talk about his devastated life right now. He pivoted, moving toward his SUV, when the front door opened and Jenny stepped outside.

"Alan, where are you going?"

He turned and faced her, the pain he was feeling evident on his face.

Jenny walked toward him and taking his arm, whispered, "Is it Mom?"

He grabbed her arm. "Oh, Jenny, no! Mom's fine." He released her arm, moved onto the porch, and sat down in one of the white rocking chairs. "It's me. My life just took a nosedive—again."

She sat down in the rocking chair next to his. "Alan, I'm sorry. I thought your job was secure since you're your six-month probationary period has been over for a while."

He answered through tight lips. "Not my job."

"Jillian?"

He ran his fingers through his hair. "I thought I was doing the right thing, but it blew up in my face—big time."

"So you two had a fight. That's part of being in a relationship with someone."

"We didn't have a fight. She's gone—I pushed her away."

"I don't understand. Where did she go?"

"Do you remember when I was asking questions about how Jillian was tolerating practice with you?"

"Yes, and you wouldn't tell me why. What has it got to do with her leaving?"

"I figured out she had been misdiagnosed with exercise-induced asthma. From a medical standpoint, there's nothing to keep her from a performance career. I shared that with her last night."

"I still don't understand. Revealing this information to her doesn't mean she's going to pick up and leave. Her life is here in Charlotte—you, her dance company, her school."

Alan leaned forward, his elbows resting on his knees and his hands positioned on the sides of his face. In a sheepish voice he explained, "I told her she had to choose between a performance career and me.

"Why did you do that?"

"I can't go through this again. After Reagan left me for touring, I just couldn't let it happen again with Jillian."

"Call her back and tell her you've thought things through, and you were wrong. Take back your ultimatum."

"I can't call her back. She came by this morning to tell me she chose her career over me."

Leaning over and hugging his neck, she murmured, "Oh, Alan. I'm so sorry."

"I guess it's just not meant for me to have a family, a special person to love. I should have gotten the message by now."

"Look at me." He raised his head to the familiar brown eyes. "I know she loves you."

"I guess loving me isn't enough to make her life complete."

"Oh, Alan, wake up! Of course it's not enough. Jillian's a talented dancer. Why would you try to take it away from her? It's part of who she is. I know how she feels. I wouldn't be the person I am if Mark had asked me to give up dancing."

"Reagan left because her career was her priority. I thought Jillian was different. She let me help her through her emotional and physical problems. She *leaned* on me—she *needed* me. Reagan didn't depend on me for anything, other than companionship."

"Men! You all can be so dense sometimes. Just because that's the way Reagan saw things, doesn't mean it's the same for Jillian. Did you give her the chance to tell you what she wants?"

"No—I just told her what I want, all of her or none of her."

Jenny stood up and stamped her foot, her hands curled at her sides. "Wrong, wrong, wrong!"

Alan stood up and began pacing. "You've got to help me. What should I do?"

"Jillian's been through so much the past several weeks, she's got to be on emotional overload after your little talk. You need to leave her alone."

"But she's going to go who knows where to build a career—I don't want her to go!"

"Give her some space. Let things settle down. I'll talk to her tomorrow and see what kind of plans she's making. In the meantime, you go to the hospital and bury yourself in your work."

"Today's Saturday, and it's not my weekend to work."

"Fine, go home. Think about how empty your life will be without her. And then think about how much happier you'll be when she's with you most of the time, except when she's dancing."

Jenny spent the afternoon sewing while she listened to Saint-Saëns "The Carnival of the Animals," the volume set low so she could hear any sound from the nursery through the baby monitor. She choreographed movements in her mind as she worked. Snipping the last thread on the apron, she held it up for inspection as the doorbell rang.

Opening the door she was surprised to see Jillian standing there with a pair of sunglasses covering her eyes on such a cloudy day. "Is it okay I came by without calling first?"

"Your timing's good. I just finished my latest sewing project and was wondering what I was going to do until Thomas wakes up from his nap. Come in."

They walked to the family room. "I made some ice tea earlier. Would you like some?"

"Yes—thanks." Jillian walked over to the sewing machine table while Jenny headed to the kitchen. When she returned, Jillian held up the apron covered with the Carolina Panthers' logo printed in a continuous horizontal pattern across the cloth. "I didn't know you were a diehard Panthers' fan."

"What can I say? I can only do so much housework while Thomas sleeps. Besides, I thought it'd be cute to wear when we host the Carolina football games this season. My major contribution is dishing out the food."

Jenny set the drinks on the coffee table. "Want to tell me why you're wearing sunglasses on a cloudy day?"

Jillian walked over to window, her back to Jenny. "They're a mess—my eyes. I've cried a lot the last few days." She took her glasses off and sat back down.

Jenny looked at her friend's swollen, red eyes and wanted to cry for her. Instead she reached over and touched her arm. "Why?"

"I've been crying because of something Alan told me. You're going to think I'm crazy."

"Let me decide what I'm going to think. Besides, it might be good for you to say whatever it is out loud. Sometimes it helps."

"Two nights ago Alan came by the studio at the end of my practice and surprised me with a picnic dinner in my office. After we finished eating, he told me he had determined the exercise-induced asthma I thought I had was a misdiagnosis. He said there was no medical reason I couldn't resume my performance career, if I wanted to."

"Jillian, that's wonderful." She wanted her response to appear genuine, didn't want Jillian to have any idea she knew some of the details. She wanted to hear Jillian's perception of the situation before deciding how to proceed to help her brother, who greatly needed it.

"I'm so torn. I want to dance—at least I think I do. It's been seven years since I've been a serious artist. But I have my school and the company to consider. I just can't run off and leave them hanging in the balance."

"But Jillian, this is your chance."

"You don't understand. Six years ago when I came to Charlotte, I had to start from scratch. My life was an empty shell. I put everything I had financially, emotionally, and physically into building my school and then the company. Six years of blood, sweat, and tears. I just can't walk away from them." She paused to take a gulp of tea, and the monitor came alive with noise.

"My sweet boy is awake. Come with me while I change his diaper."

They walked into the nursery to find Thomas lying on his back, kicking his feet and making happy sounds. Jillian stood against the door and watched as Jenny pulled him close. She kissed his neck and face. She performed a diaper change in record time before they went to the kitchen.

While Jenny settled Thomas into his high chair, Jillian collected their glasses from the family room. She sat down at the kitchen table. Jenny moved a bowl of fruit from the counter to the table.

"I wish I knew without a doubt what I should do."

Jenny popped a grape into her mouth. "Life is all about taking risks. You need to go for it. I don't mean take a contracted position in a company that will make you close up shop here and move away. Find a short-term job and do it. And then do another. I just declined a job offer from Indiana yesterday. The Northern Ballet Theater is doing a production of *Giselle*. They wanted me to dance the part of Myrtha. Mark will be on a business trip for a week during the timeframe I'd be gone. And I'm not ready to leave Thomas with someone without one of us being here, so I declined their offer. But, I could make a phone call for you and see if they still need someone."

Jillian didn't respond.

Good, she's thinking about it.

"Let me sleep on it, and I'll call you in the morning."

"Okay, now we're getting somewhere."

Jillian leaned over and hugged Jenny then kissed the baby-soft hair on Thomas's head.

"I'll talk to you tomorrow." She moved away from the table and let herself out the kitchen door.

Twenty-Four

Jillian awoke the next morning feeling better. Looking at the clock, she realized she'd slept for a full five hours. She sat up and stretched, her spirit buoyed after the long talk with Jenny. At least part of her life might be okay after all. Today she would make decisions affecting her future. As she showered, she realized she was singing. How could she be so devastated over splitting with Alan but happy enough about her dancing to be singing in the shower? It didn't make any sense. *Oh please don't let this be a sign of a split-personality disorder!* She made a quick phone call to Jenny, setting up a brunch date, then turned her attention to getting ready to visit Audrey.

Opening the door to her media cabinet, she selected two DVDs of dance recitals from her childhood she had converted from VHS tapes. She wanted to surprise Audrey during her visit today and give her a glimpse of the past she had missed. On the way to the hospital, she detoured by Java and picked up coffees and a piece of the crumb cake Audrey loved so much.

She entered the hospital room, her arms full with her offerings. Audrey was facing the window, her back to the door. "Good morning, Mom."

Audrey turned to face her, and Jillian noted her movements were sluggish. She also detected a sense of sadness as she looked at her mother's face.

"Good morning."

She deposited her packages and moved to the bedside. "What's wrong?"

"I thought I'd be going home today but I'm not."

"I'm sorry. How many more days before they discharge you?"

"Tomorrow."

Audrey struggled to recline back in the bed, so Jillian moved to help her. "I don't understand why you're so bothered. Tomorrow is just twenty-four hours away."

"No, you can't understand, unless you've been in my position."

She pulled a chair close to the bedside. "Explain it to me."

"After being here almost six weeks, I'm just ready to go home. It's been so long and—I just missed my favorite holiday."

"The Fourth of July is your favorite holiday?"

"Yes. What's wrong with the Fourth of July?"

"Nothing, I guess. Most people would say Christmas or Thanksgiving. Why is it your favorite?"

Audrey didn't respond.

"It's okay, you don't have to tell me if you don't want to."

Remaining quiet in a state of uncertainty, Audrey felt a breath catch in her chest as she began speaking. "How are we ever going to get to know each other if we don't share? The Fourth of July is my favorite because after I left you and your father, it was the only holiday I celebrated for several years. The one holiday I could enjoy. Mingled in a crowd of people, I was able to watch parades and fireworks without feeling alone. It was more of a group holiday, not personal and intimate. I couldn't celebrate Christmas or Thanksgiving for the longest time because I missed you both so much. It wasn't until I met Benjamin that I could enjoy those intimate holidays again."

"I don't understand. It was your choice to leave, so why do you say you missed us so much?"

Audrey straightened up, and Jillian slid a pillow behind her back for support. "I've rehearsed this over and over in my mind—how I would explain my leaving to you."

Jillian stepped back, putting distance between herself and her mother. "This isn't easy for me, but I'm giving you the chance now to explain it."

Grateful for the chance, she battled the threatening fear of Jillian's rejection, surrounding her like a shroud of death. She sent a silent prayer into the air. *Please help her understand my words.*

Audrey gripped the covers, her knuckles turning white as she began speaking. "I was starving—for attention and affection from your father. When we first met, I suppose because everything about us was new, I had his attention and devotion. There was a discovery process involved in getting to know and then love me. I had no idea that level of attention would decrease like it did. After we married and you were born, Ed was spending more and more time on his research. He was a good provider and a good man. But what little bit of his time he offered to our marriage wasn't enough. I had to save myself, and the only way it was going to happen was for me to leave."

Tears dampened Jillian's lashes. A sob escaped then she asked, "You didn't love me enough to take me with you?"

Unable to stand, she reached her hand out to her child. Jillian sat down at the bedside but didn't take her hand. Sharing a box of tissue, Audrey pulled one out and dabbed at her eyes.

"It wasn't about loving or not loving you. It was about survival. I didn't know where I was going, how I would manage. I just knew I had to leave or end up an empty shell of nothing. I couldn't do that to you. If I had stayed, I would have been no mother at all to you, just an unpleasant memory you would carry into adulthood. So my options were to stay and wither away or leave and look for what I needed to make me a whole person. Your father was a good man. There was no reason to take you from a stable environment into an unknown future."

"But to hear nothing from you for twenty-seven years—"

"I made a promise the day I left. I told myself if I could get up the courage to leave for a better life, I wouldn't look back, wouldn't allow myself to walk in and out of your life. I was convinced you would be better off with me out of the picture. It was torture at times, but I stuck to my guns until Benjamin died, and I was all alone again. I knew I wouldn't survive the loneliness a second time around. Then about two years ago, I hired a private investigator. That's how I found you here, in Charlotte."

"I don't know what to say."

"I know this has been all about me and what I wanted. I left you because I felt alone. Then I resurfaced in your life because I needed you so I wouldn't be alone. I don't want to lose you, but you have the option to walk away, just like I did so many years ago."

"Mom, I'm not saying this is easy, listening to your story. But I made a decision six weeks ago. I decided I wanted you in my life. I wanted it enough that it kept me from walking away when you were hurt. I'm here to stay. We still have a lot to learn about each other."

Audrey could no longer hold it together. She sobbed, taking in large gulps of air as her shoulders shook.

Jillian patted her hand. "I brought something to share with you that I hope will brighten your day. Cake and coffee—and something from the past." She pushed the over-the-bed table in place and sat her offerings on it.

"What's in here?" Audrey asked, picking up the bag.

"Something you missed about twenty-two years ago. My first and second dance recitals. I thought you might like to see my first attempts at dancing in public. It's more comical than impressive."

"Jillian, what a wonderful idea. Thank you. Will you set it up, please?" *The simplest of offerings sometimes brings the greatest hope.*

Jillian drew in a breath as she followed the hostess to Jenny's table. She settled into her seat and commented, "Good choice. The live jazz is a nice touch."

"I thought so, too."

She couldn't hold back any longer. "Did you make the call?"

"Let's at least order before we get down to business."

"Please, Jen—"

"Oh, all right. The job is yours!"

Raising her eyebrows, she grabbed Jenny's hand. "The job is mine?"

"Yes, it's yours!" Jenny repeated, nodding her head up and down and laughing.

"Whew, I don't think my day can get any better."

The waiter approached. "Sounds like you ladies have something to celebrate."

"Yes we do," offered Jenny.

"Congratulations. The brunch buffet is set up to your left. What can I bring you ladies to drink?"

"We'll have two mimosas. After all, we're celebrating."

The food was fabulous, but Jillian wasn't sure if it was because she hadn't eaten much in the last two days or because of the wonderful news. But now she had to get Jenny to agree to her plan.

"Last night I did a lot of thinking. I remembered what you said yesterday about having spare time to fill when Thomas is sleeping."

"Yes, I did."

"I'm going to need someone to take over my summer classes while I'm gone. Are you the least bit interested?" she asked as she pressed her thumb and index finger together and held them up near her squinted eyes.

"I'm not sure. I'm at home with Thomas because it's where I want to be. On the other hand, I'm getting a little stir-crazy. I just sewed an apron with Panther logos on it. Why don't you just hire someone?"

"I don't want just anyone. I want someone I know and trust."

"Thank you for that, I'll think about it. Change of subject—what does Alan think about all of this?"

She focused on her plate, not able to look Jenny in the eye. "Alan and I aren't speaking at the present time."

Jenny shifted in her chair. "Why not?"

"It's complicated. I don't know if I can go off dancing and performing and expect Alan to be sitting at home waiting on me, to be my boyfriend just when I come home. Who knows—I could come back home one day and he might not even be here."

"What do you mean?"

"Ever since you mentioned his clinic project I've been waiting for Alan to tell me about it, and he's never said anything. I wanted to ask him about it, but there must be some reason he doesn't want me to share it with me."

"It's been a couple of months since he's said anything to me about it. Maybe it didn't work out. Jenny shrugged and laid her hand on top of Jillian's. "So, you two aren't in Happyville right now. Hang in there. Things could change.

※

Days after walking away from Alan, the hurt was fresh in her mind, the pain still sharp in her heart. Relief came when her mind was focused on the preparations for her trip to Indiana. Her suitcase was packed, and she was ready to go. She saw Barbara pull up in the driveway. Jillian was out the front door by the time she stepped out of her car. Barbara opened the trunk and helped deposit the luggage inside.

"I think we have enough time to stop by the studio."

"Why do we need to go there? You know I get anxious when I fly. I need to get to the airport so I can focus and be mentally ready when I board the plane."

"It will take five minutes tops, but we have ten to spare. It's budget material you need to go over for *The Sleeping Beauty*. It can't wait until you get back. You'll have to e-mail me about how you want me to handle things."

They walked into the empty, dark studio. "I think I left it on your desk." She followed Jillian to her office. Barbara flipped on the light switch and watched as she proceeded to her desk.

"Is this it?"

"No, I remember now. I sat it on your chair so we wouldn't have to go through the stuff on your desk."

Jillian walked around to her chair and picked up the folder. "Okay, let's go." She looked up, and the Degas reproduction hit her eyes full on. She gasped. "How? I sent it back—"

"Audrey made arrangements to have it remounted on the wall."

"Barb, can you give me a few minutes alone. There's something I have to do before we go to the airport."

"Sure. I'll be waiting out front."

Jillian drew in a deep breath and sat down. Having the painting back in her office gave her a secure feeling about her relationship with her mother. *How did she always know how to make me feel better?* She tapped the screen on her cell phone and waited.

"Hey, Mom. I'm heading to the airport. I had to stop by my office to pick up some papers. I'm looking at my Degas painting."

"Good, I'm glad it's back where it belongs."

"I was upset when I sent it back, and I'm ashamed to admit part of me wanted to hurt you."

"Jillian, I understand. Sometimes we all do things that, in retrospect, we regret. Now, I think you should get going. Call me after you get settled."

"I love you."

"Love you, too."

Muscles twitching, Jillian walked into the building situated at the intersection of Delaware Street and Massachusetts Avenue. Butterflies fluttered in her stomach as she took the stairs to the second floor, which housed the studios of the Northern Ballet Theater. The space was alive with sound and movement, random and loud. Then she stepped into Studio B, where she could feel the drama-infused atmosphere as soon as she walked inside. Dancers were spaced around the room in small groups, performing stretching activities in preparation for the afternoon rehearsal.

Jillian wasn't surprised she was nervous, feeling much like she had in her late teens and early twenties when she'd faced an audition. But with maturity, he hid the jitters better, was able to keep them locked up inside. She displayed an air of confidence to the group of dancers she was joining.

Maxwell Lang, ballet master for the group, met her at the door of the studio and led her to the front of the room. He waited until everyone's attention was focused on them.

"Good afternoon, all. It's my pleasure to introduce to you Jillian Russell, who will be dancing the part of Myrtha in our production." He paused while the group applauded a greeting of welcome to the guest artist.

"Jillian comes to us from Charlotte, North Carolina—the owner and ballet mistress of the North Carolina Ballet Company. You can read the rest of her bio in the program proof. Everyone be sure you proofread your bio and give us your initials if we got it right, so it can go to the printer by tomorrow afternoon. Now, let's get to work."

Jillian became focused on the thing she thought she would never again experience, and the butterflies dissipated.

Over the years, she had not permitted herself to think about what she was missing, a defense mechanism, she supposed, that allowed her to move on with her life. But as the ensemble drew her into their group, tears of gratitude hovered behind her eyes. The chance to be submerged in the magic of bringing a story to life pulled at her emotions.

For Jillian, the afternoon sped by. If she missed a step or placement, she learned from her mistake and, like the true professional she was, didn't allow it to happen again. Lightness filled her chest as she moved across the floor, producing fluid movements that seemed effortless. It all brought a sense of satisfaction as the afternoon rehearsal ended. It was good to feel this way at the beginning of her journey, but she was smart enough to know not to expect the duration of her time here to be struggle-free. When she left the studio for the dinner break, she was sure she had made the right decision to dance again. The one thing she didn't know was if time would make the pain of losing Alan fade enough to endure the loss.

Jillian's time in Indiana passed in a whirlwind, and now their fifth and final performance of *Giselle* was underway. She was in a state of euphoria. Opening night for the Northern Ballet Theater had been a success, and she knew she had been an important part of their success. The atmosphere and experience had been positive, but now she was ready to go home for some much needed rest. She had gone full throttle the entire time, from the first moment she'd stepped foot onto Indiana soil.

She knew some degree of her success in this business was attributable to word-of-mouth communication. Over the last three weeks, she had watched others to gauge their reaction to her dancing. Only time would tell as to how far the talk would go.

She focused her thoughts on Myrtha, waiting for her entrance cue in Act II. She moved onto the stage, her chin held high and her shoulders back. She immersed herself in the role of Myrtha, portraying her to the height of her ability. She left the stage that night with a sense of accomplishment. She had stepped out and reclaimed her chance to compete in the world of ballet performers. How far would she go?

Twenty-Five

Taking advantage of the fact the chief's assistant was not at her desk, Franklin stepped over to Dr. Schuster's door and knocked.

"Come in."

"Dr. Schuster, could I have a moment of your time, sir?"

The chief picked up his glasses and, referring to a calendar opened on his desk, asked, "Witt, are you on my schedule this morning?"

Franklin shifted his weight to his other foot. "No sir, I don't have an appointment."

"I've got a busy morning. Will this take long?"

"No, sir, I have a concern I need to bring to your attention."

He pointed to a chair. "All right. Have a seat."

"It's about Dr. Armstrong, sir. I think he may be having some personal issues."

"I make it a policy never to get involved with my employees' personal lives."

"A good policy, sir. And one that is appreciated by the staff, I'm sure. But when someone's personal issues are affecting their work or may cause some damage to the hospital's reputation—"

"What are you saying, Dr. Witt."

"I'm going by past experience here, because the last time I suspected drug abuse by a coworker, at another hospital, I didn't act on it. When his life went down the tubes, I felt somewhat responsible because I didn't speak up."

"Do you have proof Dr. Armstrong is using illicit drugs?"

"No, sir, but his behavior is off, and he's doesn't appear to be taking care of himself, much like what I saw happen with my other coworker."

"How long has this been going on?"

"I'm not sure, sir. A month, maybe longer."

"All right, Dr. Witt. I'll take the appropriate actions."

"Thank you for your time, sir." Franklin walked out the door, feeling a sense of satisfaction with the trouble he'd just laid at Alan's door. He knew golden boy wasn't doing drugs. But whatever his issues, now he'd have to deal with Schuster too.

Jillian didn't realize how much she had missed her mother until she was wrapped in a secure hug in Audrey's arms. The cast had come off her ankle, the home therapy had been completed, and Audrey was now going back to the hospital three times a week for outpatient physical therapy.

"Wow, so much has happened since I've been gone. Look at you. No more cast. I like the purple color you picked for your walker."

"A lot has happened, but I still get so frustrated. I want to be done with all the therapy. I can't drive myself, and I don't like having to rely on employees and neighbors."

"Just a little more patience, Mom. Will it make you feel better if I take you? When's your next appointment?"

"I have an appointment this afternoon at one o'clock."

"Okay, let's have a light lunch, and then we'll head to the hospital."

Jillian maneuvered the walker out of the backseat of her car. She placed it in front of her mother and stood close, in case she was needed. She watched carefully when Audrey stood up and placed her hands on the handgrips of the walker. Jillian sauntered beside her as she pushed toward the hospital entrance.

Once they were inside, Audrey said, "I'll be finished by two-thirty. Why don't you go to the cafeteria and answer some of your e-mails. I don't expect you to spend your afternoon watching an old lady learn how to walk without this thing."

Jillian didn't move.

"Sweetheart, I needed a ride to get here, but I'm good to go now. Pretty soon I hope I won't need a ride either."

"Okay, I'll see you at two-thirty." Jillian turned and headed to the elevators. As she walked by the waiting room, she made a casual sweep of the area. She stopped walking when her eyes fell on Alan. He was talking to a middle-aged couple. Sharp pain shot through Jillian's chest. *Will I feel that pain every time I see him?* She couldn't move. Her vision blurred as she continued to stare. And then he looked up and saw her standing in the walkway. He touched the woman on the shoulder and shook hands with the man. *Holy cow, he is coming toward me!*

She had seen him. He couldn't leave the area without saying something to her. It wouldn't be right. As he stopped in front of her, he took in the familiar scent of her perfume. He wanted to touch her—her face, her hair, pull her into his arms. But that wouldn't be right either. "What are you doing here? Is everything okay?"

"Fine, I just brought Mom to the hospital for her physical therapy appointment. I was on my way to the cafeteria. Can you join me?"

"Can't. I'm headed to the OR. My patient was thrown from an ATV. Sorry, maybe some other time. Good to see you, Jillian." He hurried away.

Alan jerked the door to the sub sterile room open and pulled a mask out of the box on the shelf beside the sink. He tied it in place then stomped the foot control to turn on the water. Grabbing a disposable scrub brush from the box mounted on the wall, he ripped open the package and start scrubbing with vigorous strokes. *She looks so good! She looks like she's been doing fine since we split—well, good for her!*

Seeing Jillian without expecting it had rattled him. Alan tossed the pickups on the Mayo stand. "Pickups *with teeth*." His voice was full of displaced anger.

"I'm sorry, Dr. Armstrong." The surgical tech handed him the pickups he'd requested. He continued to work without acknowledging her apology. The noise in the OR remained at a minimum throughout the rest of the procedure. It was his habit to thank the staff as he left the OR, but today he swept out of the room without uttering a word.

Alan leaned against the scrub sink and pulled off his surgical cap. Jillian—his thoughts turned to her during most of his waking hours, except when he was in the OR. Now that the surgery was over, she weaved her way into his thoughts again. He missed her so much. He wasn't eating or sleeping well, and physically it was starting to show. Rubbing his head, he walked toward the waiting area to update his patient's parents. As he rounded the corner, he was intercepted by Dr. Schuster.

"Ahh, Dr. Armstrong—just the man I want to see."

"Can it wait, sir? I'm on my way to speak to my patient's family."

"Meet me in my office in ten minutes."

Alan updated the parents, cautious about being too optimistic as his patient remained in critical condition. Heading to Dr. Schuster's office, he was stopped by Franklin.

"Hey, Alan. I hope everything's okay. You're looking tired, and I'd say a little strung out. Maybe you need some time off."

"Everything's fine—just a little tired. I can't talk. I've got a meeting with Dr. Schuster."

Alan moved on before Franklin could reply. He turned the corner and entered Dr. Schuster's outer office. His stomach twisted in a knot.

The assistant looked up and said, "You can go in. Dr. Schuster is expecting you."

He couldn't get comfortable in his seat. Feeling like the kid who had been sent to the principal's office, he wondered why he had been summoned.

"Alan, is everything alright?"

The same question. "Sir?"

"I don't like prying into my staff's personal lives, but when the situation warrants it, I do."

"I'm not following you, sir."

"You've done an about-face the last few weeks. Your behavior, perhaps demeanor is a better word—well, concern has been expressed to me. And your physical appearance, you're looking a bit gaunt. So, I need you to report to employee health now and take a mandatory drug test."

"But, sir—"

"*Now*, Dr. Armstrong. Employee Health is a five-minute walk from here. The receptionist will call me after you sign in."

Alan moved in slow motion from the chair to the door.

"Five minutes, Dr. Armstrong."

"Yes, sir."

Alan had to take hold of this situation now. He'd made a mess of his life with Jillian, and he was paying for it every waking minute. His work was all he had left. He couldn't screw it up too.

Employee Health wasn't busy, not the norm for a hospital this size. Alan was relieved he hadn't run into anyone he knew and completed his task within ten minutes. The aggravating truth stared him in the face as he handed his urine specimen to the waiting nurse. It was one thing to take a random test, but a mandatory test? And now he was labeled by Dr. Schuster as someone to be watched.

He knew his drug screen would come back negative, but he had to clean up his act fast. He went to the cafeteria and forced himself to eat a sandwich and a piece of fruit before returning to make rounds on his patients. He'd make sure he got more rest, even if he had to resort to taking diphenhydramine for a few nights to assist him into falling asleep.

He began to feel a little paranoid about which coworker would have talked to Dr. Schuster about his behavior before coming to him. He could try to guess, but he'd never know for sure. Maybe they weren't speaking against him but were concerned for him, except Franklin. And then he knew—but why would Franklin do it? What would he gain from it? He just needed to release his mind from the intoxicating thoughts of Jillian and focus on other things, at least while he was at the hospital. But it was easier said than done, especially after seeing her today.

Twenty-Six

Jillian sat at her desk, deep in thought. Seeing Alan yesterday had been a shock. *How silly. He works at the hospital.* She had to face the fact they would run into one another from time to time. *He looked so thin and tired.* She wondered if he had been working longer hours while she had been gone.

At the sight of the stroller being pushed into her office, Jillian jumped up and came around to the front of the desk. "Jen, it's so good to see you and Thomas. Has he grown much in three weeks?"

Jenny pulled the stroller over by the sofa. She lifted Thomas out and handed him to Jillian.

"You tell me."

Jillian raised him up and down in the air. "A bit heavier," she answered as she pulled him closed and kissed his cheek.

"So, how was it?"

Jillian joined her on the sofa. She bounced Thomas up and down on her lap. "Amazing. Fabulous. Stupendous!"

"Would you do it again?"

"Yes." She settled the baby in her lap as Jenny handed him a small teddy bear. "I'm leaving next week for a stint in Fayetteville, Arkansas."

"That was quick. You just got home. What group is in Fayetteville?"

"The West Arkansas Ballet Group. They've been around about four years. It's a new, but ambitious organization."

"What part will you be dancing?"

"Valencienne, from *The Merry Widow*."

Jenny whistled. "Wow, a little more challenging than your last job. Will you have enough prep time?"

"I think so. I'll be gone a few days longer." Thomas started fussing. Jillian handed him off to his mother. "So how did working here go for you?"

"Good—once Anna, Sandra, and I sat down and tweaked the schedule a bit."

"Are you good to go for another month?"

"I believe so." Jenny stood up, trying to soothe the fussing baby. "It's getting close to his dinner time. Sorry I can't stay longer. Mark is having guests over tonight, so I've got to run, but I just had to stop by and see you. Would you mind strapping him into the stroller?"

She tucked Thomas back into his stroller while Jenny stuffed his things into the diaper bag. "I'm glad you came by. I hope we can see each other again before I leave."

"Me too, I'll talk to you later."

Jillian returned to her desk and the work that had piled up while she was in Indiana. A few hours had passed when Barbara stuck her head in the door.

"I'm heading out for the night. Are you ready to go?"

"Not just yet. I have a few more things I'd like to get done before I call it a night."

"Okay, I'll see you tomorrow."

"Good night. Oh, Barb, be sure to lock up."

Jillian reached for her phone, a smile on her lips. "Hey, stranger."

"I'm sorry to call, but I've got a little emergency."

Jillian straightened up in her chair, her senses heightened. "What's wrong, Jen?"

"Did we happen to leave our favorite teddy bear at your office this afternoon?"

Jillian released the breath she was holding. "Just a minute." She walked over to the sofa and moved the pillows. "Yep, I see one stowaway teddy bear behind a pillow. Is all that crying coming from one little guy, or does he have help?"

"It's all Thomas. I hate to ask, but he's so upset. Could you swing by and drop it off so we'll be able to settle him down for bed?"

"No problem. I'll see you in about ten minutes."

"Well," she said to the bear. "I guess I'm done for the night. Let's lock up and get you to Thomas before he has a major breakdown."

The driveway and street were filled with parked cars, the windows of the house all lit up. Jillian held the teddy bear in her hand. Mark opened the door before she had a chance to ring the bell.

"Come on in. I know one little guy who'll be happy to see the bear you're holding."

Jillian protested. "I don't want to disrupt your guests. I'll just let you give it to Thomas."

"No, I insist." He gave her hand a yank and pulled her into the foyer. Guiding her by the shoulders, Mark entered the family room as everyone shouted "Surprise! Happy Birthday!"

Her hand flew to her chest as she drew in a breath. She could feel her racing heartbeat.

"What's all this?" The room was filled with members of her company and friends. She surveyed the room, disappointed that the one face she hoped to see was missing from the crowd.

Barbara stepped forward. "You're a hard nut to crack. I didn't know what we were going to do if Plan B failed because Plan A—getting you to leave with me—didn't go over so well."

Jenny chimed in, "We were running out of plans." Everyone laughed.

Someone shouted, "Let's party." The room exploded with sound as the volume of the music was cranked up.

Jillian held the bear up to her face. "Poor Teddy, to find out you were just a pawn in their game." Handing the teddy bear to Mark, she asked, "How did you get Thomas to cry on cue? I don't hear an upset baby now."

"Thomas is fine. You were listening to a recording we made when we were being silly one afternoon. Man, we just couldn't get him to calm down. We thought we would record him so we could use it for torture when he's a teenager, along with embarrassing pictures."

Jenny walked up with Thomas in her arms. "And I had you strap Thomas into his stroller so I could hide Teddy behind a pillow."

"The plot thickens," Jillian said as she laughed. "I don't want to spoil your party, but it's not my birthday. Barb, you know my birthday was last week." Her voice was accusatory, not having received even a phone call from her.

"Well, it's a dual celebration—belated birthday, since you spent your birthday alone in Indiana, and a celebration to toast the rebirth of your dancing career."

She was speechless. Looking around, she realized the people in this room had, over the last six years, become dear to her. Glasses of champagne were passed around. Whoever was responsible had done things up right. The music was suspended long enough for Barbara, the person who had known her longest, to toast the birthday girl. After she finished, everyone shifted into party mode and continued past midnight. At Mark and Jenny's insistence, Jillian opted to spend the night in their guest room, rather than drive home.

She settled into the unfamiliar bed, her thoughts chasing one another in circles. She was unsure about giving up her friends and company to follow her dream. But this was her dream. She had to try. Her mind was fuzzy from the glasses of champagne she had consumed. Everything was so messed up. A few months ago her life seemed to be coming together for the first time ever, and now she thought she wanted things back the way they had been. It was too hard to figure out. Sleep finally allowed her to escape her thoughts.

The job in Arkansas had gone well, and Jillian was back home twenty-five days after she'd left to assume the role of Valencienne. Because of her trip, practice for the start of The North Carolina Ballet Company's sixth season was a few days late, not a good way to begin. If she were to continue to travel and dance, she first had to make the survival of her company a top priority. They had weathered the financial problems with the new supporters they had gained at the fundraiser. Someone that could step into the role of interim ballet mistress was needed. She had an idea and hoped Jenny would be agreeable to it.

Scrolling down her contact list, she touched Jenny's name. The call went to voicemail. "Hey, Jen. Can we meet sometime today? Give me a call. Bye."

They met several hours later at Java.

"JB, over here."

Jillian nodded and headed toward the table off to the side of the coffeehouse, away from the counter.

"I've got one low-fat vanilla latte waiting for you."

"Thanks. Where's Thomas?"

"He's getting a little boisterous with age. I thought a babysitter was a better choice today."

"I'd love to see him, but I do have something important to discuss with you. Maybe this is better." She took a sip of her latte. "I've taken another job. It's a great part, and I want the chance to do it."

"Tell me."

"I'll get to that. But my concern right now is the company. We've started practice for the new season a few days late because I was finishing the job in Arkansas. This Boston job is a little more involved time-wise because of the weight of the part.

"Okay—"

"So, I want you to assume my position of ballet mistress just through this first production of the season. Until I see how this dancing thing goes."

"JB—I'm flattered and speechless, almost."

"Well, what do you think?"

"Tell me about this part you've landed."

"While I was in Arkansas, I was contacted by Kaye Merriman, an instructor I had the second summer I studied at the East Coast Ballet Theater."

"I remember her. I never had her as an instructor, but I heard she was tough."

"She has since left ECBT and started a group in Boston. She heard some chatter about me restarting my career and was able to obtain my contact info. She's asked me to portray Gamzatti in *La Bayadère*."

"*The Temple Dancer*, phenomenal!"

"I won't do it unless you'll step into my shoes, but no pressure."

Jenny laughed. "Okay, no pressure. I'll need more information, and of course Mark and I have to have time to talk about it. When do you need an answer?"

"Two days. I have to give Kaye my answer in two days."

"Okay, I'll have an answer for you by then. Oh, I'll need a copy of your rehearsal schedules from your last production and all the arrangements that have been made so far for this production. What did you decide on for the season opener?"

Jillian sipped on her latte. "We chose *The Sleeping Beauty*."

"Love it, and I'm so excited for you. Dancing against your nemesis for the prince's heart. How cool is that?"

Twenty-Seven

Jillian dragged herself down the hall and into her hotel room. She dropped her bag on the floor and fell across the bed. Exhaustion had overtaken her body, but it felt good. It had been years since she had been challenged in this manner. She had been curious to see how far she could push herself, and today she had pushed to the limit. From the extra practice with Robert to the last minute costume fittings, she had spent twelve hours at the studio today. A hot shower and a good night's sleep would leave her fit for tomorrow's dress rehearsal.

Dancing the part of Gamzatti had been a thrilling experience. Robert, who was dancing the part of Solor, was a wonderful partner. Jillian was convinced their success as partners was, in part, due to the fact she imagined she was dancing, touching, and holding Alan. That's why she connected so well with Robert.

Her nights were miserable. She was torn about making a permanent decision. During the day it was easy to choose the dancing career because she was in the element and enjoying every minute. At night, she longed for Alan—his kisses, his embraces, and thoughts of growing old with him. All she had to do was choose him. She just wasn't ready to give up dancing, and she knew it would have to happen if she wanted a future with Alan.

The shower massaged her body aches away. Thirty minutes later she was sitting in her pajamas, waiting for room service to deliver her dinner. She reached for the phone and dialed Alan's number, eager to tell him all about her day. Before she heard the first ring, she ended the call. She missed him so much, but she couldn't talk to somebody who wasn't speaking to her. There had been no communication between them since the day she had taken Audrey for outpatient therapy at the hospital.

She wanted to blame someone for the hurt and the loneliness she was feeling. If Alan hadn't told her she could dance again, she wouldn't be here having the time of her life, but so alone at night after the dancing stopped. How could she blame him? She loved him. Grinding her teeth, her emotions became stirred as anger fed her thoughts. He had caused this upheaval in their lives. Why couldn't he accept dancing was a part of her? She remembered telling Reagan about wondering how far she would have gone with a performance career, so she had to try. Why couldn't he understand?

She dialed Audrey's number. After the fourth ring, she sat up straighter. Her muscles tensed, and her heart began to race. And then a familiar voice said, "Jillian, I'm so glad you called. How's everything in Boston?"

"Mom, are you okay? Why'd it take you so long to answer your phone?" Her muscles relaxed as she settled back against the headboard of the bed.

"I've been working on my walking. I was across the room without my cane when the phone rang, so it took me a few minutes to get to it. Sorry."

"You promised me you wouldn't overdo it while I was gone. Are you behaving?"

"I promise I'm behaving—this is my last lap tonight. Now, answer my question. How are things with you?"

"I'm exhausted, but it's wonderful. I'm so happy and grateful to have this second chance to dance. And I'm so fortunate to have Jen for a friend—to step in as interim ballet mistress so I can work out my future." She squeezed her eyes shut, and tears started to form.

"Are you spending all your time at the studio, no sightseeing?"

"I'm here to work. Besides, sightseeing's no fun alone. I miss our excursions."

"I do too. After I get this ankle's function restored, maybe I can follow you to some of your destinations, and we'll do some sightseeing. Then maybe you won't sound so sad. I know you miss him."

"I can't deny it, but what can I do about it? It's all or nothing as far as Alan's concerned."

"Jillian, let me ask you something. If I could grant you one wish, anything at all, what would your wish be? Take your time to think about it before you answer."

The phone line filled with silence, and then she spoke. "I think I'd like to dance one more day. I'd want the ability to dance without stopping for twenty-four hours. To dance all the ballets I've ever dreamed of dancing. That's what I'd want."

"Interesting—and what would you do after the twenty-four hours of dancing was over?"

"I'd take off my ballet slippers and spend the rest of my life with the man I love."

After talking with Jillian, Audrey stretched her legs out on the ottoman and settled back in her chair. She touched Alan's number from her contact list then listened as the call went to voicemail. "Alan, this is Audrey. Please call me back as soon as you can. It's not an emergency, but it is urgent. Thank you."

She closed her eyes, hoping she was doing the right thing. She didn't want to be a meddling mother, but she couldn't see any harm in moving things along between Alan and Jillian. *And they thought their relationship was over.*

The ringing of her phone jolted her from her dozing. The name on the caller ID brought a smile to her lips. "Hello, Alan. I'm glad you were able to call me back tonight."

"Are you all right? Is everything okay?"

"Thank you for asking, dear. I'm fine or on my way to being fine. My physical therapy is going well. However, I'm not sure everything is okay. I would like your help with something."

"I'll be glad to help if I can. What do you need?"

A smile spread across her face. "I want to go to Boston to see Jillian dance."

"Okay—I don't see how I can help you with that."

"I've never seen Jillian perform, and I want to be there. I will make it happen, but I only have two days to get everything together. I want you to accompany me."

"I'm sorry, Audrey. I can't do it."

This was going to be a little harder than she had first thought. "All right then, Alan, I'm calling in my favor."

"I'm sorry, what favor?"

"You know, the favor for planning Reagan's dinner party. You said you didn't know how you would ever thank me, so thank me now by taking me to Boston." She thought she heard an expletive along with a sputtering sound on the other end of the phone. "Look, dear. I want to see Jillian dance. She doesn't even need to know we're in the audience." Determination sounded through her articulate words. "I will make this trip."

Alan interrupted. "What about a travel companion?"

"It's doubtful, such short notice. Besides I would feel more comfortable if I go with someone who knows the area, like you, dear. Also, you're a physician, not that I foresee needing you in that capacity, but—another point in your favor."

"I didn't know we were tallying points."

Go in for the kill. "I don't want to miss anymore of Jillian's life, for certain not her triumphs. After almost dying a few months ago—"

"All right! I'll go to Boston. But she *can't* know we're there. Do we have a deal?"

"Deal. I'll get all the details worked out tomorrow and give you a call. Good night, Alan."

"Night, Audrey."

Why did I let Audrey talk me into going to Boston? It had been a month since Alan had seen Jillian at the hospital. He'd been so shaken from their encounter that day and the subsequent meeting with Dr. Schuster, he'd not been in a state of mind to attend her surprise birthday party. The truth of the matter was he hadn't been sure he could control his feelings around her, to pretend everything was fine when it wasn't, so he had stayed away. He'd told Jenny he had a scheduled meeting about the rural clinic he couldn't miss. It had been the quickest thought to come to his mind that sounded legitimate and she wouldn't argue about.

He had also thought about resigning from the board, but now Jenny was interim ballet mistress, and he couldn't do it. He loved his sister and wanted to support her and the company, even though it would be torture to see Jillian. He knew he was bound to run into her at events and performances. And now he was going to Boston to watch her dance. To see her do what was more important to her than claiming his love. *Man, am I messed up!*

The flight to Boston was uneventful. Audrey dozed most of the way, and Alan took advantage of the time to read one of his medical journals. Any other day he'd be engrossed in an article about pericardiocentesis after trauma, to the exclusion of those around him. But today he couldn't stay focused. His thoughts kept drifting to Jillian. Why couldn't he push this unsettled feeling away? Jillian had no idea they were coming. He wouldn't be anywhere near her like their last encounter—wanting to touch and hold her. He slammed the magazine shut. Audrey's head turned in his direction as her eyes popped open.

"Sorry, I didn't mean to disturb you."

"No worries. I wasn't in a deep sleep, just dozing. Is everything all right?"

"No." He ran he fingers through his hair. "I'm on a flight, heading somewhere I don't want to go, to see someone I need to drop from my life."

"I don't see it that way."

"Just how do you see it, Audrey?" His tone was harsh.

"You're on a discovery mission, looking for the pieces you need to fit together to make your life complete. You're here to gather information about one of those pieces."

He sighed. "Jillian."

"Yes, Jillian. How will you feel when you see her? Can you live your life without her?"

"She made the decision for me. She chose dancing over me—over us."

"You made her choose. Now you have to decide. Will it be worth having Jillian in your life, knowing she comes with the baggage of a dancing career? In the meantime, it can't hurt for you to watch her do the thing that is a big part of who she is."

The flight attendant's voice came over the intercom, instructing the passengers to fasten their seatbelts for the descent to Boston. Alan had observed Audrey leaning on her cane for support, her steps slowing as they'd boarded the plane. The walk through the concourse from the entrance of the Charlotte airport to the boarding area had been lengthy. While Audrey had dozed, Alan had made arrangement with the flight attendant for a wheelchair to be waiting when they disembarked. The flight attendant made sure they were the first to leave so Audrey could get to the waiting wheelchair without difficulty.

"You didn't have to do this," protested Audrey when Alan settled her into the chair then placed her feet on the footrests.

"You've gone to all this trouble to see Jillian dance, and it'd be a shame to miss her performance because you're sitting in your hotel room in pain. So sit back and enjoy the ride." It felt good to gripe about something, even if it wasn't the root of his agitation.

"Thank you for your thoughtfulness. I'll behave now."

He couldn't be mad at her. Because of Audrey, he was going to see Jillian tonight. So it would be from a distance, and that was a good thing. If he was going to remain in Charlotte, he would have to learn to be around her and survive his feelings for her or, better yet, let those feeling go. Or he could change his mind and join Ron in running the rural clinic.

The skycap made the transition from airplane to cab seamless. The afternoon traffic was slack, and they arrived without delay at The Harbor Hotel within an hour's time of landing at the airport. As they separated in the hotel hallway, Alan made Audrey promise she would rest until time for their early dinner at the Maritime Restaurant located in the hotel.

Alan was led to his room by the bellhop, who made sure he was comfortable and had everything he needed before he left the room. Audrey had done an excellent job with the arrangements. So far everything had been a breeze for Alan.

He rummaged through the mini-bar, looking at his choices, and pulled out a miniature bottle of scotch. He poured the contents into a glass.

Alan moved out of the room to the balcony. He stood against the rail and looked out across the harbor. It was a peaceful afternoon, lending a relaxing touch to his frazzled mind. He took a drink, wondering how he was going to right his world again. He couldn't continue on the path he was going. He'd had a wake-up call about his career with the drug-testing business. He found it amazing how one accusation could bruise a reputation. When Dr. Schuster had followed up a week after receiving the negative toxicology results, he had been pleased Alan was looking and acting like his old self. He seemed to accept Alan's explanation he was weathering a bump in his personal life and left it at that.

He needed to refocus his efforts on the deal with Ron Compton. A year ago, he would have been thrilled with Ron's offer to partner with him when he left Charlotte to start a practice in a remote area of the coast. Now the urge to do this was not as strong as it had been then. Once he settled this business of Jillian, his commitment to Ron could be solidified.

Dressing for the evening, he felt a zap of adrenaline race through his body. He was anxious about seeing Jillian. Tonight would be as good a time as any to begin the withdrawal process of emptying her from his thoughts and emotions—to remove her from his life. But what if Audrey was right? What if Jillian was the piece of the puzzle that completed his life? Could he risk choosing her, knowing she might push him aside for a full-time performance career later? A flash of heat made Alan swipe his forehead with a clean handkerchief before sliding it into his pocket. He picked up the room keycard before walking out the door.

He moved three doors down the hallway and knocked. The air here was cooler. Grimacing, he hoped their dinner conversation wouldn't revolve around Jillian.

Audrey opened her door, looking attractive for a woman her age, in a black-and-white ensemble.

"Ready for our big night?" he asked in greeting.

"I'm ready. Just let me get my bag." She returned, leaning on her cane for support.

He pushed the elevator button. "How's your ankle?"

"It's better, thank you. I'll be glad when I'm one hundred percent again."

"You know, even with physical therapy, you may never be one hundred percent."

"As we get to know each other, you'll find if I am determined enough, I will make it happen, whatever *it* is. Just something to keep in mind, dear."

With Alan's help, Audrey maneuvered to her seat in the theater. She positioned her cane on the floor out of the way. He was glad she was occupied with leafing through the playbill. He didn't feel like talking. It wasn't long before the orchestra started tuning up. The sound died away, a hush of anticipation fell over the audience.

The overture began, and Alan leaned back in his chair. Even with just a few days' notice about the trip, he had done his homework and knew Jillian wouldn't make her entrance as Gamzatti until Act II. He watched the story unfold. The dancers were good and held his attention well. And then she made her entrance. Allan shifted forward in his chair. She looked beautiful, just like a rajah's daughter, the part she was portraying tonight.

Allan had never seen this ballet before and was a little disappointed Jillian's part seemed to involve more movement with acting than dancing. But as the ballet shifted to the second scene in the palace garden for the engagement party of Gamzatti and her warrior prince, Solor, Alan's life changed. The duet performance between the two and Jillian's solo performance touched him to his core. He had always seen her dancing in practice mode, but here, in this arena surrounded by the trappings of the scenery, props, costuming, and supported by the cast, he had seen into her soul as she danced.

Alan was spellbound after that, following her every movement. He was so absorbed in his thoughts that when the house lights came up for intermission, he remained entranced in them.

"Alan, dear, would you mind? I think I should get up and stretch a bit. Could you hand me my cane?"

Audrey's discomfort was apparent when she walked. Alan was torn. Should he take her back to the hotel? He wanted to stay and watch the rest of Jillian's performance.

He wavered over his decision, but when Audrey sat down on a bench in the lobby, he knew he couldn't ignore her discomfort. "Audrey, I can tell you're in pain. I think we should go back to the hotel."

"No. I'm going to make it to the end of Jillian's performance. Afterward, I'll go back to the hotel put some ice on my ankle and take a big dose of ibuprofen. End of discussion."

She rose from the bench. He moved forward to steady her, if need be. "We've got some time before intermission is over. You can sit for a while.."

"I'm moving at a turtle's pace, so we'd better go now."

They made their way back into the theater just as the house lights dimmed. Sitting at the edge of his chair, Alan waited with enthusiasm for Jillian to make her entrance onto the stage. Her dancing was just as amazing the second half of the performance. By the time the ballet ended, Alan knew two things for sure. He wouldn't be setting up a practice with Ron, and he had made a terrible mistake when he'd pushed his ultimatum at Jillian. Now he had to figure out how to undo what he had done.

Twenty-Eight

Jenny poked her head in the door of Jillian's office. "Have a minute to talk?"

"Sure, come in and sit."

She sat down on the sofa. Crossing her long legs, she said, "You look so glum today. What's wrong?"

Jillian pushed away from the desk and leaned back in her chair. "I guess I'm tired. Just didn't know it showed."

"It's not a tired look. It's a sad, like your-joy-is-gone look."

Jillian stared ahead, her gaze focused on the Degas painting. "I miss Alan."

"So, maybe cutting him loose wasn't your best idea."

"Things were fine in Boston and Fayetteville when I was dancing. But sitting alone in my hotel room at night was awful. I was so lonely. So no, maybe it wasn't my best idea. Did you come in here just to talk about my joyless life?"

"No, I came because I have an idea I think will be an audience pleaser."

"Well, we should always try to keep the audience pleased. What's your idea?"

"On opening night, we should do a preview of the next production on our calendar. So, on opening night of *The Sleeping Beauty* we would do a scene from *Carnival of the Animals*. And you should be the one to perform it."

"A coming-attraction preview. I like it. We could do it with a plain backdrop."

"Oh no, you want to give the audience the full effect with scenery, props, and costumes. We might be a little harried to get it together this time, but there shouldn't be a problem with future productions."

"There's not much time. Do you think we can pull it together?"

"It's worth a try. Wait, I've got a better idea. You should perform the dying swan scene. It has a dark background, no props. I have a little time this afternoon I could spend on working the logistics. You should start practicing since opening night is only two weeks away. I'll check back with you later and let you know if it's going to work out."

Smiling at the idea of dancing for her company, Jillian moved away from her desk. Her smile faded as she thought about the statement Jenny had made about cutting Alan loose. It hadn't been her idea for them to separate, but she didn't know that.

Enthused about Jenny's idea, she quickly changed her clothes. After obtaining a CD of *Carnival of the Animals* from their music library, Jillian headed to Studio B. She put the CD in the player and drew in some deep breaths. She listened and began moving to the rhythm of the music. Not long into her practice, she began to question if this was what she wanted out of life. She thought back to the question her mother had asked her when she was in Boston. If she could have one wish—and she had answered, to dance one more day. She had pushed Alan aside and picked dancing. Performing had been wonderful, but at the end of the day, she was alone and unhappy until she was dancing again. She could stay the choice she had made, but one day her body would give out, and the dancing would be over. If she were to give her entire life over to dancing, she would be alone when her career came to an end.

Jillian stepped out from behind the screen. Pausing, she stared at her reflection in the mirror and was pleased at what she saw. The white costume fit her body well. "It's perfect. I can't believe you made this just for me. Thank you, Mom." She loved being able to say the word *mom*. To have a person connected to the word.

"I'm so glad Jenny asked me to make it for you. I've been anxious to do more than physical therapy. It was my pleasure."

Jillian turned around to face her mother. "Still think exciting things happen backstage before *curtain up*?"

Silence filled the air.

"Mom, are you okay?"

"Yes, dear. I was just thinking about where I was this time last year, not geographically, but emotionally in my life. And I have to say I'm happier now than I have a right to be." Tears shimmered in her green eyes as her voice began to quiver. "I love you so much, Jillian, and I'm so happy to witness the renewing of your dance career. I'm a proud mom." She laughed. "I should have a tee-shirt made that says *Proud Mom of a Professional Dancer.*"

Jillian lowered her head. She reached for Audrey's hand and said, "Let's sit for a minute. I'm so happy you're a proud mom, but I'm not sure how long it will last."

"What are you talking about?"

"I've made a decision that involves giving up my dancing career. Tonight will be my last performance."

"I don't understand. I thought you missed performing."

"I did miss it, and I do love performing, but I love Alan more. I want to be Alan's wife, and if that isn't scary enough, I think I want children—even knowing I'll be a basket case the whole pregnancy. I'm sorry this will be the only time you'll see me dance."

Audrey put her arms around her daughter. "Sweetheart, it's not your dancing that makes me proud. It's the wonderful, brave woman you are that makes me a proud mom. And to be honest, this won't be my first time to see you perform."

"Now I don't understand."

"Well, you see, I came to Boston and watched you perform on opening night."

"You were there? Why would you do come to Boston and not tell me? And how in the world did you make the trip on your own? You were still using a cane."

"I wasn't alone. Alan accompanied me, at my request. I pushed him into coming. You did an amazing job, and I'll always remember how beautiful your dancing was that night. It's getting late. I'd better go find my seat. Just keep in mind, things have a way of working out."

Jillian pulled Audrey into a tight embrace. "Thanks, Mom. I love you."

Audrey stopped at the doorway and, giving a light touch to her lips blew a kiss in her daughter's direction.

Jillian moved in front of the mirror, checking her reflection one last time. She touched her headpiece, making sure it was secure. How appropriate it was that she was ending her career portraying a dying swan.

From house left, David stepped onto the stage, wireless microphone in hand, into the circle of light waiting for him. The curtains remained closed.

"Good evening. It is my pleasure to welcome you to *The Sleeping Beauty*, the sixth season opener of the North Carolina Ballet Company.

He paused as the audience erupted with applause.

"We've made a few changes this season you may note when you read through your program. We are starting a new tradition tonight, which you will experience at all of our opening nights in the future. Prior to *curtain up*, in a prelude performance, we will give you a glimpse of a scene from the next production on our calendar. So tonight, it is my pleasure to welcome our founder, Jillian Russell, to perform the dying swan scene from *Carnival of the Animals*.

David exited the stage, and the audience again responded with applause.

Carnival of the Animals music began. Jillian glided onto the stage in her snow-white costume as the stage lights came up, mixed with blue lighting to help set the night scene effect. The music had a sad quality to it that matched her mood. She was in her world now and reigning superior, a product from all the years of hard work and practice she had endured. Bending and circling with fluidity, extending and bending her arms in wing-like fashion, giving the demeanor of a swan to her audience.

Jillian executed the choreographed movements with precision and grace, showing evidence of the degree of her artistry. At the end of the scene, she floated to the floor as she covered her head with her *wings,* dying away as the music ended. She remained in hold as a piece of herself died, tears threatening.

After an appropriate amount of time, she came upright and presented a graceful bow. Moving downstage, she bowed again, catching movement in her peripheral vision. She knew the traditional bouquet was about to be presented. Surprise claimed her heart as Alan walked toward her and placed the beautiful arrangement of pink roses in her arms. She had just assumed David or some other board member would do the honors. She bowed a final time then allowed him to take her arm.

He escorted her to stage left and leaned down close to her ear. "You are the most beautiful ballerina I've ever seen."

The electric jolt from his touch reminded her of the first time he had had such an effect on her. A smile formed, knowing this would not be the last time she would experience his touch on her skin.

Backstage was alive with movement, the *curtain up* preparation for Act I of *The Sleeping Beauty* was in progress. As professionals, the group was keeping the noise level to a minimum. Alan pulled Jillian to the back wall to avoid colliding with the busy dancers.

He kissed her. "You are a most talented and graceful dancer."

The kiss had both surprised and taken her breath away. It pleased her he chose to kiss her in such a public place. She moved her head back. She had ached for his touch and his kisses. "Thank you, Mr. Armstrong. I'm glad you enjoy my dancing."

"You should continue to share your gift." He kissed her again. "In fact, I insist that you do—you should continue to dance."

Jillian opened her mouth to speak and could feel her chin tremble.

"I refuse to discuss this with you. I know how much performing means to you."

Her mind raced, searching for the meaning of his words. And then it all became clear. Her stomach clenched, and she stepped back, creating space between their bodies. She couldn't believe what she was hearing. She had been prepared to put her career aside—again—for a man she had known for less than a year. Ready to give her whole heart and life to this man, but before she had been able to tell him how she felt, he had tossed aside their chance at a wonderful life together. She was finding it hard to breathe, but she was not going to let him see her struggle. Jillian turned and ran away in the direction of the dressing rooms, feeling physical pain in her chest as her heart shattered.

Alan reached out to grab her arm, but Jillian was too quick in her retreat. He moved to follow and almost collided with his sister.

"Wasn't it the most wonderful performance? Is Jillian changing?"

He ran a hand through his hair. "I swear I don't understand women."

"What's wrong?"

He began pacing to work off his nervous energy. "I was ready to propose, and she just ran away."

"Propose?"

A costumed dancer rushed up and interrupted. "Sorry, Jenny, we have a wardrobe malfunction, and one of the fairies is freaking out."

"I'll be right there." She turned to Alan. "I have to go. *Curtain up* in two minutes. I'm sorry you're upset—we'll talk later, I promise."

The curtain went up, and the prologue began. Audrey sat in the audience with Mark, David, and Ann. Her eyes weren't on the stage. Instead, she focused on the two vacant seats at the end of the aisle that had been left for Jillian and Alan.

Ten minutes into the performance, Audrey noticed the seats remained empty. She was pleased with herself for convincing David to pass the chore of flower presentation to Alan. She knew, if she could just get them together in one place, they would take it from there. It seemed obvious her plan must have worked. The seats remained unoccupied. Her smile faded as she watched Alan settle into the seat at the end of the row alone. Where was Jillian? The performance continued, and Audrey wondered if she should leave to find her. Perhaps she was helping with something backstage. This was Jenny's first performance as ballet mistress. Maybe Jillian had decided to stay backstage for support. She observed Alan's profile. He sat rigid in his seat, the exact opposite of someone relaxed and happy.

After what seemed like an interminable amount of time to Audrey, the house lights came up for intermission. She hurried back to the dressing area, searching for Jillian. Audrey found her in her robe, huddled on the sofa, knees pulled up to her chest. Her eye makeup was smeared from crying.

Jillian jumped up when Audrey entered the room. "Oh, Mom!" She wrapped her arms around her mother.

"What is it, honey?" She guided her to the sofa.
"It's over. Alan doesn't want me." Fresh tears threatened.
"What makes you say that? Did he say it's over?"
Jillian blew her nose. "Not in those words. He insists I continue to dance—and if it's either him or dancing and he's telling me to dance, then I guess it means he doesn't want to be with me. I guess he made my decision for me."
Audrey's forehead wrinkled into a frown. "Are you sure that's how he put it?"
"Yes, Mom, I'm sure."
She needed to get these kids together to sort things out. "Can I help you fix your makeup? Intermission will be over soon."
"I've never done this before, but I'm going home. I have a migraine starting, and my medication's at home. Jenny's here to handle things. I just need to go home. Would you please tell her for me?"
"Of course I will. Are you okay to drive—the lights on the road?
"It's just starting. If I go home now and take my medication, I'll be fine."
"I'll call you tomorrow." She paused at the door. "Are you sure you don't need me to drive you home?"
Jillian was already pulling on her sweatpants. "I'm sure, but thanks for worrying about me."
Audrey moved through the crowd of people, looking for Alan. The air was energized with excitement over the well-received performance. It was nice Jillian had gone to the expense to recognize the company's hard work with a celebration. It was a good morale builder. She had told her this was a tradition she had started after their first opening performance. It helped to carry the enthusiasm of the group through to the final performance. It was too bad she hadn't been able to stay.

Seeing Alan talking with David away from the crowd, Audrey moved toward them, although she wasn't sure what she was going to say.

"Hello. David, I think Ann was looking for you. I'm not sure where she is now, but maybe you should find her."

"Thanks, Audrey. I'll talk to you later, Alan."

After David stepped away, she studied Alan's face. "You look as unhappy as Jillian, and I simply don't understand what's going on."

"Audrey, I like you a lot. I think you're a wonderful person. I just don't want to talk with you about Jillian, not right now, anyway."

"I think maybe I know something about Jillian that you don't. If you knew, you wouldn't be acting the way you are."

"I'm not following you."

"Would you mind if we find some place to sit? My ankle is throbbing."

⁓

They moved from the stage without talking until they were seated in the theater.

"I'm sorry your ankle is still bothering you. We don't have to talk right now if you'd rather go home."

"No, you need to hear this because it will change your life—unless I've misjudged you."

Tightness squeezed his chest. Frustration from the confusing events of the evening took hold of him. He ran his hand through his hair. "Enough, Audrey! Tell me what I don't know."

"I was with Jillian tonight in her dressing room before her prelude performance. She told me this performance would be her last."

"Why would she say that?"

Audrey placed her hands on his cheeks. "Because, dear boy, she wants to spend the rest of her life with you."

"She actually said those words?"

"Yes, she did."

He jumped up from his seat. "I've got to go to her. Where is she?"

"She left at intermission. She was getting a migraine and needed to go home to take her medication."

"Well, I'll just—"

"Alan, please sit down. I think you need to leave her alone."

"I think I should check on her."

"No, she's asleep by now. I told her I would call her in the morning."

He began pacing in the aisle, his mind reeling with this new information. "Don't bother, I'll go by in the morning."

"Alan, listen to me. She won't want to see you. She thinks you were telling her to continue dancing because you don't want to be with her."

"I never said that. Why would she think so?"

"Her reasoning is you gave her an ultimatum—you or dancing. Now you're telling her to dance, she thinks you don't want her."

Sliding his hands in his pockets, his pacing slowed. "When I saw her dance in Boston, I knew I couldn't ask her to give up performing. But I want her in my life, and I've come to realize it will have to include her dancing. What should I do?" He ran his fingers through his hair.

"Leave her alone."

"How will leaving her alone solve anything?"

"Leave her alone for now. She's overwhelmed. As her mother, I want to know—what are your intentions toward my daughter?"

"I want to marry her. I don't want us to spend any more time apart."

"Now then, all you have to do is figure out some very special way to propose. But give her a day or two to settle her mind down."

He bent down and hugged her. "Thank you for making me listen"

"You're welcome. And remember, I'm on your side."

Alan watched through the window of the studio, the music seeming to entice Jillian to dance. How could he have ever asked her to give this up? She danced as though her body had been made just for this purpose. After watching her perform in Boston and then again two nights ago, his heart had reconciled what his eyes and mind had known since the first time he'd seen her dance in this very studio. Jillian would never be complete if the joy of dancing was taken from her.

He didn't wait for the music to end. Opening the door, he broke the spell.

Jillian turned around and drew back. "Alan!" Her hand pressed against her chest as her breathing became labored. "You scared me! How did you get in here? The entrance door was locked."

He moved toward her. "Jenny knew you were here alone and gave me her key. I had to see you."

"Why? I got your message the other night—we're done." She turned her back and picked up the remote. She touched a button to stop the music.

He touched her shoulders and turned her to face him. "That's why I had to see you. Backstage the other night, I didn't do a good job of saying what I wanted you to hear."

Her shoulders remained tense.

"Can we sit for a minute—please?" He led her over to the bench against the wall.

Sitting down, she laid the remote on the bench beside her. She folded her hands in her lap, her head downcast.

"Jillian—I think you're a wonderful dancer. It has taken me a while, but I've finally realized dance is an integral part of who you are. And if I asked you to give it up, I'd be destroying a part of you. I couldn't do that to you—to us."

When he received no response from her, he continued. "I saw Audrey after the production was over. She told me you had intended the prelude performance to be your last dance because you wanted us to be together. Is that true?"

She looked up. "Yes, but then you were insisting I continue with my career, and I knew you were throwing us away." Tears ran down the side of her face.

"And that's where I messed up. Before I said you should continue to dance, I should have told you how much I missed you and how much my life has sucked while we've been apart. I couldn't understand why you turned and ran away."

"I left because I thought you were throwing us away. I couldn't bear for you to see how much you upset me."

She started sobbing. He pulled her into his lap against his chest and stroked her head. Her ragged breathing and crying calmed, and she wrapped her arms around his neck.

He placed a light kiss on her ear and said, "When Audrey told me you were willing to give up dancing so you could spend your life with me—well, I've never had anyone do something like that. I was overwhelmed, and knew I had to make you understand how I feel. Then Jenny stepped in to help. She told me you were here and gave me the key." He moved her away from his chest and looked down into her eyes. "Jillian, I adore you. I want you to be my wife."

"Oh, Alan!"

He cupped her face in his hands and kissed her soft, full lips then pulled back with abruptness. "I've never been good at reading minds. Was that an answer?"

She laid her head against his chest and pulled him close. "I want to be your wife, more than anything. But I can't if you're not going to share your whole life with me."

He pushed her away, staring into her eyes. "What are you talking about?"

"Your rural clinic. The first day we spent together you mentioned it was one of your goals. Through bits of conversation with Jen, it seems your plans have been progressing, but you've never once mentioned it again to me. How can you ask me to marry you if you're not willing to share such an important thing as moving to a rural area?"

"For one thing, the last few months of your life have been drama-filled, not needing any more pressure. And for another, I've made a decision about my role in this project. I'm willing to plan and offer my financial support to the effort. But since you stole my heart, my plans to leave Charlotte have dissipated."

"Oh." Confusion remained in her eyes.

"Now, we'll work out the logistics about your traveling and dancing. I might even take time from work to go with you on occasion."

"Would you?" She traced his chin with her finger. "I like the idea, but once we have children, we may have to rethink that part of the equation."

He stood up and eased her feet to the floor. "What are you saying?"

"I'm saying I think we'll make beautiful babies." She wrapped her arms around him. "I'm saying when I was alone all those years mourning Lily, the only way I thought I could keep myself from repeating the hurt was to refuse to have any more babies. But I've come through all that, with your help. And now I feel different about getting pregnant. She picked up the remote and resumed the music. Taking his hand, she said, "Dance with me, Mr. Armstrong."

Pulling her close, he replied, "For the rest of our lives."

About the Author

In 1977 Rachel earned her Bachelor of Arts degree in Music Education and taught music for ten years. After the birth of her second child, she returned to school and in 1991 earned her Associate of Applied Science degree in Nursing and passed the state boards for registered nurses. She has been a labor & delivery and antepartum nurse since that time.

Anticipating her retirement from healthcare, Rachel decided to write her first novel at age fifty-seven. For years she had experienced scenes of heroes and heroines rambling about in her thoughts and spilling into her dreams. So it was a no-brainer she should attempt to capture these thoughts on paper.

Rachel resides in a suburb of Atlanta, Georgia with her husband of thirty-seven years. She has three adult children, who help spoil their Labrador retriever. She is a member of Georgia Romance Writers, Southeastern Writers Association and is a PRO member of Romance Writers of America.

Clean Reads
ALL STORY, NO GUILT